ACT of Betrayal

The Second Chances Series - Book 3

Marsha R. West

ACT OF BETRAYAL
©2017 by Marsha R. West

Cover Art© by Charlotte Volnek

Editor, Joy Clintsman, Big Sister Edits LLC

Formatting by Stacey Blake, Champagne Book Design

Print and e-version published by MRW Press LLC, and orignially released September 2017.

ISBN 978-0-9989415-2-3

ACT of Betrayal

The Second
Chances Series
· Book 3

CHAPTER ONE

Thursday, August 25

“I’m sorry, ma’am. Your card has been declined.” The waiter’s words stung Devon Moore. Her stomach did the dropping thing like when a police car’s flashing lights showed up in your rearview mirror.

She glanced at the two people sitting with her then back to the waiter. “There must be some mistake, Ricky. My business card should have plenty of space on it. Will you try the card again, please?” She shot him her brilliant smile, the one guaranteed to get whoever to do whatever she wanted.

“If you’ve got a problem, Devon, I can pay for our lunch,” offered Sam Jenning, a middle-aged, gray-haired man with a slight paunch, the CFO of the cosmetics company Devon hoped to buy.

Not what she wanted at all. They’d come to the ultra-posh Dallas restaurant to sway the opinion of the CFO and the president, Millie Swanson, about the wisdom of selling out to Devon. Having them pay threw a wrench in her plans.

"Not necessary, Sam. My card should be accepted. I'm sure it must be some problem with the computer." Devon took another sip of her wine, barely registering the nutty taste. This would be fine, wouldn't it? But, twice before, she'd had this situation with her card arise. Drawing in deep breaths to ward off a sweating nerves attack, her fingers tapped the wine glass waiting for the waiter to return. He approached the table with a troubled expression on his face.

"Ms. Moore, I re-ran your card, and it was declined again. I'm sorry." The young blond waiter with a blush spiking his cheeks looked more embarrassed than Devon, which said something. She swallowed twice before she forced down the lovely salmon salad threatening to come up into her throat. The subdued chatter of other patrons and an occasional clink of silver or crystal filled the silence at the table.

With a flip of her hair over her shoulder, Devon reached for her purse and pulled out her card case. "I can't imagine what the problem is, but use this one." She held out a personal credit card, which she hated using for business lunches because she preferred to keep her personal and business accounts separate. Couldn't be helped this time. She couldn't let Sam pay for their meal.

Devon forced a chuckle while fighting her gag reflex. "I'm sorry about the confusion, Sam, Millie. Must be a glitch somewhere. I do have the resources to buy your company. I think we'd all be pleased with the results of merging our two small firms."

"I must confess, Devon, at first, your proposition didn't interest me much.

However, as you've talked I've envisioned having more time to travel and hang with my grandkids, and I'm seriously considering this move." Millie Swanson, in her late 60s and an early entrant into the makeup business in Dallas, had lost only a bit of her edge.

Sounded like she'd appreciate the extra freedom and being out from under the daily grind. Devon looked forward to the day she'd have more time to travel. She'd always had the money to travel and been on some memorable trips in the past, but now taking off when she had the full weight of responsibility for the business resting on her shoulders, didn't make sense. She chose to stay close.

"Here you go, Ms. Moore. No problem with that card." The waiter beamed as he handed Devon the black folder with her card and the bill in it. She signed, the scratch of the pen on the paper irritating, but she ignored the sound and smiled at him when she handed him the container and the pen. "Thanks, Ricky. Lovely service as always." He nodded and backed away.

Devon leaned forward and with effort dug deep for her 100-watt smile. "Millie, I'll get my attorney to draw up a proposed contract. You and Sam go over the document with your lawyers, and let's see if we can't work out something mutually beneficial." Devon's voice sounded firm and unwavering despite the jumping jacks going on in her stomach. What had happened to her business credit card? She could hardly keep from leaping from her chair and running out of the restaurant to demand an explanation from her head accountant. Hardly the best way to continue to sell this deal to Millie and Sam. She needed to appear cool, calm, and in control.

Millie rose and extended her hand, her voice deep and commanding. "I'll expect to see the papers then, Devon. Maybe something can come of our meeting."

Devon stood, shook the woman's hand, clasping her left one on top. "I'm optimistic, Millie."

"Sam, I'm heading back to the office? Are you?" Millie slipped her purse strap over her shoulder.

"No. I've got a dentist appointment. I'll see you in the morning." He shook hands with both women and made his way from the restaurant. His expression expressed his lack of desire to hurry off to the dentist.

"Thanks for lunch, Devon. I expect to hear from your lawyer." Millie left the same way Sam had.

Devon dropped back into her chair, the stiffening running out of her legs like sand through a sieve. After a few sips of water, she patted her mouth with the crisp white napkin and then made a quick stop in the ladies' room. With a deft touch, she reapplied lip liner and lipstick. With the additions to her mask, Devon walked briskly to the exit. Talking to Karen Johnson, her accountant, topped her list of to-dos when she got back to her office.

The drive from downtown to her office took about twenty minutes. She'd been lucky. Depending on the traffic, the trip could take as much as three-quarters of an hour. She cranked up the AC enjoying the feel of icy cold air on her face. Thank God for AC. How did people manage to live and work in Texas before this brilliant invention?

Her cosmetics business was in a small two-story building in a strip shopping center near White Rock Lake. On good weather days in the fall, winter, and spring she made a point of walking partway around the lake every couple of days. Walks in the summer were problematical. She'd melt or have a heat stroke. Besides, she had the fundraiser this evening for the local women's shelter, an event she never missed attending and supporting. Her psychologist had encouraged her participation, seeing it as a way of reclaiming her strength and helping others who'd gone through what she had. Devon should've started those sessions many years earlier, but then maybe she'd not have gotten into the cosmetics industry or created her company.

After parking in her designated spot in the garage, she made her way into the office. The buzz of hard work filled the space, and she took only a moment to smile at staff members on the way to her corner office. She settled her large purse in the credenza behind her rich oak desk, sat, and picked up the phone to call her head accountant.

"Karen, can you come in here please?" The woman assured her she'd be right there.

Devon rose and paced behind her desk, pausing to enjoy the view from the windows. She'd worked hard to build the company. What in the world could be wrong with her credit card?

"Hey, Devon. How'd the meeting go with the folks from Swanson Cosmetics?"

She turned smiling. "I'll be asking our lawyer to draw up a proposed contract, and I'm optimistic we'll reach an agreement. I hit Millie at the right time. She's ready to be a full-time granny." Devon crossed the room and closed the door.

"Have a seat, Karen." Devon gestured to a chair, and she settled behind her desk cluttered with files. Despite her best efforts, she couldn't keep papers under control. Time to get her secretary, Liz, in to wrangle the mess into some sort of sanity.

Karen's eyebrows rose. "Your expression is crinkled. Is something the matter?"

Devon ran a hand across her forehead, smoothing out the wrinkles. "Perhaps. My business credit card was refused again at lunch today."

"You're kidding. This happened a couple of months ago. Maybe a glitch with their machine occurred."

"Didn't seem so. I had no problem using my personal card. You've advised me not to use my personal credit card for business to help keep the accounting straight. I adhere to that, except today. Sam offered to pay, but I couldn't let him do that." Memories of her discomfort at the card debacle caused her to swivel her chair back and forth. She made herself stop and folding her hands on top of her desk, attempted to look like she was under control.

"No, I completely agree. Let me do some checking about the balance, Devon, and I'll get back with you. I made a payment at the end of the month. We have a $300,000 credit line on there. I can't imagine what's happened."

"Thanks, Karen. I'm leaving early this afternoon to get ready for the gala tonight."

"I'll bring you up to date tomorrow morning then. Have fun at the party." Karen left the office.

Devon swiveled in her chair again, worrying her bottom lip. How could this mess with her funds have happened? Karen was smart. She'd figure out what caused the problem.

Devon buzzed her secretary, "Liz, help!" She'd know what that meant and would come in an instant.

Her secretary, a sharp gal who'd been with her from the earliest years, stuck her head around the door. "Ah, yes. I see the need for a clutter cleaning."

Devon laughed despite her concern about her credit card. Liz, in her early forties and only two years younger than Devon, always brought a smile to her face. She was a whiz at organizing and problem-solving.

For the next thirty minutes, the room was filled with the sounds of papers and files being picked up and moved and file drawers opening and closing, as Liz picked up every piece of paper on Devon's desk and made her decide what to do with it. In a file? In the recycle? In the shred container? When they were finished, Devon's desk again appeared neat and in order. She heaved a sigh of relief as stress flowed from her body.

"Thanks, Liz. Not sure why I can't manage to keep up with my papers on my own." Devon smiled at her desk. "Such a feeling of accomplishment. You know how I like that."

"You have a lot of other stuff going on, and you can't stop and deal with the papers as you go along. Lots of folks are like that. People who don't have someone to help them out are flat out of luck. You, on the other hand, have me." Liz laughed.

"And I'm conscious of how lucky I am, too." Devon lifted her large turquoise leather bag from the credenza. "Okay, I'm heading home to get ready for the fundraiser. I'll see you in the morning. Leave whenever you'd like."

"Thanks. I may take you up on that. The weather is hot, but

I can shop first, and then chill by the condo pool with a glass of wine."

"Enjoy." Devon sailed from her office and drove to her home in Highland Park to get ready for the fundraiser. She put the credit card out of her mind and planned to have fun for a good cause.

CHAPTER TWO

Friday, September 2

"Bailey, honey. Get a move on or you'll be late." Devon poured coffee over her third large cup of ice. The only way she drank the brew in the summer. And summer in Texas could last all the way into October. Moving slowly after last night, she was grateful she'd long ago decided to dress in black and white with only a touch of color. Decision-making became a snap. Last night Bailey had attended her first Shelter fundraiser, and they'd stayed late.

"I'm ready." Bailey, in her school uniform, stepped into the kitch-en, reached for an apple from the bowl on the counter, and slung her backpack over her shoulder. "What are you waiting for?" She winked at her mother.

"Ah to be young and unfazed by late hours." Devon chuckled, as she picked up her large purse and made for the door to the garage.

"You may not be young, Mom, but you're not old." Bailey settled into the front seat of the SUV and fastened her belt.

"Thanks for those kind words."

"And you looked good last night. Several people commented on what a pretty mom I had."

"They were saying how lovely you looked and how you took after me. Thanks for going along with me last night." She patted her daughter's shoulder. "I'm sure you could've been someplace else."

"I had fun dressing in my royal blue gown. Not strapless, like I wanted, but I got lots of compliments."

"Of course, you did, Bailey. Devon tried not to put too much emphasis on her daughter's good looks, choosing to focus on her brain and her skills, but denying her daughter was a beauty was point-less. Dressed as she had been last night she could've easily passed for someone in college. She'd used a light hand on the makeup, but wow. Devon's heart swelled with pride.

"You can't argue with what a good cause it is." Bailey took a chomp from her apple and wiped the juice with a napkin. "Some of the stories those women told…well I had to bat my eyes to keep tears from falling."

Devon reached across the gear-shift and patted her daughter's hand. She had a big heart besides being a beauty. In exactly fifteen minutes, Devon turned into the front drive of the high school Bailey attended. "What time do I pick you up this afternoon?"

"I've got cheerleading, and Linda's mother will bring us both home."

Devon leaned over and gave her daughter a quick kiss on the cheek, grateful they were close. "Well, then. Have a great day, and I'll see you this evening."

Bailey had dealt with the divorce well. She seemed to understand her parents both loved her, but not each other.

"Bye, Mom." Bailey closed the door and hustled toward the old red building. Devon sat for a moment more, but cars piled up if you didn't keep moving, so she moved. Besides, she was eager to get to work and talk with Karen.

But Karen had to wait, several of her developers insisted on meeting with her about a new product they were hot about. How could she say no to hearing about a better under-eye corrector than the company already had?

The numbers on the digital clock read eleven when Devon fi-nally made room for Karen in her schedule.

"So, what'd you find?" Devon settled behind her desk and ges-tured to Karen to take the seat on the other side from her

Karen sat and set a folder down on Devon's desk, her eyebrows worried into a frown. "We appear to have some missing funds."

"What?"

"Yeah. I made these printouts of the business credit card activity."

The pages rustled as Karen scooted them over to Devon who put on wire-rim reading glasses to see the numbers better. She hated this part of the business. Not the fun part at all. "You'd better explain what I'm looking at, Karen."

"Sure. I hate to tell you this, but the bottom line is our $300,000 credit line is maxed out. That's after I made a $50,000 payment at the end of last month. So, in two weeks, $350,000 has gone missing."

Devon ran her fingers over the figures as if she could read braille and somehow, she'd be able to sense from the squiggles, but she couldn't. "Damn. This is not good. Any idea of what happened?"

"Well," Karen looked at Devon then cast her gaze back at the papers. "Only a couple of us have access to this card. You. Me. And your ex-husband." She met Devon's gaze head on. "I didn't take it."

Devon sighed and rested her forehead on her hands. "No. I didn't think you did." She looked at her accountant. "Not for a moment."

"And if you took it, well, Devon, it's your company's money," Karen shrugged her shoulders.

"I didn't take it, either, Karen." Devon shook her head; her lips took on a firm straight line.

Karen shrugged again. Her fingers twisted in her lap. "I don't know what to say.

Devon dropped her head into her hands again and rubbed her forehead where a shooting pain grew. Good grief. Karen had been too kind to point out the obvious. "Guess we're left with Franklin, who I apparently didn't remove from the account."

"His name is on a half-dozen withdrawals for sizable amounts over the last several weeks. I'm sorry. I should've paid more attention."

"No. This is my fault, Karen." Devon straightened her chair. "I screwed up by not taking his name off the account. Franklin has tons of money; it never occurred to me he'd need any of mine." Devon rose and paced behind her desk. She fiddled with the tie at the neck of her white silk blouse and paced the length of her office. What the heck was going on?

"I don't mean to butt in, but have you seen or talked to him lately?" Karen shifted to stare at Devon.

"I don't consider you're butting in at all, Karen." Devon faced her head accountant. "The divorce has been final for over six months. I see him when he occasionally picks up Bailey for a weekend, but no long talks since our lawyers settled everything. He hasn't lived in the house for almost two years. Guess I'll have to have a chat with him." She made her way behind her desk and sank into the chair. "I'd better tell the development department to hold up on their new product, and we shouldn't use the business credit card until we get this straightened out. Thanks, Karen."

Her accountant nodded. "Of course. You'll tell me if you need me to do anything?"

Devon nodded and swiveled her chair to stare out the windows. The soft sound of the door closing told her Karen left the office. Why would Franklin have needed those funds? If he needed money,

11

an idea hard to imagine, why didn't he ask? She'd have given him a loan. They shared a child together for heaven's sake.

Devon pulled the keyboard toward her and emailed a message to her developers telling them to put a temporary hold on plans for the new product. She'd get this straightened out, and then they could get back to business. Lifting her cell, she punched in a text message to her ex-husband. "Meet me at the house in an hour. Important." This meeting needed to happen when Bailey wasn't at home.

Devon met Franklin, a senior in college when she was a mere freshman at SMU. The best friend of her sorority big sister's boy-friend, Franklin made her feel special and loved, and they married as soon as she graduated. She'd been dabbling with makeup for a while, and he supported her opening her own cosmetics company. Helping women look good gave Devon a sense of purpose. A lot of long nights and weekends, hiring good people, and luck had contributed to the success of her company.

They'd both been busy, and thankfully, her parents had been able to take up the slack with Bailey. While she owed Franklin for his support in helping get the business started, he didn't have the right to take money from her company.

The ache in her head made her reach for pain meds in her purse. She didn't get these headaches except when she faced a confrontation. During the months of negotiations to finalize the divorce agreement, she'd taken more than her share of these little pills. Looked like she had one more confrontation ahead of her. "Liz, I'll be out for a couple of hours."

"Okay. I'll handle all your calls."

Forcing a smile, Devon strode to the parking garage.

Devon glanced in the large mirror hanging in the dining room of their Highland Park home. She reapplied her lipstick and fluffed her dark red hair, which fell past her shoulders. Her slim black skirt, matching jacket, and white silk blouse looked professional, feminine, but not sexy. She never wanted to do anything to appear sexy. The chimes at the front door made her catch her breath. She had no fondness for Franklin except as Blair's father, and he'd better give her a darn good explanation for what happened to all the money.

She walked into the entryway. Franklin's reflection came through the cut glass on the door.

Her hand paused above the knob. She sucked in a big breath and yanked open the door. "Hello, Franklin." He stepped into the entry way. Heat smacked her in the face before she could get the door closed. "Thanks for stopping by on such short notice." She turned and led him into the living room, her high heels clicking on the hard wood floors.

His heavier steps echoed behind her. "Your curt message sur-prised me. Is Bailey all right?"

"She is." Devon sat in one of the large burgundy wingbacks arranged in front of the stone fireplace. She gestured, and Franklin sat across from her. Her fingers gripped the chair arms. She crossed and uncrossed her leg, then planted them firmly on the floor. Might as well jump right in.

"Franklin, I'm missing money from my business credit card account."

"Really? How much?" Franklin's face expressed curiosity. Like he had no idea about what she was talking.

"$350,000." She held his gaze.

"Damn. That's quite a bit. How'd you misplace that? You need to be more careful with your money, Devon. Your accountant, what's her name?"

"Karen Johnson," Devon supplied through almost clenched teeth.

"That's right, Johnson. She's never been good enough to keep things straight. You're too softhearted for business. Because she needed a job, didn't mean you had to hire her." He crossed one leg over the other, straightened the crease, and eased back in the chair, as if he had not a care in the world.

Devon leaned forward, resting her hands on her knees. "Franklin, only three of us have access to the business account."

"And that would be?" His eyebrows rose in question.

"Karen, me," she paused, "and you."

Franklin waved his hand. "Just what I've said all along, Karen is no good."

"Karen didn't take the money," she stated in her sternest voice.

"And you know she didn't because?" Still, he sat relaxed and untroubled.

"She told me."

"Oh, Devon, Devon. How naïve. And you believed her?" He switched legs and did the same business with the crease in his pants.

"Yes. I did."

"So, you borrowed from your own account, Devon? What did you need the money for, and why didn't you come to me? I could've helped."

Anger burned up Devon's throat. "Well, as a matter of fact, Franklin, I'm wondering what the reason was you needed the money."

"What? Are you suggesting I took the money?" He rose from the chair and paced across the room. "Are you nuts? I don't need your money. Seriously, Devon. Is this why you asked me to come by, interrupting my busy day?"

She rose and stepped in front of him. "Did you take the money, Franklin?" She had to ask him point-blank.

"I'm offended you'd ask." He moved past her. "If you don't have anything else, I'm leaving. Have a good day, Devon." He crossed the room, opened, and then closed the front door with a slight thump.

The starch went right of her Devon. She reached for the back of the nearest chair, missed. Her trembling legs couldn't hold her up, and she sank to the floor. She closed her eyes and drew in several slow, deep breaths. Franklin didn't exactly deny he took the money. He only got all huffy that she suspected he had.

What was her next step? To begin with she got up off the floor and walked to the kitchen. She needed iced tea in the worst way and fixed a glass. The cold fruity liquid trickled down her dry throat. The caffeine gave her a bit of a punch, and the cold helped cool her blood.

Carrying the glass back into the living room, she settled into the high-backed chair, retrieved her cell phone from the pocket of her jacket, and punched in Addie's name. One of her best friends since meeting at camp when they were in elementary school, Addison Greer lived in Fort Worth and had recently married a homicide detective, Mike Riley. Between them, they'd have advice for her. Middle of the afternoon, Addie, the Executive Director of Cowtown Theatre could be busy right now, but she'd get back to Devon as soon as possible. That's the kind of friends they were.

"Devon?"

"Yes, Hey, Addie. I'm glad you answered. Do you have a spare moment? I need to pick your brain about something."

"What a coincidence for you to call, Devon. Mike and I were talking last night about the last time we'd seen you. It's been too long. Can you come to the ranch tomorrow evening? We'll cook out. You can spend the night. We'll have a chance to catch up."

Hearing Addie's words gave Devon a boost. Things didn't seem quite as dark. That's what good friends did for you.

"Sounds like a great idea, Addie. Thank you."

"What's up? Tell me why you called." She laughed. "We'll help you fix whatever."

Devon swallowed a couple of times. How awful to have to accuse your ex-husband of stealing, but that's what she was about to do.

When she finished talking, the silence on the other end spoke of her friend's shock. Addie, never at a loss for words, didn't fill the void.

"Addie, are you there?"

"Yes, Sweetie. Can I talk with Mike about this?"

"Of course, I don't mind."

"Maybe he'll have some suggestions of what you need to do first."

"I'd welcome y'all's ideas. I'm at a loss for what steps to take."

"Well, then we're still expecting you to come over tomorrow night. I'm sure we'll have some suggestions by then."

Devon breathed easier at the idea her friends could provide her with practical solutions. "Sounds lovely to get away from this mess for a while. I'll see if Bailey wants to stay with my mother."

"Jeremy and Elizabeth are away at college, but bring Bailey if you'd like."

"I'd like to keep this from her if possible."

"I understand. Hang in there. You can count on us."

Devon disconnected, sighing. She was doing something. Not much. But something.

CHAPTER THREE

Friday, September 2

Late in the after noon, Brett Townsend closed a folder and pushed it to the corner of his desk for his secretary to file. He kept most everything on his computer now, but the little old lady client didn't do emails, so he used paper for all the documentation for her accounts. Sad her grandson attempted to take advantage of her the way he had. Some families weren't worth the trouble of having them.

His cell pinged. He read a message from Mike Riley, a homicide detective friend in Fort Worth. *Do you have time to talk?* Brett typed *Yep.*

Wonder what this was about. He and Mike had crossed paths on a case last year. Mike looked for a murderer. Brett worked the financial angle. The guy had landed life in prison and was lucky not to get the death penalty. His cell buzzed.

"Hey, Mike. What's up?"

"Thanks for taking my call, Brett. Let me get right to the point. Know how busy you can be. My wife Addie's best friend, Devon Moore, has a problem, and you are the best candidate to help her." Mike explained the situation, and Brett listened and made notes.

"Can you see your way clear to come to the ranch tomorrow evening? Devon will be more comfortable meeting you here for the first time than in your office."

"She lives here in Dallas, you said?"

"Yes. Your location and the fact you're the smartest guy I know with financial stuff is why I thought of you. Can you come?"

"Hang on a minute." Brett checked his phone calendar. He was supposed to eat supper at his partner's house, but he could reschedule. "Sure, Mike. Thanks. Look forward to seeing you and meeting Addie and her friend."

As soon as they disconnected, Brett began an internet background search on Devon Moore and her ex-husband Franklin. His fingers flew across the keys and in moments articles and pictures popped up of the couple at various fundraisers in Dallas and even a couple in Wichita Falls. Wonder what the connection was in that town?

The man had been married to a real beauty. What was wrong with him to let her go? Or, maybe she was a shrew and drove him nuts with her nagging. Apparently, she had her own skin care company, which appeared to be successful. He found pictures of their daughter connected to Highland Park High School. Looked like she had inherited her mother's looks and red hair.

Time to reconnoiter. He reached into his pocket for his keys He stopped at the receptionist's desk. "Sylvia, I'll be out for a couple of hours. Might or might not return."

"No problem, Brett. See you whenever."

In the garage, he climbed into his 4-wheel drive SUV. He didn't always need the extra control, but he didn't want to need maneuverability and not have the feature.

He drove toward the White Lake area of Dallas, easily locating the modest building housing Blair-Moore Cosmetics, Inc., part of a strip shopping center. The company seemed to take up two floors with part of the second being used for parking. Employees must love that perk especially during the spring storms known to lash Dallas and all Northcentral Texas. From there he followed his GPS directions to Moore's house in Highland Park, a large two-story colonial with large columns on the expansive front porch. A circular driveway took up only a small part of the front yard. Giant oak trees, and well-trimmed lawn, like many of the other houses in this neighborhood.

Looked like she got the house in the divorce or her company did well enough she could afford to continue to stay there on her own. Meeting the beautiful Devon Moore Saturday night and learning about her problem ought to be intriguing.

Saturday, September 3

Early on Saturday evening, the traffic on I-30 was crazy. Oh, not like LA crazy, but Brett hated this drive either direction. Repairs continued for one part or another of the roadway all the time and people drove like maniacs, zipping in and out of lanes as if they were the only ones on the road and their destination should take precedence over anyone else's trip.

A certain anticipation hit his stomach when he thought about the evening ahead. He suspected the feeling didn't have everything to do with the meal and everything to do with meeting Mike's new wife's friend. Devon Moore had peaked his interest.

Brett followed I-30 through town. About fifteen minutes on the west side of Fort Worth, he took the turn leading to Mike's Ranch. He couldn't see the house from the road, but as he crested a hill, the homestead came into view sitting in a copse of oak trees, their limbs and leaves waving in the wind. He pulled into the circular drive and parked behind a Cadillac. Looked like Devon Moore had already arrived.

The smell of grilling meat hit him as he stepped from his SUV and his mouth watered. The front door swung open before he got there.

"Welcome, Brett. Glad you could come." Mike Riley held out his hand.

"Thanks for asking me." Brett grasped the extended hand. "Love that hickory smell."

"I've got the grill heating up. We're having steaks. Hope that's all right."

"No arguments from me. The Cadillac out here must be Ms. Moore's?"

"Yep. Come meet her."

Brett followed Riley into his house. A lovely woman with long black hair, wearing tailored blue jeans and an orangish shirt greeted him, "Welcome to the ranch."

"You must be Addie."

"You're a detective." The woman chuckled.

"Well, I try."

"Here you go, Brett." She handed him a beer. "Mike told me this was your poison of choice."

"He's right about that. Thanks." As he tipped the beer back, he caught the eye of a gorgeous redhead. He slowly lowered the bottle. "Pardon me. You must be Addie's friend, Devon Moore." He extended his hand hoping she'd reciprocate. For some reason he couldn't understand, something about the woman drew him in. She flat out took his breath.

"Yes, Mr. Townsend, I'm Devon Moore. Pleased to meet you." She shook his hand, but much too briefly for Brett's liking. He wanted to hold on to her smooth, soft hand.

"Let's have a seat." Addie led them further into the large room with wood floors and a giant fireplace. Even unlit, the massive stone-work highlighted the room making it seem warm and welcoming.

Brett waited while the two women sat on the sofa. Addie leaned back pulling one leg up under her. Devon sat forward on the edge of the couch, rolling a glass with white wine back and forth between her hands. He settled into one of the two large leather chairs on either side of the fireplace. While he'd prefer to be close to her, this position gave him a better chance to study her face. She might not have any reason to lie, but he liked to cover all his bases.

"Should we jump into this before supper? I'm afraid we'll ruin this great meal Mike is throwing together." Devon raised her glass and took a quick sip.

"Hey, I don't throw together a meal. I'm a chef. This takes effort."

"Sorry, Mike. I didn't mean to demean your talents." Devon rose, and faced the empty fireplace.

"Hey, lady, just teasing." Mike took her shoulders and swiveled her around.

"This is the easiest meal. Potatoes in the oven, I've put the steaks on the grill, and we'll have salad, which I do kind of throw together."

Devon's smile didn't reach her eyes, but she nodded at Mike. "I do appreciate y'all having me over here and giving me a chance to meet Mr. Townsend."

"Brett, please. If your story may take a while, and it seems it may, why don't we wait until we sit down to eat? Otherwise we run the chance of ruining Mike's steaks by making them cook too long. I've heard rumors they're the best."

"You're right there, Brett. His steaks make for some good eating." Pride in her husband lit up Addie's face.

"How long have you and Devon been friends, Addie?" The two beautiful women intrigued Brett.

"We met when we all attended a camp in East Texas after second grade. None of us—Kate and Kim are our other two friends—had met each other before then."

"Several years of camp solidified our friendships." Devon took Addie's hand in hers. "We get together several times a year for a weekend, but now, of course, social media makes keeping in touch easy."

"We all, except for Devon, went to Maine for Kate's wedding. Such a beautiful state and the wedding was perfect."

"Why didn't you go, Ms. Moore?" Brett leaned forward to make sure he got her answer.

Devon glanced at the others, took another quick sip of her wine, before setting the glass on a side table. "I suspected a problem with my money but didn't know what. I had concerns, but now, I've learned it's much worse."

"I'm sorry, hon," Addie squeezed Devon's hand.

"Let me check these steaks." Mike rose. "Addie, pull the potatoes out of the oven, please. We'll be eating in less than five minutes." He opened the back door and stepped outside.

The aroma of hickory flavor filled the air, making Brett's stomach growl.

"Brett, will you top off our drinks? Devon, come with me to get those potatoes ready to go." Addie rose and moved toward the kitchen. She slipped an arm around Devon's waist.

The women were close. Brett rose and began refilling their wine glasses. Devon seemed like an okay person. He wouldn't mind helping the gorgeous redhead. She wasn't dressed all frou-frou, but wore black jeans, boots, and a white shirt. A large turquoise hung around her neck on what looked to be black leather. Her long red, curly hair flared out around her head and down to her shoulders. He wouldn't mind sinking his hands in the mane.

Devon smushed the potato before she removed the foil. Steam

spiraled upwards. Excitement built in her middle, surprising her. An attractive, in a wavy blond hair, blue-eyed kind of way, private investigator Brett Townsend appeared as tall as Mike, well over six feet. No time for this complication. She quickly finished uncovering the potatoes, placed one on each plate, and set the plates on the large eat-in kitchen table.

"I've got sour cream, butter, bacon bits, cheese, and chives. Y'all can fix these to suit yourselves." Addie placed a Lazy Susan in the center of the table with the additions.

"Coming through." Mike shoved open the back door and entered holding a tray with two fillets and two T-bones.

The sizzling and the hickory aroma made her mouth water and her stomach growl. Worry had kept her from eating much lately.

"Hope I've cooked these the way everyone likes. Addie, yours is well-done." He grimaced as he speared the small steak, which he placed on her plate. "Devon, yours is medium."

"Thanks, Mike. We've never understood Addie eating a steak cooked until it's like leather." Devon smiled as she teased her friend.

"Thanks," she threw over her shoulder as Brett held a chair for her. He'd dressed casually in jeans, a blue shirt, boots, and a sports jacket. After laying the napkin in her lap, she took it back up to twist and then refold the fabric. Dropping all this on Addie and Mike embarrassed her enough without also telling a perfect stranger what she feared happened.

She gulped her wine and determined to hold herself together. Going through the automatic motions, she fixed her potato, as if making it exactly the right way was the most important action in her world.

Brett cleared his throat drawing her gaze to his. "Ms. Moore, why don't you start at the beginning. When did you first suspect, you had a problem?" He added a large spoonful of sour cream to his potato.

"Several months ago, my business credit card wouldn't work.

My accountant checked and found a payment hadn't been posted in a timely fashion. Then the card was rejected two other times." She stirred her potato with the ingredients she added, no sour cream but all the other options. "Most recently the card was declined after a luncheon meeting with people who owned a cosmetics company I hoped to buy."

"Oh, my gosh, Devon. How embarrassing! How awful for you." Addie's expression meant to comfort Devon did.

"Thanks." She forced a small bite of the fluffy white stuff into her mouth, struggling to swallow.

"Have you been able to determine how much is missing?" Brett put a piece of steak in his mouth. "Damn. This is good, Mike."

Mike nodded at the compliment, clearly believing the praise justified. Would she be able to eat any of the steak? Devon struggled to chew a piece. She barely managed to wash the small bite down with a sip of wine before managing to mumble, "It's at least $350,000."

"Wow!" Addie, set down her fork and faced Devon.

"Yeah. When Kate got married, I didn't know how bad things were, but I'm glad now I didn't make any unnecessary expenditures."

"Wise to be cautious, Ms. Moore. Definitely better safe than sorry to state a cliché."

"Given I'm spilling my financial guts to you, you can call me Devon."

"Thanks." He nodded and then ate for several minutes. No one spoke, focusing on the meal.

"Who has access to those funds? Do you have an idea who took the money...Devon?" Brett met her gaze.

She liked the way her name sounded when he spoke. He seemed to focus all his attention on her and her problems. And that's exactly what she needed right now.

"Besides me, only my head accountant and," she paused,

"apparently, my ex-husband."

Brett leaned forward. "Your ex-husband? How did that happen? Well, not the divorce, but how did he access your funds?"

Devon glanced at Addie, Mike, and then back to Brett before answering. "Total lack of forethought on my part. Franklin had never accessed the business account the whole time we were married. I'd put his name there in case something happened to me. He's always had plenty of money. I had no reason to suspect he'd do something like this."

"You're sure it's not your accountant?" Brett raised his beer bottle and tipped.

"I trust Karen with my life and my business. When I confronted Franklin, he tried to place the blame on Karen and my stupidity for hiring her."

"Devon, you confronted Franklin?" Addie glanced at Brett. "That's not her strong suit. I'm proud of you, sweetie." Addie raised her wine glass in Devon's direction.

"May not have been the wisest action to take, Devon. Now you've alerted your ex-husband you're suspicious." A frown wrinkled Brett's forehead.

"I thought he'd have some reasonable explanation and a plan to return the money. He totally stunned me when he didn't accept responsibility. He didn't exactly deny knowledge, but he redirected the focus." Devon rubbed a hand against her temple where a pain throbbed. "What do I do?"

"If you give me permission to access your files I can do a bit of digging to see if we can tell where the funds went." Brett took a swallow of his beer then set the bottle on the table and stared at her, waiting for her response.

"How much are your fees, Brett. Since my financial life is in an upheaval, could we do a contingency deal or something—"

"Let's not worry about payments right now, Devon. I'll check out the situation because Mike's my friend. Addie's important to him, and you're important to Addie. So, let's not talk about fees."

Devon fought the tears forming. "I'm grateful." She turned her gaze to Mike and Addie in turn. "Grateful to all of you."

"I'll clean up in here. Y'all take your drinks into the family room area, and you can continue the discussion." Addie rose and took her plate and Brett's from the table.

"I'll help." Mike picked up his own plate and Devon's.

Addie certainly had a catch with the homicide detective. Well-deserved considering all she went through with her first husband. Before Devon rose, Brett took her glass and poured more wine. She smiled. "Thanks. I'm spending the night. No worries about drinking and driving."

He followed her into the family room area. "What's your opinion, Brett? Am I a lost cause? Will I have to sell my business?"

A small smile flashed and then disappeared. "Don't believe so, but let's imagine what could happen." He gestured to the sofa.

"I need to walk. Thanks. You can sit." Brett settled into the chair he'd been in earlier. "So, what could happen?"

"Let's say I find proof your husband—your ex-husband—took money from the company. He's arrested, charged, and stands trial. Then depending on the outcome of the trial, he may face jail time. After all that, you may or may not get back your money."

Devon paced faster in keeping pace with her racing heart. Poor Bailey. How embarrassing to have your father arrested to stand trial for theft.

"Do you want him sent to jail?" Brett cocked his head at her.

Devon dropped onto the sofa, set the glass on the end table, and literally wrung her hands.

"Devon, do you want him sent to jail?"

"No, no, not really. I want the money back and no more thefts. I want to keep my business, but I don't need Franklin sent to jail."

"Let me investigate the situation." He consulted his phone

calendar. I've got to finish up a project on Monday, but I could be at your office on Tuesday, September 6. How does the date work for you? I'm sure you'd like to get this cleared up soon as possible."

Devon nodded. "That will be perfect. Thanks, Brett. How do I explain your presence?"

"You can call me an auditor doing a standard check on the IT system."

"Can I tell Karen?"

"No, let's keep this between the two of us." His hand waved back and forth.

"Okay." She nodded and extended her hand. "I can't thank you enough."

"Well, let's wait to see what I find out." His handshake was firm and gave her confidence.

Later the same night, Devon settled into the guest room at the ranch. From her big bed, she stared out the window at bright stars in the dark night sky. No moon. Made it easier to see the fireworks when someone shot them off for an early Labor Day celebration.

Despite the comfortable bed, she tossed and turned. She fluffed her pillow and attempted to shove away her problems. Any success she had at that was because investigator Brett Townsend filled up most of her mind. An odd reaction on her part. She seldom noticed good-looking men, but something about him drew her. He seemed smart and capable, and that's what she needed right now. Good thinking on her part to plan to spend the night and not drive back to Dallas tonight. Those extra glasses of wine had taken their toll.

How long before Brett found out anything? Would whatever he found help? What was going on with her ex-husband to cause him to take money from her company? Could he have done that? Stolen from her? Her stomach twisted with sharp pains. She hoped not.

She hoped none of this affected her daughter in any way. She hoped the situation could be quickly and quietly resolved.

Rolling her back to the window and the beautiful stars, she hoped she'd fall asleep before morning.

CHAPTER FOUR

Sunday, September 4

Franklin stared down the fairway. This shot was important, symbolically, if not for the game. Henry Logan, a wiry man, lived and breathed golf. One of the trappings of his wealth he enjoyed and not because it was something he was supposed to like. Franklin had to pretend the game of golf held any importance to him. He'd rather have been out shooting his rifle. He swung. The ball sailed through the air.

They had a warmer than normal fall day to be knocking the ball around, but the breeze made the temperature tolerable. In Texas, you played golf on all but the hottest days unless you were a wimp.

In the circles in which Franklin ran, appearing a wimp was out of the question. He surreptitiously wiped the sweat from his brow while Henry teed up.

"Not a crappy shot, Franklin. You almost made the green. You been practicing?"

"Just lucky, Henry."

Logan took his swing, and the ball soared over the grass to land on the putting green. "Now that's what I call a great shot," Henry congratulated himself.

Franklin followed his client toward the golf cart.

"You got any positive news about the gas leases?" Henry fixed Franklin with an icy stare as he crawled in the cart.

Franklin squirmed in the seat. What could he tell Logan? We're losing our shirts on that company. No, not yet anyway. He expected the last batch of dollars he'd skimmed from Devon's company to tide them over. As soon as OPEC cut their production, and prices rose, their company would start pumping again.

"We'll be okay, Henry. Have faith."

"I don't have a lot of faith, Franklin, or only as much money as I have. That's been shrinking. I won't be happy to lose any more. You got it?"

The gaze Henry shot Franklin curdled his insides. Best not to mess around with Henry Logan. He'd come up the hard way and had made millions. He valued what those millions did for him.

Franklin nodded. "Yeah. I got it, Henry. No problem." He sure as hell hoped there wouldn't be a problem. In a few days, OPEC would meet. All the speculation pointed to the decision they'd cut production. They'd better for his sake. He didn't see how he could dig into Devon's company any more with her already suspicious.

Tuesday, September 6

Devon rose early not because she was eager to see the investigator again. No, no way, but she did want to get to the office before he got there. Bailey had left for an early morning cheerleading practice. With hopes of going to nationals high, the team scheduled extra practice time.

When Devon climbed out of her car in the garage of her cosmetics company, the tall, blond investigator already leaned against the wall next to the door. He wore khakis and a sports jacket. No tie. But most of her employees dressed on the casual end of the spectrum.

"Well, you're an early riser, Brett." Devon extended her hand. "Thanks for coming in."

"You're welcome." He briefly shook her hand. Have you decided how to explain me to your staff?"

"Yes. You're a new IT guy here to make some updates to our equipment, and you will perhaps have to get on everyone's computer. How does that sound?"

"Works for me."

"I went ahead and told Karen Johnson why you're here."

"She's your head accountant, right?"

"Yes." Devon tightened her hand on the bag. He'd told her not to, but she couldn't exclude Karen. He probably doubted her decision.

"And you trust her completely?" His eyebrows wrinkled into a frown, questioning her judgment.

Just what she suspected. Well, she'd set him straight. "Of course. She's the one who pointed out the losses to me."

"Well, let's go see what we can find out and hope you didn't make a mistake."

"This way." Devon led Brett through the glass door into what she thought of as a classy, soothing, environment. Lots of light flowed from the floor to ceiling windows. Decorations were in shades of turquoise, her favorite color, and beige. Devon predominantly wore black and white because in her mind the colors went with the job and looked professional. Aside from admiring glances from the women she introduced to Brett, no one seemed to find anything odd she'd brought in an IT guy.

She knocked briefly on her accountant's door before opening

and sticking in her head. "Hey, can I interrupt you?" Devon led Brett in and made the introductions.

Karen Johnson came around from behind her desk to shake Brett's hand. "I'm happy to meet you and relieved you've come. I hate to admit I can't get a handle on this missing money."

"Well, I'll leave you two together if that's okay. You'll be talking over my head. I'm not fond of technology only what it can do for us."

"I'll get back to you as soon as we find what's going on." Brett had already focused on Karen and her computer.

"Sure." Devon smiled at Brett and Karen before leaving them together already engrossed in *techno-speak*.

When she returned to her office, Devon slumped behind her desk and swiveled her chair toward the windows. The partial view of White Rock Lake, normally soothing, didn't work today. How long would Brett's detective work take? Would he be able to find out what had happened to her funds? Was Franklin seriously stealing money from her company? If so, what the hell should she do? All the same questions she'd mulled over during her restless night at Addie and Mike's ranch. And still, she had no answers.

Thursday, September 8

Devon spent the morning looking over reports from the development department. The new product looked promising. Such a shame not to be able to bring this to her customers. She shoved the file to a corner of her desk and got ready to leave for lunch with her mother by adding an extra touch of blush and lipstick. Devon told her secretary, Liz, she'd be out for a while and then hurried out to meet her mother.

They met at the Coffee Pot Café, one of her mother's favorite lunch spots. They tried to eat lunch together once a week but had missed last week because her mother and father had been out of town on a trip. Devon, eager to catch up, hoped she'd be able to keep her mom in the dark concerning her worries about the company and Franklin and the money. Tough task.

Her mother, a tall, slender woman who didn't appear to have reached 70 years, arrived at Devon's table in a swirl of her favorite flowery scent. Devon had always liked it, and the scent suited her mother well. Miriam Blair emulated everything good about being a socialite, a hardworking volunteer for important causes, not interested in gaining glory for her work. The feeling she got when she helped someone in need kept her doing good works.

"Hey, Mom." Devon rose and kissed her mother on the cheek. "You're looking great. The cruise must've agreed with you and Dad."

"Oh, sweetie, we saw beautiful scenery and had perfect weather. Altogether an incredible trip." Miriam settled into the chair across from her daughter, chuckling. "Great shopping too, but even more I loved the snorkeling in the sparkling turquoise waters. You would've enjoyed the trip, too."

"I'm glad you and Dad had a good time." The waiter stopped by their table with water glasses and tool their order. Not a long process, since Devon and her mother ate there often and frequently ordered the same thing. Tomato basil soup and half an egg salad sandwich on rye bread.

"The pictures you sent were beautiful." Devon squeezed two lemons into her tea.

"The Caymans are amazing. You'll have to visit there sometime."

"Maybe, but not on a cruise. I'm not a great sailor."

"We ran into Franklin one day while we were shopping in town. Had you heard he'd be there when we were?"

Devon stalled by taking a bite of her sandwich. "Umm. This is my favorite."

Her mother stared at her across the table. "Before the divorce, you could've come with him, and we could've hung out together lolling on the beach and shopping in the quaint stores." Her fingers played with her napkin.

"No, I hadn't heard, but then we seldom talk about anything but arrangements for Bailey to visit him." Why had Franklin gone to the Caymans?

Their food arrived and conversation circled back to Bailey, her grandmother's pride and joy. "All Bailey talks about is the possibility of the cheerleading squad qualifying for nationals. I guess because last year's squad went, they feel a lot of pressure to do well enough to go, too."

"They haven't heard yet, but they're optimistic and working hard." Devon took a spoonful of the soup, the flavors exploded on her tongue. Nobody made tomato basil this good.

"Finals will be in Nashville again, right? I assume you're going." Her mother sipped her iced tea.

"Yes. Will you and Dad be able to come? Bailey mentioned she'd love for you to be there."

"Of course. What's the date? I'll put it on my calendar."

"The week following Christmas. We could fly out together and get rooms at the Gaylord where the girls are staying."

"I'll check with your father, but count me in either way. I'll get all of our tickets."

"That's not necessary, Mom. I'm doing well."

Her mother smiled. "I know, sweetie, but count this as an extra Christmas gift. Shall we splurge on dessert?" Her eyes scanned the small one-page menu.

"You can, but I've got to get back to work; I hate to hurry you."

"Don't worry about me. I'll keep myself company with a piece of their coconut pie. I can go work off the lusciousness at the gym later." Her mother laughed, and Devon leaned over and kissed her on the cheek.

"Enjoy. Check with you later about Nashville. Glad you enjoyed your vacation in the Caymans."

Her mother ordered the pie while Devon exited the café. She'd have loved the pie, too, but couldn't fit in a trip to the gym, and her mother, right as she often was, believed the only safe way to enjoy a pie or any dessert was to exercise afterward.

When she entered her building, she looked around but didn't see Townsend or Karen. Guess they were tied up. Better get to the Swanson Cosmetics contract. Money questions existed right now, but at some point, she expected to be able to buy the firm. She told Liz to hold all her calls, set the fifty-page document on her desk, and popped on her reading glasses. Fifty pages. Were her lawyers paid by the word?

A soft knock drew Devon's blurry eyes from the document.

Liz stuck her head in the door. "Hey, it's past going home time. You're pulling a late one."

Devon yanked off her glasses and ran her hand over her eyes "Oh my God! My vision is blurry. What time is it anyway?"

"Seven. You've been at this all after noon."

Devon stood and stretched her hands over her head. "Gosh, this is tedious, but I'm almost finished and better to swallow the document whole than piecemeal where I could forget what I'd already read." She settled into her chair. "You run on, Liz. I'll only be here another thirty minutes or so."

"You sure? The building is almost empty. The IT guy is still working."

"Of course. We've got good lighting, and this is a safe neighborhood. In the old days, I frequently left the building last after everyone else."

"You're worth a lot more now than then." Liz smiled but shook her head. "Don't stay too late. See you in the morning."

"Sure. Thanks, Liz." The door closed and Devon's stomach

growled. She'd worked through supper. Probably should've had the pie at lunch. Five more pages and she'd head home to eat supper. Her mother had picked up her daughter today. Maybe Bailey had made supper. Devon should've called her earlier; Bailey was probably worrying. She tapped her daughter's name on her cell.

"Hi, Mom. You okay?"

"Sorry, hon. I got caught up in paper work. I'll be home in about 45 minutes."

"Okay, but I make no promises on how good your warmed-up supper will be." They both laughed. After the divorce, taking turns making supper had worked out well for them. Tonight, had been Blair's turn. She'd become a quite competent cook, her grandmother a good influence. Devon hated she'd missed her daughter's latest concoction.

After disconnecting, Devon picked up her red pen and went back to the contract. Thirty minutes later, she sighed and closed the document. Finally. She'd pass on the documents to her lawyers to have them make the final changes, awaiting time to move on the deal. The contract went in her left land bottom desk drawer. She stood, picked up her purse from the credenza behind her chair and left her office, flicking off lights and closing the door as she went.

She pushed through the outer door, her quick steps clicking on the garage floor. Glancing around, her car appeared to be one of only two parked in the garage. Must be Brett Townsend still working. The sooner he found something the better.

The garage took up extra space on the second floor. Franklin hadn't wanted her to use the space for parking. He'd wanted her to lease out the area, but she was convinced her employees valued the parking perk. No worry about rain, hail, or ice and snow. Many a time, she'd been grateful she didn't have to scrape the snow or ice off her windshield. And she and her employees had sailed through the last hail storm unscathed.

Just as she got hold of her keys, the lights in the garage

flickered and went off. Huh. What caused the malfunction? Devon glanced over her shoulder but didn't see or hear anything. No worries. Her keys had a small light attached. She clicked the button on and pointed the beam toward her car.

The sound of steps pounding toward her jerked her around, her breath quickening, her blood pressure zooming. A solid dark mass slammed into her, knocking her keys from her hands. She landed hard on the concrete floor. Pain shot from her rear and her elbow. Her heartbeat accelerated as she struggled to get a breath. A hand yanked her hair, and warm breath caressed her cheek. Oh, God. Did he plan to rape her?

"Get me the money. Tell Franklin to get me my money."

The man let go of her head, which landed with a thud on the concrete. Devon saw stars, and the garage danced around on rollers. The sound of steps running away brought a sense of relief, but she lay there struggling to get her brain to work. What should she do now?

Slowly she reached for the back of her head. A lump. Blood covered her hand when she moved it in front of her face. Her eyes briefly closed, but she couldn't lie here. Phone. She should call the police. What happened to her phone? She rolled to her stomach and struggled to get a knee bent under her body to help her stand. Pain seemed to radiate from all over at once. Her head spun.

What had the guy said? Tell Franklin.... Maybe the best choice didn't involve calling the police. After all, she couldn't describe the guy except to say he was strong.

Slowly she dragged herself upright—well, sort of upright—she leaned against her car. More steps filled the night. She stumbled around the back of her car and crouched there, barely balancing.

"Damn. Where are the lights in this place?"

Devon recognized the voice of the investigator, Brett Townsend. Thank God. "Brett." Her voice squeaked. Take another stab at this. Wouldn't do for him to leave without seeing her. "Brett." Better. Louder.

"What? Who is it?"

"It's me, Devon."

Fast steps brought Brett through the gloom until he appeared not far from her.

"My God. What happened to you?" He set down his brief case and rushed to her side. "Hey, you're bleeding. Did you lose your balance and fall?" He helped her stand.

She grimaced. "No… someone slammed into me and knocked me over. Can you…can you help me find my keys? They're under the car, and I can't reach them. If I have the keys, I can get home"

"Sure." He squatted down then flattened himself on the garage floor and reached under the car. Standing up he brushed off his pants and jacket but kept hold of the keys.

"Your head is bleeding, Devon. You should go to an emergency clinic and have them check you out."

"No. I want to go home. My daughter will be worried. I told her I'd be home fifteen minutes ago."

"Well, let me drive you."

"But my car…"

"I'll pick you up in the morning. We're coming to the same place. But what you should do first is call the police."

"The police? Right." She nibbled her lip. Waiting for the police to come would make her even later to get home to Bailey and her head hurt like the dickens.

"I want to go home…and I accept your kind offer to drive me."

The frown on Brett's face sent her the clear message, in his opinion, she'd decided wrongly about the police.

"Well, you need to send a message to your employees tomorrow about what happened. They need to be put on alert."

"And I'll get the lights fixed asap, too."

"Okay." He nodded, slid a strong arm around her waist. "Let's get you home."

CHAPTER FIVE

Thursday, September 8

Her mom should've been home twenty minutes ago. Bailey had turned the burner way down, but the soup continued to bubble. She stirred the thick broth again and cut off the heat. If Mom didn't show up soon, Bailey would plunk the pot in the fridge. Heating up soup later always made the taste better anyway.

Ever since the divorce was finalized, her mother had worked longer hours. Dad provided child-support, and the company did well. She shouldn't be worrying about money. Maybe it was about being in control, important to her mother. Before long, Bailey expected to get her own car and not need to rely on Mom or Mimi for transportation. Her friends were great, but at some point, you wanted to be able to pay them back.

After Bailey put the lid on the soup and set it in the fridge, she paced to the front of the house. Pushing aside the closed drapes, she drew back. A strange car parked in the driveway. Who could be here this time of night? She peeked out again. Oh, my god. Mom. Bailey open the front door.

"What happened?" Her feet hardly touched the stairs to the sidewalk. "Are you all right? Is that blood?"Bailey's heartbeat kicked up, and she'd almost squealed the last question.

"Yes, sweetie, but no need to worry." Her mother clung to the arm of a tall, well-built blond man. Who was he?

"Bailey, this is Brett Townsend, the new IT guy at work." Her voice quavered.

"Hello, Bailey. We need to get your mom inside. I tried to convince her to go to an emergency clinic, but she refused."

"Be quiet, Brett. I'm all right." Her mother used her "Don't-worry-about-me" tone. On several occasions since the divorce, Devon used that tone to her mother. Bailey's grandmother rolled her eyes like a teenager and went on doing what she'd intended.

"Mom, that's blood trickling down your forehead. You can't be okay." Bailey glanced at the man supporting her mother. "She hates doctors. Follow me." Bailey led them up the stairs to the porch and inside. She closed and locked the door behind them. "Come on. We'll go to her bathroom. She's got first aid stuff there, and blood will be easy to clean up from the tile."

"My ever-practical daughter."

"At least she's still got her sense of humor. Are you able to give her first aid? Fix her head?" She glanced at the man as she settled her mom on a bathroom chair. "I don't do blood well."

"She doesn't. We'll be dealing with her throw-up if she tries to help. I can manage." Devon let go of Brett's arm, attempting to stand on her own, but she swayed and clutched his arm again.

"You can't see this, Devon. Let me clean up the wound first, and we'll tell how bad the gash is. I've have experience with first aid." "Whew. I'll leave her to you then while I get soup on the table."

Her mom and the man both nodded. After one last look, and when he seemed to be competent to care for her, Bailey escaped to the kitchen.

Good grief. What happened? How bad was her mother hurt? Had she been in a car wreck? Had her car been towed? Who's this Brett guy? Good looking for sure, but what's mom doing with an IT guy? Bailey's mind circled around and around. Not a patient person, she wanted to see right this minute her mother was all right. Maybe she shouldn't have left her in the bathroom with a strange man. Geez, what had she been thinking? He could be hurting her right now.

She set a bowl on the table and wheeled around heading to-ward her mother's bedroom, nearly plowing into her and the strange man in the hallway.

"Sorry. I got worried about you being alone with a stranger."

"Understandable. It's been a shock for all of us." Brett helped Devon make the trip to the kitchen and settled her in a chair at the table. "Your mother's been telling me about your culinary skills."

Blair's face turned a light pink color. Brett smiled. Probably a result of her strawberry blonde hair. Not the same shade as her mother's, but the skin tone easily blushed.

"Well, I—"

"Don't be shy, Bailey. You are a good cook. Whatever you prepared for tonight smells wonderful." She leaned back in her chair, not able to hold herself up.

Brett had seen enough of Devon Moore to realize she always had an upright posture.

"Can I do anything to help?"

"Oh, a man who offers to help. Good deal, Mom. You ought to keep this one around." Bailey's laugh filled the room.

"Bailey." A dash of pink splashed across Devon's sheet white cheeks.

"I've got this, Mr.…"

"Townsend, but you can call me Brett." He dropped into a chair at the end of the table close to Devon to be near to help if necessary.

While they ate Blair's thick and savory soup, Devon explained what happened. She appeared to be leaving out something. A pause now and then made him wonder. Humm. Why would she leave out anything? She included the scary part about the lights going out and the man shoving her down. Had she told them all? Maybe she knew more about the missing money than she'd indicated. Hard to believe a wife, all right to be fair an ex-wife, didn't have some idea of what her husband did with the finances.

As practical as her mom claimed her to be, Bailey went to the main point. "Get the lights fixed, Mom, and you need to hire an off-duty cop to be there after dark." She pointed her spoon at her mother. "Or maybe you could come home at a decent time."

"This has been an ongoing argument with us for a while." Devon covered her mouth with her hand to stifle a yawn, but her mouth flew open wide anyway. "Guess I'm heading to bed. Sorry to be such a bad hostess."

"No worries, Mom. I can manage the hostessing duties." Devon nodded. "I know, sweetie." She started to stand, but couldn't pull it off by herself.

"Let me help." Brett moved to her side and supported her. "Staying awake long enough for a bath would help the aches and pains. Do you have a standard pain reliever, Bailey?"

"Yes, I use a lot of OTC stuff because of cheerleading, which is more athletic than people realize."

He nodded. "Let's get you back to your bedroom, Devon. Can you help her get ready for bed, Bailey?"

"Yes. Do you mind waiting around? Maybe help yourself to another bowl of soup."

"No ganging up on me, you two." But Devon's soft voice held little strength to protest much.

Brett nodded. "Sure. And I'll take you up on seconds on the soup."

The excellent soup with rich broth, big chunks of chicken and carrots and potatoes and onions satisfied his hunger. Brett had finished the second bowl by the time Bailey returned to the kitchen.

"How's she doing?" He cared about what Devon's daughter had to say. More than he expected. More than he should.

"She's out like a light. Barely got her undressed and into bed. No way possible for her to stay awake long enough to take a bath. How about some iced tea or coffee?"

"Coffee if you have it."

"Won't take but a couple of minutes."

"What grade are you in, Bailey?"

"I'm a junior, a young junior. Not driving yet. I hate the situation." She set a cup in front of him. "Anything in your coffee?"

"No this is great." He sipped and sighed. "Soup and coffee. What else do you cook so well?"

"A number of things. Mom and I share the chore." Devon put her fork on her plate. "We alternate. She cooks when I'm late, and I cook when she's running late, like tonight."

"Sounds like you've come up with a good plan."

"Tell me more about Mom."

"If I can. Should we compare notes?"

Bailey settled at the table with her cup of coffee. "What happened to Mom tonight?"

"Not a lot more than you heard, but I suspect she didn't tell us everything. Not sure why, a hunch."

"You're not an IT guy, are you?"

"Yes and no." He sipped the strong brew, drew in a breath and let it out. "I can't tell you everything. It's your mother's story to tell, but best to be on alert for anything unusual or not what you're used

43

to seeing."

"Like strange men or strange cars showing up at the house?" She pinned him with a narrowed glance.

He chuckled. "Well, you do have a point. Your mom's car is in the company garage. She shouldn't have driven home by herself."

"How did you show up at Johnny-on-the-spot time? For being only an IT guy you were working late."

"You're right to be leery, Bailey." He leaned forward and reached his inside jacket pocket. Her eyes grew large. "It's okay. I'm getting my ID."

He handed a small leather folder across the table to her. She glanced at what he held, at him, and then she took the card case.

"This lists you as a partner i n Foster Security Company. I thought you were an IT guy. Did you lie to Mom?"

"Devon knows who I am." He took the folder back and returned it to his jacket pocket.

"Is there some problem at her company?"

"Again, your mom's story."

Friday, Sept. 9

Devon limped down the front porch stairs to Brett's car. Would he notice? She couldn't get over how much her body ached. Bailey wanted her to stay home for a day, but she couldn't. Too much to do. Addressing the garage security to make sure her employees were safe took precedence over everything else.

"I can't tell you were run over by a Mac truck." Brett held open the passenger door.

"Gee thanks, I think." She'd taken special care with her makeup this morning, but still better she'd left before her mother came to get Bailey to take her to school. It had never been easy to hide things from eagle eye Miriam. Devon gritted her teeth as she doubled her body to climb into the seat. She had a long day ahead if her pain continued at this rate. She'd taken two Ibuprophen at 6:30. Ten-thirty before she could take more. Seemed a long time away.

"Are you sure you have to go in to work this morning? Even waiting until after lunch would help." Brett competently steered the car down the street and into the traffic on Mockingbird Lane. He probably did everything competently. She was such a long way from competent right now. Her body had deserted her. She dug deep to pull her thoughts together.

"First on my to-do list is to get maintenance to check out the garage lights. Then I'll follow up on Blair's idea to hire an off-duty policeman to cover in the evenings until everyone has left." Paying for the officer might be a trick. Her hands gripped as Brett hit the breaks to let in an idiot not following the signs. Her head hurt, and her hips did too where she'd hit the concrete.

"Let me arrange for your evening security coverage for the garage. That's one task off your plate."

Better not nod. Devon cast her gaze in his direction. "Thanks." She made herself draw in deep breaths and let them out slowly. As soon as she took care of maintenance and got the lights fixed, she'd have to drive home. Her body ached like she had the flu or had been in a car accident. To top it off, despite sleeping like the dead last night, she had no energy.

What should she do about Franklin and the message the attacker left? She didn't want to deal with her ex-husband at all, but what choice did she have in this scary situation? A sigh escaped as she remembered the good years with her husband. They'd been a happy couple with their precious new baby girl. Franklin adored Bailey and helped care for her.

Things changed somewhere along the line. Franklin made some new friends and focused all his attention on making more and more money. He also spent more and more money. At first, he'd been supportive of her cosmetics company then he resented any money she spent on the business as well as the time she spent working there. He became distant, and they grew farther and farther apart.

He refused to go to counseling when she suggested it, and she'd seen how useful her visits with the psychologist had been for her issues.

That had been the last straw. His unwillingness to work on their marriage meant they didn't have a marriage. For all that, the divorce was amicable. She'd left him as an advisor to Bailey-Moore Cosmetics because he was a smart businessman.

"You okay, Devon?" The rumbling words drew her abruptly from her thoughts.

"Yes. Thinking."

"The office is ahead toward the end of the block." She pointed and he wheeled into the parking garage, but couldn't get through the gate.

"You have a card or something?"

"Yeah, sorry. Here." She unsnapped her keys from her purse and handed them to Brett. "It's the little rectangular thingy. I should get one for you while you're here on the job."

After a quick swipe, the bar rose, they entered the garage, and they proceeded to the second floor. He parked near her car. Devon couldn't suppress the shudder racing through her body as she took in the area where she'd been attacked. The lights weren't on, but the sun filtering through the openings cut the dimness.

"Let me help you." Apparently, she'd cut out for a moment. Brett had gotten out and come around to her side of the car. Gathering her strength, she took his hand and clambered from his car.

"Thanks." She held on to his arm as they made their way to the entry into the main offices. If she gave him the wrong idea, she'd clear up any misunderstanding later, but for now, she needed the extra support.

"Hey, Devon. Did you have car trouble last night?" Liz had a worried expression on her face as she greeted them at the entrance. "When I arrived, your car was parked in its regular place, but you weren't here."

"Not exactly car trouble, Liz. Come into my office, and I'll explain." Not relinquishing her hold on Brett, she made her way to her office and sank carefully into her desk chair. "Thanks, Brett. You'll find the off-duty officer for me?"

"What?" Liz's artfully plucked eyebrows rose almost to her hairline.

"Check with Karen about how we'll pay for it."

"You got it. I'll be in touch." Brett gripped her shoulder before heading for the door.

"What happened?" Liz moved closer, her intent clear. She'd stand there until she got her answer.

Devon explained, leaving out the assailant's words.

"Wow!" Liz dropped into the chair in front of the desk. "Who'd have thought we'd have security issues here. What can I do for you? Have you seen a doctor? Are you in pain?"

"Get hold of maintenance." Devon ignored the wash of words from her secretary. "We've got to get the lights working asap. Then I'm drafting a note to the staff about safety issues. For the foreseeable future, no one should leave by themselves."

"You haven't called the police? Why?"

"Frankly, I hurt too much to talk with the police about the event last night and now too much time has gone by...well it's not like there'd be any evidence of anything. A lone man zipped in and out. It was all over and done so fast I didn't have a chance to process the event."

"What did he want? He didn't take your purse or car."

"No, he didn't, Liz. I don't have any answers, that's why I didn't call the police. Probably one of those random happenings. Now, will you get with maintenance about the garage lights?"

"Sure thing." She rose. "Tell me if you need anything else." She slipped through the office door.

Devon dropped her pounding head into her hands. The pain ricocheting like a pinball machine made her stomach queasy. Maybe she should have gone to the emergency clinic…No. She'd be okay. She needed to rest. That's all. As soon as maintenance assured her the lights were working again, the safety note went out to the staff, and Brett had found an off-duty officer for this evening, she'd head home.

Well, this wasn't getting the note written. Devon raised her aching head amazed to see fifteen minutes had gone by. Good grief. She was practically useless. Sliding the key board toward her, she powered up her computer and got to the safety note for the staff. Preparing the brief message didn't take her long. She emailed Liz and asked her to send the attachment out and to post a hard copy by the door to the garage as an extra reminder not to leave alone.

"Hey, Devon," Liz stuck her head around the door without coming in all the way. "Maintenance came right out. They fixed the flipped fuse, and we're good to go."

"Thanks, Liz. I emailed you the safety note for the staff."

"I'll get right on it."

"Liz."

Turning back to Devon. "What can I get you?"

"Will you see if you can find Mr. Towsend? I'd like to talk with him."

"Sure. Need anything else?"

"No thanks." All Devon wanted was to go home and lie down.

She also needed to talk with Franklin, but she needed to be in much better shape before she tackled him. Never go into what could be a tough situation from a position of weakness. And clearly, that's where she was right now.

A tap on the door drew her attention from the troubling question of Franklin.

"Come in." Boy, not her usual strong voice.

"How're you doing?" Brett swung into the room and took a seat in front of her desk.

"Hanging in." With great effort, she stretched a smile across her face. "Were you able to find us some extra security for the evening?"

"Sure did. Name's Lopez. He'll get here at 4:45 and stay until there are no more cars in the garage."

"Great. Thank you, Brett. I couldn't bear any of the staff being attacked."

"Not likely for anyone to return if this was random, though."

He cocked his head at her, apparently not quite believing her story. She should've figured some reason for the attack.

She shook her head and then winced. Not a good choice. "No, not likely, but better safe than sorry as they say."

Brett nodded. "You sure you're not leaving anything out of your story? The guy didn't say anything. Ask you for anything?" He paused. When she didn't respond, he continued. "Odd he didn't take anything, you know?"

"Well, if he'd planned to, he didn't get a chance because you came. Thank you, seems inadequate to express my appreciation for what you did."

"Glad I could be of help."

"Why were you working so late last night? I never thought to ask. Have you found out anything?"

"Karen told me about something she found interesting, but had to get home to her family and didn't have time to follow up, so I stayed."

"Well?"

"Nothing definitive yet, but you may have lost more than Karen first found. It's more like $500,000, with a withdrawal as recently as last week."

Thankfully, she was sitting. Devon's legs shook, and her hands trembled. This was way worse than she imagined. If they couldn't get back the money, this would kill the deal to buy Swanson Cosmetics, and worse than that, paychecks could be in jeopardy. Dear God. Did all of this have something to do with Franklin? She couldn't put off talking to him until she got stronger. She had to get to the bottom of this right now.

"Are you all right, Devon?" Brett asked. His eyebrows crinkled downward into a frown.

"No. No, I'm not all right. I'm going home to rest. You and Karen keep plugging away. Tell me as soon as you get more info."

"You can't drive home, Devon."

She pushed to her feet, resting her hands on the desk. "Oh, I most certainly can and will."

He rose. "Let me take you."

She couldn't do that. She needed her car to go talk with Franklin.

"No, I'm okay. Or I will be when I get home to rest. I'd prefer you continue working here."

Devon awkwardly tugged her purse strap over her head. Using her shoulder, she angled through the door to the garage with Brett hot on her heels still trying to convince her not to drive.

In the end, she won and drove out of the garage for a confrontation with her ex-husband.

CHAPTER SIX

Friday, September 9

Devon steered her car toward Franklin's office, all the time wishing her body didn't ache. She hoped meeting with him in his office where he couldn't easily walk off, increased her chances he'd come clean. Her stomach churned. Her head ached. As if a baseball player swung his bat at her head, aiming for the bleachers. The pounding worsened rather than improved, caused by either the incident last night or her fear of confrontation. The clock in the car read 11:00. Did she take her pills at 10:30? She couldn't remember, but she shouldn't be hurting this much if she'd taken them thirty minutes ago. Maybe she should've gone to the emergency room.

After parking in the office building garage, she reached into her purse for meds and washed the pills down using the small bottle of water she kept with her all the time. She glanced at herself in the driver-side vanity mirror.

Good grief! She looked pitiful. She didn't want to look pitiful. She wanted to look strong and brave. More lipstick always made her feel stronger. After carefully applying the liner and lipstick, she looked again. Needed a bit of rouge. Yes, makeup always made her more comfortable in her own skin. Crawling from the car, she determined to stand straight and tall, no matter how bad she hurt. If she walked slowly, she wouldn't limp.

After stepping into Franklin's office, she stopped at his secretary's desk.

"Hello, Jessica."

The gray-haired Hispanic woman had been with Franklin for many years. She rose. "Ms. Moore, did Mr. Moore expect you?"

"No, but it's important I speak with him. Now. Please tell him."

Something about the way she'd spoken to Jessica got the woman moving fast.

Devon gritted her teeth. She had to hold herself together long enough to get through to Franklin. What was going on with him?

Franklin's secretary returned from the office and held the door open for Devon. "He'll see you now, Ms. Moore."

Devon brushed past the secretary. He damn well would see her. The door closed behind her.

"What's going on, Franklin?" She stood like an oak with roots planted deep. She'd not leave till she got to the bottom of this. The fingers of one hand clutched the strap of her bag like a lifeline.

Franklin pointed his finger at her. "You don't look good. Are you all right?"

"No. I'm not all right. Some goon body-slammed me in the garage last night. My head is pounding like a kettle drum."

"I'm sorry. Do you need to sit down? You don't appear too steady on your feet. Did he take anything?" He stood in front of his desk.

As much as she needed to sit down, giving into her weakness wasn't an option.

One hand gripped the chair as pictures from last night flashed through her brain. "No, he didn't take anything. He gave me a message. A message for you."

"What?" Franklin moved around to the back of his desk.

"He said, *Get me the money. Tell Franklin, to get me my money.*"

"Oh, my God." He sank into his chair and dropped his head into his hands. "Did you call the police?" She understood his muffled words. And his words scared her.

"No. I didn't. But Franklin, tell me what's going on. Talk to me."

"Thank God!"

"Franklin," she moved to in front of his desk, planted her hands on her waist, and her feet shoulder-width apart. "Tell me what's going on. Now. Or I will go to the police."

"Shit."

Devon stepped back, shocked at his language. He never swore or cussed. She used blue language way more than he did.

"You better sit down, Devon. I have to tell you this story in my own way and time."

A slight moan escaped as she lowered herself into the large leather chair. Her heartbeat accelerated. Her hands trembled so she gripped the arms, not wanting to see how much he'd rattled her.

"I'm listening."

"You were always a good listener, Devon. I should've talked to you more often."

No words came because her mind whirled with possibilities. None of them made her optimistic about a good resolution.

"I lost a significant amount of money for a couple of my clients. One of them took exception. Told me I should've known oil prices were about to tank. To cover the loss, I borrowed from your company."

"You borrowed? Did you ask? Have you returned it? That's what borrow means. Franklin, you didn't borrow, you stole. You stole not only from me, but from my employees as well."

So much worse than she'd imagined. Could she turn her ex-husband, her daughter's father, into the police? With a trial and jail? My God.

"I intended to replace the funds before you noticed, but OPEC hasn't cut back on production as expected to drive up the cost of oil. Had they done what we all expected, everything would be fine--the company I'd invested my clients' money in and me. No need to borrow from you. My clients would be fine. We'd all be fine."

"Well, what do we do now? How much do you owe?" Could they borrow money on her house or his business?

"Over half a million."

"Dear God!"

"Yes, it's quite significant, and thus your visitor last night. I'm sorry about that, Devon. Never meant you to get hurt." The fingers of one hand tapped on his desk. The other rolled a marble back and forth. It's what he did when something bothered him.

"So, what are you going to do?"

"Maybe it's time for a trip to the Caymans. Remember? We went there for our honeymoon."

Devon's heart ached. Those were good times. Special times. Their room number, a combination of their birthdays. They took the numbers to be a good omen for many years of happiness. Well, they got more years of happiness than many did.

"Can you beef up security around your business and the house for a while, until I get this settled?"

"I've already added an off-duty police officer. He'll be there from 4:30 until everyone is gone." She scooted forward on the chair. "Could we be in danger at the house?" Her stomach clenched with fear for her family.

"I don't know, Devon." His face looked haggard like he was lost. "Bailey." She shot from her chair and wobbled across his office with awkward steps. "Oh, my God. How can I keep her safe?"

"I'm sorry, Devon. I never meant for you to be involved."

"Not involved?" She stopped and stared at the man who'd been her husband. "You stole from my company! I'm involved."

Franklin didn't say anything, but his face turned gray. He always wanted to appear to be in charge and on top of things. This must be killing him. But she had a responsibility to keep Bailey and her parents and her company safe.

"Do you have a plan for making up the money, other than stealing from my company?"

"I've got some money in the Caymans that could keep them off me."

"In the Caymans? When did you set up an account there?" Each question made her head pound more. How could they manage this god-awful situation? Regardless how much she disliked this, the situation involved her.

"I started squirreling away a couple of years ago. Keeping funds from being taxed, you know."

"Why didn't you use the Cayman money first, Franklin, rather than taking from my company?"

"Th is was only supposed to be for a short time, D evon. I had good advice OPEC planned to cut production. Th e company would make up the loss, and I could replace your funds before you ever noticed. I'm sorry you got hurt."

"I'm sorry you found yourself in this situation. However, Franklin, you need to understand if they come after my parents, Bailey, or me, I will call the police. I'm giving you a short time to find a way to fix this. I won't let us live like this with a threat over our heads."

Friday, September 16

Franklin paced his office. A week had passed since Devon had first confronted him about the money. Her behavior took him totally by surprise. So unlike her to confront about anything. She'd been hacked at him without realizing exactly how much he'd siphoned from the company. If she'd known, she'd have probably gone directly to the police. And scared. She'd been scared. A smart woman. Losing the money scared him, too. Never occurred to him Henry Logan would physically threaten him, certainly not through Devon. Franklin shook his head at how out of control everything had become. He'd made a bad investment and then made more bad decisions in trying to fix the situation.

Pulling into the parking area at the country club, he determined to get some sort of deal worked out with Henry, which didn't include accessing the funds in the Caymans. Franklin had put away money to make sure Bailey had plenty for college, wherever she wanted to go. Sure, Devon's business and his had been doing okay, but better safe than sorry. Because he and Devon had fallen out didn't mean he didn't love his daughter.

"Good afternoon, Mr. Moore." The maître 'D welcomed him into the Men's Grill. No women allowed. The smell of grilled meet and cigar smoke greeted him.

"I'm meeting Mr. Logan. Is he here yet?"

"No, sir. How about your regular table by the windows? It's available."

"Yes, thanks." Franklin settled himself in his chair looking out on the golf course greens. He loved this club and all the membership stood for. He'd arrived. He was somebody people looked up to. He refused to let go the trappings of wealth and importance he'd worked so hard to achieve. He wouldn't let Logan win.

"Can I get you anything, Mr. Moore?" The waitperson had come to the table while he'd been mulling his options.

"Maker's Mark, neat."

"I'll be right back with your drink."

Franklin drummed his fingers on the table. An idea had popped into his head...absurd and scaring him. If Logan didn't respond positively to Franklin's idea of a delayed payout, then he'd be forced to give more consideration to this bizarre idea.

"Here you go, sir." The server in a green vest with gold accents set Franklin's drink on the table.

"Thanks. Bring another right away." He gulped back the drink and shook his head at the burn down his throat. He should've sipped, but needed the courage for the coming meeting.

Franklin twisted the glass around and around on the table. He had to convince Logan to give him more time.

"You got here before me." The wiry man in the tailored suit pulled out a chair, settled himself, arranging his long legs out in front of him.

"Yes, for once. How are you, Hank?" Better to be less formal and use a friendlier tone. "You want a drink?" The young man arrived with Franklin's second and eyed Logan to see if he wanted anything.

"Sir?"

"Maker's Mark."

"Yes, sir."

The waiter disappeared. Hank Logan stared at Franklin, and he began to sweat. Better to take charge. Franklin leaned back in his chair like he didn't have a care in the world. He could act this part and convince Logan to give him more time.

"I've got a proposition for you, Hank."

"I don't want a proposition, Franklin. I want all my money. And I want the money sooner rather than later."

Crap. He's playing hardball.

The waiter returned with Logan's drink. "We won't need to see you for a while." Logan didn't make eye contact with the server, dismissing him as a nobody.

He took a sip of the booze and set the glass on the table. "How do you plan to get me my money?"

"Hank, I've explained about OPEC. They were supposed to cut

production, which would've jacked up the price of oil. We'd have made back what we lost. And the bucks would've been rolling in fast."

"Not my problem, Franklin. I don't care what hoops you jump through to get my money. Just so long as in the end you return my money." Logan steepled his hands and leaned across the table. "Didn't you get my message?"

Franklin jerked and spilled his drink on the glossy table. Logan must be talking about what happened to Devon. His fingers tightened on the glass. He nodded.

"Unless you want something like what happened to your wife to happen to your daughter, you'll do whatever is necessary to get me my money. You don't have much time." The man took the last swig of his drink, rose, and stalked from the dark wood paneled room.

Franklin dragged a hand down his face. What options did he have? Could he kill Logan? His fingers drummed on the rich wood table. He wouldn't know how to begin. He could research the specifics on the internet, or he could hire someone to kill the greedy bastard, only he didn't have the money to do that.

"Mr. Moore, do you care for another drink or are you ready to order lunch?" The waitperson picked up Logan's glass and Franklin's, setting them on a tray.

"Yes. Bring me another whiskey and a burger and fries." His fingers clamped on the arms of the chair as he considered another option. Not one he'd have ever considered before. Extreme times demanded extreme actions.

CHAPTER SEVEN

Monday, September 19

Brett closed out the files on his computer in the office Devon had set up for him in her company. He and Karen had finished all the checks they could run. The evidence seemed to support the contention Devon's ex had stolen a significant amount of money from his ex-wife's company. The question now, what was she willing to do? Talking to the police seemed to be the best bet. They had the evidence to get a conviction.

But Bailey's face popped into Brett's mind. A neat young woman who'd apparently handled the divorce well. The question now was, how would she react to her father being arrested, tried. and maybe sent to jail?

Brett didn't envy the tough decision ahead for Devon. She lived in a big expensive house in her daughter's school district. Keeping Bailey in her school would be important to Devon. What about moving and starting over? He shook his head, picked up his phone, keying in her name in his favorites folder. His information would help her make make her decision.

"Hello, Devon." She'd answered on the first ring.

"Brett. How are you? Any more info for me?"

"Yep. Are you at home or running errands? I didn't see you in your office."

"I'm home. Bailey's at cheerleading and not due home for another hour. Can you stop by?"

"Yeah. Probably easier for you to hear this without Bailey around. Be there in fifteen minutes." He disconnected, drew in a deep breath, before picking up his car keys and heading to the garage. He nodded to the off-duty policeman who'd come on at 4:30, liking the sense of security. Too bad Devon had to take those steps when her office was in an otherwise safe part of town.

Fifteen minutes later, Brett entered Devon's circular driveway. She stepped through the front door and again, he wondered what had made her ex-husband turn away from this beautiful woman. Standing on the porch, she twisted her hands in a wringing motion, her eyes crinkled, and her brows turned down. Clearly worried.

He left his SUV and carrying his briefcase he walked up the stairs.

"Thanks for coming. I've got coffee. Okay with you?"

"Never say no to coffee." Brett followed her into the high-end kitchen with all stainless-steel appliances, and a large island with a sink facing a sitting area. Devon filled two mugs.

"You take the brew straight if I remember right."

"You do indeed." He took a sip. Hot and strong exactly the way he liked it. He liked that about her—she seemed to take note of people's preferences.

"Can we sit here?" She indicated the island.

"As good as any." He set his cup on the counter and his case on the empty stool next to him before holding a stool for her. He settled himself onto one right next to her.

She folded her hands around the mug. "So, what do you have?" She glanced at him and away as if she really didn't want to know. And she probably didn't want to hear what he had to tell her.

He laid out papers on the counter in front of her. Proof backing up his words.

Devon's gaze fell to the papers and then seemed to glaze over. She flipped aside the papers with her fingers. "Use your words. I can't take in all the figures. They make my head hurt."

He sighed. "Okay. Here's the bottom line. Your ex-husband, Franklin Moore, has siphoned money from your company using your business credit card to take out cash. He's been taking money over six months and has embezzled $500,000."

Devon sat in her kitchen, her fingers squeezing the cup in front of her. She couldn't bring herself to meet Brett's gaze. How embarrassing. What kind of woman had a husband who stole from her? What must Brett's opinion of her be for being oblivious about something so important? He'd probably assume she must know, but she didn't. Oh, my gosh, what could she tell Bailey?

A tear slipped out of one eye and trickled down her cheek.

"Ah, Devon." Brett leaned toward her and caught the tear.

"I'm stupid." Still, she couldn't meet his gaze and faced away.

He reached out and faced her toward him. She let him, not having the will to take any action on her own.

"Not stupid. Maybe too trusting. Maybe too expecting of folks to be honest and caring like you are." He tipped up her chin and wiped a tear falling from her other eye. "You'll get through this. You're a strong woman."

"Thanks, but it's hard to believe right now." She fought the tremble in her lips. "Did you figure out what he did with the money?"

"Looks like he lived on some of it. May have sent some to an account in the Caymans. Some may have gone into a client or two's accounts."

She shook her head. "I can't believe any of this."

"Devon." Brett took one of her hands in his.

She looked at their clasped hands then at him.

"Did you leave out anything in the story about the guy who knocked you down in the garage?"

She tried to remove her hand, but he hung on. "Why do you ask?"

"It was a strange incident, Devon. For some random person to attack you in your own garage and not take anything? It's odd."

She sighed. "Guess your knowing doesn't matter now. The fact is Franklin stole from me. After the guy knocked me down, he said tell Franklin he wanted his money. I guessed Franklin owed him money. I didn't talk to the police because I was certain Franklin could explain everything. If we could handle the situation privately, that would be better for everyone. Especially Bailey."

She yanked her hand from his, "Oh, my gosh!" and leaped from the stool and paced around the kitchen island. "What will I tell Bailey? She loves her father. Franklin was a better father than a husband."

"She didn't blame you for the divorce?"

"At first maybe a little, but she's a smart girl, and she realized her father and I hadn't been happy for quite a while. We worked hard to make sure she understood we both still loved her, just not each other."

"So now for the hard question. What do you want to do? Go to the police? I've done enough of these types of investigations to recognize we've got enough evidence to have him arrested. He will stand trial. Juries are never a sure thing, but I believe he'd be convicted."

Devon stopped moving and faced him from the other side of the island. "I don't want to lose my company, so I've got to get the money back. I must be sure we'll be safe. I can't imagine

Franklin would do anything to put Bailey in danger. But…"

"What can I do for you?" Brett leaned across the bar toward her. "Come with me to talk with Franklin. Bring your papers." She gestured to the ones on the table. "He likes figures and numbers, and he'll understand we've got him. I need him to fix this problem. I can't stand the idea of Bailey finding out."

"Finding out what, Mom? Are you okay?" Bailey stood in the doorway.

Devon backed up a step. Her gaze flew to Brett then to her daughter. "I... uh…I'm having some problems at the company. Th at's why I invited Brett."

Bailey dropped her bag on the stool Devon had sat in earlier. "So, what's up?"

Franklin took the street leading to the country club for one more meeting with Henry Logan. His dear friend Hank. He chuckled low in his throat. What a crock. He picked up the drink in the cup hold-er of his Mercedes. Th e whiskey burned his throat. He'd take the Dutch courage to do what needed to be done. Before climbing out, he reached into the glove compartment and hefted the gun, stuffing the revolver in the waistband of his pants. He left the car in the lot and made his way through the tennis area. Grunts, oofs, the thump of rackets hitting balls, and skidding sounds of feet on the court met his ears. Much better time of year to play the game than the dead of summer, but the players wiped sweat from their brows, despite the breeze ruffling the tree leaves. Fall had yet to arrive in Texas.

He made his way to the pool, closed for the season, which made an excellent spot for a quiet talk. Th e only occupant of the area, a gray-haired man in stylish sports shirt and slacks bearing a sharp crease, sat at a table with a drink before him. Either he'd brought the glass outside with him, or he was such an important member of the club the staff made sure he got what he wanted.

"Wasn't sure you'd come, Franklin."

"What makes you say that, Hank?"

"Oh, I don't know, maybe because you're in big trouble without enough cash to cover your obligations. Obligations some people would run out on."

"I've had a few setbacks, Hank, but nothing I can't manage."

"Are you telling me, you've got my money now?"

"Not exactly."

Hank huffed out a breath. "Apparently, you don't care for your ex-wife."

"What are you talking about?"

"Did your pretty redhead get over her little incident in the garage? We can make another visit if you'd like, but then again, maybe because she's your ex, she doesn't matter. I've always heard you talk highly of your daughter. Don't you care for her either?"

"You're threatening my daughter?"

"Just saying stuff happens to teenagers. They aren't always as careful as they should be."

Franklin struggled to get his breath. He'd never shot a person before, but he gripped his hands together in fists to keep from pulling out the gun and shooting Hank Logan in the chest as he sat there right now. Not a good idea. As much as he wanted to, the pool area while deserted, seemed too public.

"You'll get your money, Hank, but I…I need a little more time."

"That's what you said last time, and I still don't have my money. And Franklin, I'm tired as hell of waiting. Whatever happens is on you." Henry Logan rose, shoved in his chair close to the table, patted the back once, and walked away.

Franklin swiveled his head looking everywhere, expecting to see Logan's hired thugs coming out of the bushes to drag him off. Relief swept through him when only the waiter appeared.

"Can I get you anything?"

"Whiskey, neat. In fact, leave the bottle."

The server nodded his head and walked away.

So now what? Franklin didn't have the money. He still had the fund in the Caymans, but he wanted to keep that for Bailey. He had to do something to keep her and her mother safe. The waiter returned with his bottle and the glass. "Thanks."

The pool lights came on as did some of the grounds lights. This was a fancy club; all the old-time wealthy folks from Dallas were members. He had lots of fond memories of bringing Devon here during the early years, showing off his beautiful wife. Later when Bailey came along, she became one of the popular kids, excelling on the swim team. Her gorgeous strawberry blonde hair made her a standout.

He threw back a shot and poured himself another. When had his life all gone south? Devon got caught up with her company. Bailey got busy with friends and school activities. They stopped doing things as a family about the same time he'd become involved with Henry Logan and money became more important than anything in his life.

He'd hate anything happening to Bailey or Devon for that matter. The only achievement he could claim up to now was to resist the temptation of dipping into Bailey's college fund. He was glad he'd squirreled away so much in the account. He needed to make this problem go away before he gave in and took his daughter's college money, too. He needed to be a man. If he were gone, he'd force Logan to eat his losses, and he'd leave them alone. Yeah. Neither Devon nor Bailey had Logan's money, which was flat gone, lost down the speculative drain of a gas well. Logan would have to leave them alone. He'd have no reason to go after them.

What about the funds in the Caymans? He'd have to figure out a way for Bailey to get that. Devon didn't realize he'd moved the money in Blair's college fund there. He finished off a drink and poured an-other. How could he get the information to them? Once he figured that out, he'd leave. He was determined to find a way to keep his family safe.

Bailey stared at her mother and the handsome blond man. Brett Townsend, the IT guy who worked for a security company. What the heck was going on? "So, what are you afraid for me to find out, Mom?"

"How did cheerleading practice go, Bailey?"

"What? You think I'm easily sidetracked? What's going on at your company? I'm a big girl, and I can hear the truth. I'm sure the reality won't be as bad as I'll imagine if you don't tell me." She crossed one arm over the other. Her mother would recognize her determination from earlier confrontations.

Devon looked at Brett then at Bailey. "Okay, sweetie." She reached out her hand, and Bailey took hold of it. "Come sit down."

Well, maybe this was more serious than she'd first thought. Her mother's eyes looked pinched around the corners. They never looked like that. Bailey enjoyed people going on about her mother's beauty. If she ended up being half as pretty, she'd be a happy camper.

"We've had a bit of a set back at the company. We've lost some money."

"Lost money? As in sales got recorded wrong?" She looked from her mother to Brett.

"Sort of, honey." Her mother glanced at Brett. "He discovered we've got some money missing. A loss we can't account for."

Bailey cast her gaze between the two adults. Brett didn't say any-thing, but his expression seemed sad.

"What exactly are you saying, Mom?"

Devon licked her lips. "It appears someone borrowed money from the company. I expect them to return it, but for now, we'll be a little strapped for cash."

"What do Mimi and Granddad say about this?"

Devon closed her eyes. "I haven't told them yet, but I will."

"What's the bottom line? Do I need to stop shopping? Oh, gosh. Do I need to cancel my plans to go to the cheerleading tournament in Nashville in December if the team gets the invitation? Is college off the table?"

Her mother chuckled. "My bottom-line daughter. Let's start with cutting back on the shopping. Hopefully, we'll have the problem worked out before you have to take either of those other actions."

"So, we could take those steps?"

"I'd hope not, but I want you to be aware of the possibilities."

"Okay. Thanks for treating me like an adult, Mom."

Devon hugged Bailey, and her daughter slung her backpack on one shoulder and headed out of the kitchen. "See you in the morning, Mom. Night, Mr. Townsend."

"Good night, sweetie." Devon's heart swelled and ached at the same time.

"Good night, Bailey." Brett leaned back in his chair, "Boy, she is one mature young lady."

"Yeah, she is. I couldn't be prouder."

"You didn't say anything to her about her father."

"I'm still hoping I won't have to. Oh, Brett, what can I do?" Devon dropped her head onto her arms on the counter. Brett's hand fell on her shoulder. He'd moved next to her. His heat suffused her body and brought comfort. Something else, too, perhaps.

"It will work out, Devon. What's the worst that can happen?"

She sat up and faced him. "Oh, a number of things I guess." She swiped at her eyes and brushed her hair back from her face. "I lose my company because Franklin can't make up the money. Bailey finds out her father is a thief. The bad guys come after Bailey or me again." She squared her shoulders and clenched her hands into fists. "I'll do anything to keep her safe and her relationship with her father intact."

"Those may be mutually exclusive. The only way to keep her safe may be to file charges against her father."

"Surely not. There must be some other way."

"Well, before Bailey came in, you'd asked me to go with you to visit Franklin. Let's start there. Maybe when he sees the evidence, he'll figure out how to make the missing money right."

Devon drew in and let out a long breath, and then she nodded. "Let's start there. The police are the last resort."

"Shall we hit up Franklin tomorrow morning?"

"Yes, sooner is better than later. The longer this all drags on, the crazier I'll get and the more chance Bailey will find out about her father."

"I'll pick you up here at 9:45, okay?"

Devon nodded. "Yes, thanks, Brett. I appreciate your support." She took his hand and didn't let go as they walked toward the front of the house.

"Good night, Devon. We'll get this worked out." He leaned in, briefly kissed her on the cheek, and walked through the front door.

Devon raised her hand to the spot Brett had kissed. What had he been thinking? Probably didn't mean anything. He'd only kissed her on the cheek. Did she want the kiss to mean something? Perhaps she did. Devon locked the front door, set the alarm, and wandered into to her room on the ground floor. The room she'd moved into when her marriage fell apart. A room in which she now pictured Brett Townsend. Good grief. She'd taken leave of her senses.

CHAPTER EIGHT

Monday, September 19

The chainsaw buzzing through his head made Franklin nearly puke. He must've passed out sitting by the pool. The sunrise brought pain to his eyes but also jerked him from his whiskey-induced sleep. He stumbled to his car and made his way to his condo, grateful no one from the club had found him. Bad enough he'd lost his shirt in the downturn of oil prices, he couldn't stand to look like a bum, too.

After a shower and several Alka-Seltzers, he still felt like crap. But not for much longer. He'd figured out what to do. He sat down at his computer and typed a letter to Devon and one to his daughter. Blair's was the tough one. He wanted to make sure she knew he wasn't deserting her. He'd do anything to keep her safe. This was the only way. He put the letters in an envelope addressed to Miriam Bailey, Devon's mother. She'd prepare Devon and Bailey before they read them. With him out of the way, there'd be no reason for Logan to come after them. Then whenever OPEC limited production like they'd been supposed to do three months ago, Logan's wells would start pumping again and he'd get his money back. Franklin walked downstairs and dropped the envelope into the mailbox box on the street. Then he walked back to his car and pulled it out of the garage.

After driving around for an hour, he stopped at a liquor store and bought a bottle of his favorite whiskey. Might as well go out feeling good. He drove to the wooded area bordering the country club. From his pocket, he removed his wallet, which held pictures of the family. He fingered a special one of Bailey he'd taken in the back yard. The sun sparkled and shimmered off her hair. Sighing, he put away the pictures. She was the one accomplishment he was proud of.

He finished half the bottle of Whiskey before stumbling from the car. No reason to ruin his beautiful Mercedes. He tugged the gun from his waistband. His insides curdled. Could he do this? He'd read if you held the gun in the right place, you wouldn't feel a thing. And how else could he protect Bailey and Devon? He'd racked his brain for any other way to protect his daughter, but nothing. He had nothing. He was out of options. Saddened, but determined , he drank one time more from the bottle, put the barrel of the gun in his mouth and....

CHAPTER NINE

Tuesday, September 20

Brett entered the circular driveway in front of Devon's stately home, kicking himself every which way from Sunday. What had he been thinking last night to kiss her on the cheek? How lame. If he was going to kiss the woman, he should've kissed her on the lips. Well, it happened, and if he got the chance again, he'd kiss her like a real man. Except he shouldn't be thinking about a client this way. Besides, for all he knew, she could be involved in some way with the money disappearing.

He hadn't found any evidence of her involvement yet, but why else would she be so damned determined to protect her ex-husband. Odd. Most exes were ready to drill their former partner. He needed to keep his distance. If he could.

He climbed out of his car and trudged up the stairs to the columned porch. Before he rang the bell, the door swung open.

"Good morning, Brett."

There she stood, her glorious red hair swinging around her shoulders. She wore a white silk blouse, revealing a hint of cleavage, black slacks, and ankle boots. Slipping her arms in the sleeves of a blue-green jacket, Devon closed the door, turning the key in the lock.

"I hope I didn't keep you waiting."

"You didn't. Let's go."

Brett followed her down the stairs and opened the car door for her. She scooted into the passenger seat, apparently having recovered from the encounter in the garage. He caught a scent of vanilla maybe. He needed not to notice. She seemed eager to get this settled. Guess he'd withhold judgment. "Should you call your ex?"

"No, let's utilize the element of surprise." Her mouth formed a straight line.

"Where should we start?" Brett buckled the seat belt.

"His condo. If he's not there, we'll go to his office."

He didn't say anything as they made their way to Franklin's condo. She limited her comments to giving directions to the gated community. Lush greenery filled islands between buildings all with garages under the units.

Devon glanced at him. "I have the code for when I pick up Bailey. She hasn't been staying with him much this year, but the first year we were separated, she went every other weekend. Sometimes, Franklin would drop her at my house and sometimes, I'd pick her up here." She pointed to the right. "His condo is around this way. It's number 211."

Brett found a visitor slot near Franklin's condo. He got out and walked around as she wedged open the car door. He reached out his hand, which she took. He wanted to hold on, but let go when she dropped his. She led the way to the front and rang the bell. She rang again. Brett banged on the door. Still no answer.

Devon huffed out a sign. "I guess we'll have to find him at his work. I wish we'd intercepted him here. More private. Oh, well." She shrugged. "Let's go." She plodded toward his car, her lips in the firm straight line he'd noticed before.

Brett inserted the key and started the engine, driving out through the gate. "You'd still rather not call?"

"No. I'm sure we'll find him at work. You know where his office is?"

"Yes. Take us about twenty minutes from here."

"Not bad for Dallas." Her fingers twisted the chain strap of her purse.

"That's true."

"Do you live near the security company?"

That's a good sign if she's interested in where he lived.

"I'm lucky. My house is east of the North Tollway and south of Mockingbird. On a good day, I'm at work at Foster Security in only fifteen minutes.

"You have a house? Not a condo?"

"Yeah. I live in what had been my aunt's house. She and her brother lived there for fifty years. It's a small, red brick bungalow. The whole thing would easily fit inside your house, but I like like the family continuity."

"I like that, too, Brett. Do you have any other family?"

"My father was in the Air Force, and we moved around a lot. Ten different places before I graduated from college."

"Oh, my."

"It wasn't all bad because I have an older & younger brother. We were a team."

"What about your parents? Where do they live?"

He gritted his teeth before answering. "They were killed in a gangland killing. Wrong place at the wrong time."

"I'm sorry, Brett." She rested her hand on his arm. Her tone of voice showed sincere concern for his loss and brought comfort.

He nodded. "Thanks. They died a long time ago."

"Do your brothers live here?" She removed her hand and

73

brushed her hair back. He wished she'd left it on his arm.

"My older brother Jim lives in Tampa, Florida. He's got his own security company. Our younger brother Teddy lives in Houston and works for an energy company. I've tried living in both places, but the humidity and sameness of the temperatures make me nuts. I like seasons, even as crazy as the ones we have here in Dallas."

She chuckled. He liked the way her eyes crinkled when she laughed.

"You're right about that. We can have all the seasons in one week. How did you end up in Dallas?"

"My dad was stationed for several years at Carswell Air Force Base before the name change to the Naval Air Station Fort Worth Joint Reserve Base. Quite a mouthful."

She chuckled. "Indeed."

"We visited Dallas for Cowboy games. After trying Tampa and Houston, I visited Dallas and Fort Worth, which is nice, but a bit too laid back for me."

"It definitely has a small-town feel. Addie loves living there."

"Yeah. Mike Riley does, too."

"Guess all kinds of places for all kinds of people. Franklin's building is up ahead. We can park in the garage."

Brett helped her from the car and rested his hand on Devon's lower back as they made their way into the office building. "Which floor?"

"Twelve. Franklin always wanted to be higher in the building, but despite handling a lot of money, his company doesn't have many employees, and he's tight with a buck. He couldn't justify the higher rents for the higher floors."

Brett tapped the button, and after the doors opened, they stepped into an empty elevator whose burnished walls reflected them. If he'd worn a tie, he'd have checked if it hung straight. They glanced at each other once, but then stared at the numbers. The ping announced the floor, the door glided open without a sound, and they stepped out.

"This way." Devon led him to the right and to glass doors with engraved words. *Franklin Moore, Investments.*

"Nice." Brett opened the door for her. They entered a reception area with comfortable looking dark leather chairs. An older Hispanic woman sat behind a large desk.

"Good morning, Jessica." Devon addressed the secretary/receptionist.

"Ms. Moore. Are you looking for Mr. Moore?"

"Yes. Can you tell him I'm here? This is Brett Townsend. Jessica Lopez."

She nodded. "Well, I'd be happy to, but Mr. Moore hasn't come in yet."

"Oh?" She glanced at Brett, her eyebrows turning down.

"Mr. Moore had an early meeting this morning, too, Ms. Moore. I canceled when he didn't get here. He's never shown up. He's not answering his phone, either."

"Unusual." Devon cut a glance at Brett.

"It seemed so to me." Jessica nodded agreement.

"If you hear from him, ask him to call me, please."

"Certainly."

Devon sipped her iced tea at the Deli near her office. When Brett mentioned lunch, this place popped in her mind first. Lots of healthy salads for her, but filling food for him. They hadn't talked on the ride from Franklin's office. Devon's mind whirled with possibilities.

"Could something have happened to him?" She set down her glass.

Brett gestured to give him a second. He had taken a large bite of an enormous Ruben sandwich and couldn't answer. He took a swallow of his soft drink and wiped his mouth with his napkin.

"Damn, this is one great sandwich. How come I've never known about this Deli before?"

She smiled. "Can't imagine. The store's been here about 40 years. What about Franklin? Is he okay?"

He nodded. "Probably. Yes, the guy who he owes money to came after you, but it makes no sense for them to go after Franklin. They'd eliminate the possibility of ever getting their money."

"That's oddly comforting." She toyed with her salad, using her fork to move the bits of lettuce around. "I haven't loved Franklin for a long time, Brett, but he's Bailey's father, and I wouldn't want anything to happen to him. And she would be hurt."

"I understand why you haven't already called the police, but I believe you should."

"That's a last resort kind of thing. If he'd just give me my money back, I'd be happy."

"Understandable. How long can you manage without it?"

"Three months is the max before I'll have to start laying off employees. Instead of buying Swanson Cosmetics business, I could be selling mine." She shuddered. "I'm not sure if I can survive the loss. I've put my life into building the company. I believe in quality skin care and how it can improve a woman's self-esteem. I've seen how much of a difference the right skin care regime can make in many women's lives."

"Can you keep your house?"

"No, probably not. We could move in with my parents for a while. They'd welcome us and, they don't live too far from Blair's school. Gosh, I hope I can keep her there until she graduates."

Brett took her hand, rubbing comforting circles on the back. "Don't borrow trouble. You may not be forced to do that."

She squeezed his hand. "Hope not. I hate feeling stupid. I like to be in control. And I'm not now. Why didn't I take his name off the company's credit card? Or pay more attention to the stupid printouts. I should've caught this before we found ourselves in such a bad situation. Karen feels just awful that it all got by her."

"I hate to see you beating yourself up over this. Sometimes bad things happen. No one's fault, Devon."

"Thanks." She removed her hand from his. Not good to depend on him. He had another life, probably a woman friend. Yeah, he'd kissed her last night, but just on the cheek. More like a brotherly kiss. She tamped down the feeling of disappointment. What did she really know about him?

He understood numbers. Karen raved about his quickness in grasping the intricacies of their system. He was a friend of Mike Riley. Addie wouldn't let Mike steer her wrong. Devon let out a long breath and straightened in the booth. Brett had to be one of the good guys. "I need to go back home and pick up my car and head back to work."

"Well, I've got to return to your company, too. Pick up and pack up. I'll drop you at your house, you can get your car, and I'll follow you to the office."

"Thank you."

"I'm almost finished with this, and we'll take off." He went back to his sandwich making short work of it.

Brett threw dollars down on the table, stood, and held her chair for her. She liked the way he rested his hand on the small of her back. Her father walked with her mother that way. Not something Franklin ever did.

After a short drive in companionable quiet, she climbed out of his SUV and walked through her house then to the garage. Brett waited for her while she backed out, and he followed to her office building. After parking in the garage, they parted company, Brett going into the office he'd been using and Devon into hers. She called Liz and Karen to come see her. Not a conversation she wanted to have, but she couldn't put it off any longer.

"Hey, Liz, Karen. Close the door and come take a seat." Devon perched on the edge of her desk. Her staff members she considered friends settled into the chairs in front of her desk.

"What's up?" Karen asked.

"Some of this you're aware of, Karen, but Liz you aren't. My ex-husband has," she paused clenching her jaw, "borrowed money from the company. I'm not sure when or if he'll be able to replace it."

"Oh, Devon. I'm sorry. How much is it?" Liz leaned forward in her chair.

"$500,000." Sounded to Devon like she'd shouted the number. Such a lot of money.

"Wow!" Liz looked at Karen. "This is bad, isn't it?"

Karen nodded. "Yep." She leaned toward Devon. "What do you plan to do next?"

"I'm starting by telling both of you. You're as close to our employees as is anyone. I may have to let people go. If we come to that point, I need input from you about who we'll hurt the least." Devon clenched her hands at her waist. Her stomach tightened into a knot. She was afraid she'd be sick, and she hadn't done anything yet, only considered the possibility. Hopefully, she wouldn't have to take that step.

"Give me some time to see if I can find areas we can cut our expenses before we start cutting employees, Devon."

"Thanks, Karen, but we're personnel heavy."

"And we have this building. You could sell it and get a chunk of money. It would probably raise enough to carry us through tough times." Karen offered another cost cutting suggestion.

Devon rose, crossed behind her desk, and looked out the windows. "I started the business in a small store front. We could go back to that."

"Let's see how much inventory we have on hand. Possibly we can shut down for a period to save money."

"Not a benefit to our employees."

"If you sell the building," Karen tapped her fingers on the arm of the chair, "we'll have enough money to continue paying employees at least a partial salary while you search for another, smaller location."

"Those are all good ideas, Karen."

"Your employees love you and working here." Liz always the upbeat member of her staff.

Devon whirled from the window to face them. A ray of hope shooting through her.

"I bet they'll be willing to take a small cut," Liz volunteered.

"Grateful to hear, Liz. Thanks. I'll work on a memo asking everyone to come to a meeting later this week for some announcements. Maybe by then, we'll have something concrete to offer them. Uncertainty kills morale."

"You don't think Franklin will return the money?" Liz asked.

Devon shook her head. "I don't know, doesn't seem likely at this point. We need to be prepared for the worst. Please, let's keep this from the rest of the staff until I have something concrete to tell them. One last thing, let's keep Franklin's involvement out of it, too. Th at will narrow the chances of Bailey finding out about her father."

The two women looked at each other and then at her before nodding.

"I like your idea of selling the building and finding something smaller, Karen. I'll drive around to see if I can find any likely properties. If we must do this, I'll get a realtor, but right now I need to take action."

"Sounds good, Devon. Hang in there. We'll get through this." Devon took comfort in Liz's positive attitude. "Thanks. We'll talk later."

She hefted her large purse to her shoulder and walked to the garage. Looking for new locations provided a welcome escape.

Two hours later, she walked back into her business, a page filled with likely property possibilities for her company, pleased and not as negative as she'd been before leaving.

Devon plunked her purse into the drawer in the credenza behind her desk and settled into her chair. Liz knocked once before sticking her head around the door.

"Devon, sorry to interrupt you after you just returned, but there are some police detectives to see you." She almost whispered the words. "Can you see them?"

"Of course." Devon stood.

Liz held open the door for two plainclothes detectives to enter.

"Mrs. Moore?" A heavy-set man in a rumbled sports jacket stepped into the office followed by a tall, wiry guy in a gray suit.

"Yes, I'm Devon Moore."

"I'm Detective Spenser and my partner, Detective Sanchez." The first man looked to be in his fifties, the second in his late thirties.

Liz closed the door behind them as she left.

"What can I do for you?" Devon looked between the two men.

They glanced at each other, and then Spenser said, "I'm sorry to inform you your ex-husband, Franklin Moore was found dead earlier today."

Devon's legs literally gave out, and she sank into her chair. "What? That can't be." And yet, she hadn't been able to find him this morning when she and Brett went to his condo and office. Hadn't she wondered then if he'd been all right?

"Ma'am, we believe he may have taken his own life. Can you suggest any reason he'd have done that?"

"Oh, dear God." Devon dropped her head into her hands. Tears filled her eyes. She brushed them away as her stomach tightened into painful knots. What could she say? If she mentioned the stolen money, then Bailey would find out. Better not to mention her company's missing money or anything about him owing money to one of his clients. She raised her head, wiping her eyes with a tissue she took from the box on the corner of her desk.

"Are you sure he killed himself?" A shudder shook her body at the idea. Imagining the pain engulfing a person enough to cause them to take that final step made her nauseated.

More likely, the client had killed him, but Brett said that didn't make sense if they wanted their money back.

"We won't know for certain until after the autopsy, but that's what appears to have happened."

"Where did you find him?" Was she grizzly to ask?

"A country club worker found him on the edge of the club grounds. You're unaware of any reason he'd take his life?"

Devon sat straighter and curled her hands together in her lap. Decision made. "No, Detective, I'm not. Our divorce has been final for six months, and we'd been separated for a couple of years before that. I don't keep up with Franklin but to exchange information about our daughter." More tears spilled out. Poor Bailey. She'd be devastated.

"In his wallet, you were listed as next of kin. Is there anyone else we should contact?" Detective Sanchez asked.

"His parents are both dead. He has two brothers one in Dallas. One in Houston. I've got their addresses if you need help locating them." Devon ran a hand over her eyes then reached into her center drawer and retrieved an address book. Her hand shook as she flipped through the pages. She should get Liz to put these all on her computer. Like that's important to her life now.

She slid the book toward the detectives. Sanchez jotted down the info in his notepad.

"Thank you, Ms. Moore. We'll contact them. Will they handle the funeral arrangements?"

"I...I don't know. I assume so." She ran fingers over her trembling lips.

"And you can't offer any reason Mr. Moore would've wanted to take his life?" Detective Spenser cocked his head at her, searching inside hers.

Devon shook her head, but couldn't put any more words together.

"We may have more questions for you later, Ms. Moore. We're sorry for your loss." The two detectives left her office leaving the door open behind them.

Liz popped in followed by Brett. Devon had never been as glad to see anyone as Brett right then.

"What did the police want?" Liz asked.

Brett crossed to her side and laid his hand on her shoulder. "You've been crying. What's wrong?"

Devon glanced between the two people. Her face scrunched together into the awful way she did when a full-on cry engulfed her, and the tears fell. Brett eased her up and into his arms.

After what seemed like a hundred years, she got enough control so instead of sobbing, tears only dropped down her face. They were for many things wrong. Upper most in her mind was Blair's loss of her father, the situation her company was in, and the likelihood of no chance to retrieve the money Franklin had taken. Fear the police investigation would reveal the reason Franklin took his life, and how the revelations about her father's actions would hurt Bailey. The list went on.

What if the client came after them now? Devon's primary concern now had to be keeping her daughter safe.

"Devon, honey. Tell me what's happened." Brett's arms around her took her to mountain cabins with a roaring fire and a brook gurgling by. Such comfort, and he'd called her "honey." Devon wanted to stay in his embrace.

"I'll get you a cup of coffee, Devon." Liz headed toward the door.

"Thanks, Liz." Devon's spoke i n a scratchy soft voice. She stepped back from Brett, took his arm, and led him to the sofa where they sat.

"Liz said the police were here. What's going on?"

"Two detectives reported finding Franklin's body in the woods on the edge of the country club. They believe he killed himself."

"Oh, Devon." Brett's hand came up, and he massaged her neck. "That's rough. Are they sure?"

"They'll have to wait for the autopsy to be certain." Devon shuddered. She sounded like a character on a TV show. Her whole world had turned topsy-turvy. Her brain had nothing on a run-away Ferris wheel. At any moment, she expected to be flung off into space.

"Have you told Bailey yet?"

"No. Oh, dear God. How will I do that?"

Brett squeezed her shoulder. "You're strong. You'll manage, and so will she. I'll help in any way I can. Did the detectives ask if you had an idea of any reasons for Franklin to commit suicide?"

She nodded."

"Did you tell them about the stolen money or our belief he owed a client money?"

She shook her head but didn't meet his gaze. "Keeping Bailey in the dark is my priority."

"You may not have any choice. The detectives' investigation will probably uncover the reason. Devon, finding out what has happened will help Bailey understand why her father killed himself. Otherwise, no telling what conclusion she'll come to."

"I hadn't considered that. Where do I begin?" She rubbed a hand over her forehead.

"What time does Blair get home from school?"

One hand rubbed her forehead. "What day is it?"

"Tuesday."

"She should be home right after school today. My mother will pick her up."

"You should tell her sooner than later. What if she hears a rumor from a friend who's heard a news report?"

Devon nodded, but still, she sat there. She took a couple of deep breaths and blew them out. "Okay, will you please ask Liz and Karen to come in?"

"Sure." Brett rose and left her office.

Devon wanted to alert the staff. She particularly wanted Liz and Karen to keep the story quiet about the trouble with the company. Working through all the details of Franklin's death and the funeral and being there for Bailey had to take top priority. Then she'd turn her attention to the company.

Bailey got out of her grandmother's car. "Thanks, Mimi. You won't have to do this too much longer. I should get my license soon and a spiffy new car. You'll get back some time for yourself."

"But I love picking you up, you, silly girl." Her grandmother, who always dressed well and kept trim with her many trips to the gym, laughed. Bailey couldn't ask for better role models than her mother and grandmother.

"Yeah, I like it, too, but time to move on. New experiences lie ahead."

"Tell your mother I'll call her, and we'll schedule a supper. Your grandfather hasn't seen much of y'all in a while."

"Will do." She hoisted her backpack and smiled at her house. Special to be home right after school. She loved cheerleading and her other after school activities, but she had a history test coming and needed to spend some quality time with her notes. Bailey climbed the front steps and glanced at the swing on the porch. Lucky to live in such a great place for sure. Oh, theirs' wasn't as big as some of her friend's homes, but with only her mother and her living here, they didn't need a palace. Now a car? A sexy, hot, red car? That was dif-ferent. She'd start on the car campaign tonight.

"Hey, Mom, I'm home," she hollered as she went through the front door. "I'm going up to change, and then I'll be back for a snack."

"Bailey." Her mother's voice called from the den. "Can you come back here first?"

"Sure." She laid her backpack on the bench under the rear bay window, which provided a view of the back yard. No pool, like at Mimi's, but nicely done. "What's up?"

Her mother sat on the sofa. She held out her hand. "Come sit by me, sweetie."

"What's happened?" Her mother's appearance shocked Bailey. She dropped onto sofa next to her mother. Her mother whose eye makeup looked smudged. Her mother who never had a hair out of place, much less having issues with her makeup.

"Mom?"

"I have something to tell you, Bailey, something bad." Her moth-er looked away then squeezed her hand tight.

"I said goodbye to Mimi. She can't be the problem. Is Granddad all right?"

"I'm sorry to tell you, Bailey, and there's no right way…your father is dead."

"What?"

"Sweetie, the police came to my office to tell me."

"Was there an accident? What happened?"

"I'm afraid he killed himself."

"Oh, no. That can't be." Tears filled her eyes and trailed down her face. She dropped her head into her mother's lap and sobbed. Her mother's hand on her head comforted, but her upended world would never to be the same. Time passed, and finally, she sat up.

"What happens next?"

"What do you mean?"

"Well, I guess there'll be a funeral or something." Her mother nodded. "Will the uncles manage all the details, or will we?"

Her mother let out a long huff of air. "I'm not sure yet, sweetie. The police were contacting your father's brothers. I'm not next of kin. You are, of course, and your uncles. I'll be in touch with them. I'm sure they'll include you in the plans."

"Good." Her mother's hand threaded through her hair, the repetitive motion comforting. "Do Mimi and Granddad know?"

Her mother shook her head. "I haven't had a chance to tell them yet. I wanted you to hear first from me before you picked up the news from social media. In fact, let's leave the news off this evening."

"Okay."

"I'll tell the school you won't be in for a couple of days."

"Thanks. I'm going up to my room, now if that's okay."

"Sure. I'm here for you, to talk with anytime about anything."

"Thanks, Mom." Bailey, nodded, picked up her book pack, and then stopped and reversed. "How are you doing?"

"I'm sad, Bailey I haven't loved Franklin in several years, but I did, and we had you together. Yeah, I'm very sad." Bailey kissed her mother on the cheek and wandered toward her room.

She stretched out on her bed. What made her dad do something so awful? Didn't he love her anymore? Oh, she got the concept he and her mom weren't in love, but she'd always believed them when they told her they both still loved her. Had they lied? Had she done something wrong?

She curled into a ball, cuddling her stuffed panda her dad gave her when she turned five. Tears leaked from her eyes and on to the bear.

Thursday, September 23

A couple of days after she learned of Franklin's suicide... Devon shuddered at the word...her mother called and asked to stop by. Odd, her mother usually popped in unannounced. Had something else happened? She couldn't stand it if something were wrong with either of her parents.

How could she deal with anything else? She was barely

managing to keep things together and be strong for Bailey.

A tap on the door preceded her mother using her key to come in. "Hey, dear. I'm here."

Devon met her mother in the entry hall. She looked like her beautiful self. Her mother worked out and watched what she ate, had never smoked nor been a sun-worshiper, and looked years younger than she was. "Is Dad all right?"

"Yes, dear, why ever do you ask?" She dropped her sweater on the bench in the entry hall, carried her purse, and led the way into the living room. She settled on the off-white sofa and patted the seat next to her. "Join me, Devon. How are you holding up?"

Devon shrugged. "As well as possible, I guess." Her mother acted not like her usual self. Something was up. Devon sat next to her as requested. "So, what's going on, Mom?"

Miriam reached into her purse and removed a long envelope. "This came in the mail today. It's from Franklin."

"What?" A cold shiver ran down Devon's back.
"Two letters, more like notes, one for you and one for Bailey. You should read them."

Devon reached her hand toward the envelope. Her fingers trembled as she removed the two pages. She read her name on a folded sheet and Blair's on the other one. She dragged in a deep breath and let it out before opening the page with her name, letting her gaze skim the short message before reading the words out loud.

Dear Devon,

I'm sorry. I don't normally use those words, but I'm afraid I've done some stupid things. I love Bailey and regret putting her and you in danger. This is the only way out. Remember our honeymoon in the Caymans and our room # there? Check it out. Please don't hate me. Franklin

The Caymans? What in the world? Devon glanced at her mother, whose sad expression made Devon's heart ache.

"Read the next one, dear."

Devon opened the one with Bailey's name scrawled in her husband's unique script.

Dear Bailey,

Know I've always loved you. You're the best thing your mother and I ever did. Have a good life. Love, Dad.

"My poor daughter. Should I show this to her, Mom?"

"I think so, dear. The message will comfort Bailey to read her father had her in his mind at the end."

"And still he killed himself. Poor man." Devon put the letters in the envelope. "Thanks for bringing these, Mom. When did you get them?"

"In today's mail. You needed to have them immediately."

"Yes. Thanks." Devon scanned the two letters. Notes really. "My God. He must've have been unable to see his way out and in so much pain he decided to kill himself."

"Can I help by staying when you tell her?"

Devon squeezed her mother's hand. "No, thanks. I'll manage I hope. Bailey is upstairs catching up on some homework her friend Linda brought over after school."

Her mother leaned over, put her arm around Devon's shoulders, and kissed her on the cheek. "Let me know how the talk goes. And if you need me for anything...."

"Thanks, Mom. I always need you." She walked her mother to the entry, closing the door firmly after Miriam left and leaned against the solid wood. She straightened up and made for the stairs. May as well get this over with.

After climbing to the top, she tapped on her daughter's door. "Bailey. Can I come in?"

"Sure, Mom."

Devon entered her daughter's room done in pink, lavender, and green. Bailey leaned against pillows propped in front of the head-board, cuddling the panda her father had given her.

"How're you doing, Bailey?"

"Okay, I guess. But I ache," she gestured to her chest, "in here."

"I don't know if this will make any difference in how you feel. It's a note from your father." Devon sat on the edge of the bed and held out the folded sheet.

Bailey sat forward and reached for the paper. She hastily opened and skimmed the few words, dragging in a short breath, tears squeezing from her eyes. "Geez, mom." She grabbed another gulp of air. "Did he write you one, too?"

Devon nodded. "Yes."

"What did yours say?

"He apologized. Your father never did that in all the years we were together." Devon wiped a tear struggling to escape. "And some stuff about the Cayman's and our honeymoon. He didn't make much sense."

"Life is pretty crazy, Mom."

"Yes, it is, Bailey, but we'll be all right." Devon gathered her precious daughter into her arms and rocked her, praying she'd be able to protect and support her daughter through this loss.

CHAPTER TEN

Tuesday, September 27

The service held on Sunday at the funeral home's chapel had been well attended by Franklin's associates and many of Devon's friends. Even though a week had passed since her ex-husband killed himself, she felt like she was caught in a nightmare, one she prayed to wake from soon. Thus far, Devon hadn't. Her parents had been wonderful, helping with Bailey and going with them to pick out the casket, which cost money she didn't have. What could she do? Franklin's brothers washed their hands of the process. They'd been led down the yellow brick road too many times by Franklin. Devon had no idea what Franklin did to bend her brothers-in-law out of shape, but accepted planning the service fell to her and Bailey.

When she talked with Addie about her questions about their situation, Addie had suggested she get Brett to untangle the financial knots of Franklin's business. Devon wasn't sure why she hadn't thought about the idea herself. He'd attended Franklin's funeral and offered condolences and his help. She felt uncomfortable asking him to dig into Franklin's money and investments again, but his will had listed Bailey as the sole beneficiary, so they needed to find out where she stood.

Franklin's lawyer surprised Devon when he called to tell her Franklin had named her as the executor of whatever estate remained. Addie's suggestion made sense. Brett was a forensic auditor. If anyone could untangle all the lines, he could. Not to mention, it didn't make sense to start over when Brett had a head start with the work he'd already done on the accounts.

The little flutter of excitement because she'd see him at her house for supper seemed inappropriate somehow. Couldn't put her finger on why. She and Franklin hadn't been a couple in many years. Still...

Bailey chose to hang out at Miriam's. Being with Mimi and Granddad would do her good while Devon and Brett talked. Keeping her daughter from learning about her father's dealings was important to Devon. She'd added a touch more lipstick and fluffed her hair right before the doorbell rang.

"Hey." She swung open the front door to find Brett standing there in jeans, boots, and a leather jacket. Broad shoulders and blond hair such an excellent combination.

"Can I come in?" His smile tilted up one corner of his mouth as if he was aware she'd been ogling him.

She drew in a deep breath, catching a whiff of his aftershave. Ah, nice. She stepped back. "Yes, please." She must appear nuts.

He followed her into the kitchen. "How are you and Bailey holding up?"

"Eehh. Devon waggled her hand back and forth. "She gets up every morning and puts one foot in front of the other, but quieter than usual. Me, too. Would you like a glass of wine or beer?"

"I'll take a wine, please."

He towered over her. And good looking. Get a grip, girl. He propped himself on one of the bar stools, one foot on the rail and one on the floor. "A Cab, if you have it."

"Sure. Won't take me but a minute." She expertly opened the wine and poured a glass.

She set the wine in front of him then poured a Chardonnay for herself. Guess she'd have to get used to drinking this instead of the Champagne she preferred. "Thanks for coming. Addie suggested I talk with you about Franklin's finances. I hoped supper would make the talk easier."

"It smells great in here. What'cha cooking?"

"Pot roast. You struck me as a meat and potatoes man. My mother used to cook this for us for Sunday dinner. She used her crockpot, and when we came in from church, we were met by this mouthwatering aroma."

"Kind of like now." Brett smacked his lips together. "I can't wait." His laughter rolled out making her join in.

"Well, all right then, let's get busy." She took the lid off the crockpot, selected a fork and large spoon, and maneuvered the roast out of the pot onto a large platter. Hunger-arousing aromas filled the air as she ladled out the potatoes and carrots around the meat.

"The roast looks and smells fantastic, Devon. I didn't figure you for a cook."

"Oh, why not?" She served up the plates and set them on the table. "Thanks." Brett held her chair for her.

"Don't take this wrong, but you're beautiful and all about makeup and your company. I didn't see you in this domestic setting." He took a bite of the roast. "Boy, did I blow that. You're an awesome cook. That's about the best roast I've ever tasted. I don't need to save any for Bailey?"

"Glad you like it. She's eating with my parents. I didn't want her around to accidentally hear any of our conversation."

"Don't you think at some point, Bailey will need to hear the truth?"

"Why should she. The information will only hurt her. It's bad enough her father committed suicide without finding out he'd stolen from me and who knows who else."

Devon set her fork on her plate and took another sip of wine before heading into the whole mess.

"Brett, please go over Franklin's finances, completely. You already found he'd stolen the $500,000 from me, but I want to be certain nothing else—other time bombs—are hidden away to blast apart our financial lives. We need a sense of security."

"I'll be happy to do that, Devon. I told you I'd help anyway I can."

"Yes, I know. And Addie convinced me you meant what you said."

"She mentioned you were the executor of Franklin's will. Were you expecting the will to name you?"

"Not at all. I figured one of his brothers would have the respon-sibility. Apparently, they'd become estranged and they wanted noth-ing to do with planning the funeral or anything. Can I get you more roast?"

"Everything if that's okay." He held out his empty plate.

She rose chuckling. "Of course. Glad you're enjoying the meal." After filling his plate, she picked up the wine bottle. "More?"

He nodded. She refilled the glasses and set the bottles on the table. "So how do we begin?" She dropped into her chair.

"I need to get into his office."

She nodded. "Franklin's attorney gave me the keys. At some point, I'll have to close the office. Doesn't make sense to pay rent for longer than necessary."

"Did his attorney have any of his passwords?"

"I didn't think to ask. My guess is they'll be in his office somewhere."

"They aren't essential. I can still get in, but the work will take longer. You'd probably like all this settled sooner than later." He shoved away his plate and patted his flat stomach. "Wow. I haven't eaten a home cooked meal that good in…since the steak dinner at Addie and Mike's."

"Bless your heart. You don't have some cute woman hanging around wanting to cook for you?" Now, why did she ask that? She knew all right.

"Nope. Not in a long time. I stay busy with work. Hours are weird. It's been my experience women want someone more regular. That's not me. I'll work until I get the job done, and then I take off for a week or two."

She smiled at him over her wine glass. "I can see how planning social engagements would be difficult."

"What about you? Anyone since Franklin?"
"Are you kidding? Huh-uh. I split myself between Bailey and the company. Of course, my parents help with her anytime I need them. The business can be all-consuming, especially while we worked on making a deal with the Swanson Cosmetics Company. Franklin was a workaholic, too. It was the way we did life."

She stood and took their plates and set them in the sink.

"Let me help clean those up."

Devon twisted about and stared at him. "Wow. Franklin never offered to help. I'm stunned."

"My mom brung me up right," He used an exaggerated Texas twang and looped his thumbs through his belt loops.

She laughed. "That's nice. You make me laugh, Brett Townsend."

He moved next to her at the sink and turned on the water to rinse the plates. His arm brushed hers making goose bumps pop up. Oh, my.

"My mother also insisted we run water over the plates if we

didn't take the time to put them in the dishwasher, but she expected us to do the pre-wash either way. No water and we'd catch her bad side."

Devon stacked the dishes in the dishwasher and then put the crockpot in the refrigerator.

"Not many leftovers, I'm afraid."

Devon smiled at him. "Not a problem. I'm glad you enjoyed the meal as much as you did." She picked up her glass. "Let's go sit in the living room."

Brett followed the beautiful redhead into the front room, his brain barely registering the soft pastel colors covering the furniture and the dark wood floors. She'd bypassed the room when he entered, leading him directly to the kitchen. Devon Moore completely cap-tured his attention. No one had in a long time.

She settled into a high-backed chair sitting at an angle to the fireplace. He took the companion one. Homey. Wait a minute. Where was his little head going? Remember. Client. Don't. Mess. With. Clients. Yeah, right.

"When could you begin?" Devon wearing what he guessed he'd call a sun-dress baring her arms and emphasizing her small waist, crossed one leg over the other, swinging it in a slow arc, an open toe sandal dangled from her toes. She held her wine glass in both hands rolling it back and forth.

"I finished up a short project yesterday, so I'm all yours." Maybe not the best choice of words. He rushed on. "When can you get me into Franklin's office?"

She nodded. "Why don't I meet you there at ten in the morn-ing? I have an early meeting with my staff planned. I'm obligated to give them a heads-up we could be facing rough waters."

He leaned forward. "You haven't had any other unusual happenings since you got the after-duty police officer?"

"No. We've experienced no further issues. And we've made a company practice now for no one to walk out of the office alone."

"Good." He sipped his wine. "In your opinion, could we still have trouble about the mon-ey Franklin owes? I mean, they wouldn't expect anything from me, would they?" Her beautiful green eyes grew large, her brow furrowed.

"Well, let's hope not and in the meantime, be vigilant."

She shuddered. "Okay. I need to fill in Mom and Dad more to make sure they keep an eye open for anything unusual."

He leaned forward. "And still you're determined not to tell Bailey?"

"Yes. She doesn't need to deal with this."

It seemed a mistake to him, but as both the mom and the client, she called the shots. "Okay. You're the boss." He set his empty glass on the coffee table. "I'd better get a move on. You have an early morning tomorrow." He walked through the house toward the front door. "Thank you for dinner. You're quite a chef."

She laughed. "Oh, no. It's the crockpot. I'll see you in the morning."

She held out her hand, and he grasped it between both of his. He wanted to kiss her again, but not on the cheek this time. Probably not appropriate, but boy he wanted to pull this woman into his arms. He refrained but with regret and stepped through the door onto the porch.

"Lock up."

She smiled. "I will."

He went down the steps, nodding at the sound of the lock clicking into place. He climbed into his car and drove down the street. Her neighborhood of large houses seemed safe, and many of the houses had cameras. Unfortunately, Devon's did not. He'd talk with her about that to see if he could get her to consider installing them.

He wanted to understand more about Franklin Moore. What kind of man lets someone like Devon get away? She was smart, a good daughter and mother, ran a successful business. And beautiful. Don't forget beautiful. The long, red hair and green eyes. Well, they did something to him. The creamy skin. He wanted to run his hands all over every inch…. Okay, stop, bud. You've got work ahead of you. Back up. He drew in a deep breath and let it out.

He'd check with Mike and Addie for more info on both Devon and her dead ex-husband. He pulled into the driveway of his three-bedroom bungalow. He'd inherited the house from his great aunt, and he'd gutted almost everything, doing major renovations, replacing the small garage with one big enough to hold two cars. He enjoyed the hard, physical labor of pulling up the old carpet and refinishing the hardwoods, but farmed out the electrical and plumbing updates and the AC replacement. Best to stick with the stuff he was good at.

Numbers and computers were also his passion. He'd enjoy applying those skills for Devon's benefit.

CHAPTER ELEVEN

Wednesday, September 28

After a restless night of waking up several times trying to figure out how her life could possibly get worse, Devon rose and straightened the tangled covers on her bed. Grateful to be up, she ate a hasty breakfast and then poked her head in Blair's room to make sure her daughter had gotten up. "I've got an early meeting, Bailey. Don't go back to sleep."

Bailey rolled out of her bed. "See. I'm up. Don't worry about me."

Of course, Devon did worry about her almost grown daughter. How could she not? Bailey had a good head on her shoulders, but she was a teenager, and they didn't always make the best decisions. Devon shook her head at her musings as she drove into the garage for her company. She was lucky to have Bailey and thankful her parents were in good health and could help with her. But Devon loved her company, had worked hard and made sacrifices for its success made her stomach churn. She grabbed her bag, straightened her shoulders, and stood tall. Better get this show on the road. Maybe one of her employees could provide some ideas to help.

Wearing a black suite with her favorite turquoise pin on her lapel, a white silk blouse, and her black high heeled pumps, she pushed through the outside door, entered her domain, and forced a smile. "Good morning, Liz. Could you remind our employees we need to meet in the presentation room in ten minutes?"

"Sure. It's time, huh?"

"Yes." Devon went into her office, dropped into her chair, run-ning both hands through her hair. This meeting would be rough. She dreaded having to tell the employees, but with the possibility of the company going belly up, she owed it to them to be prepared. Other companies kept their eyes on her chemists. She'd heard of the offers. She'd hate to lose any of her staff, but treating them fairly demanded she share, so they didn't miss out on an opportunity.

God forbid a time came when her company might not exist. Her stomach cramped, and she reached for a couple of antacids. No, she wasn't looking forward to the next thirty minutes. Stopping in front of the mirror, she reapplied her lipstick and touched up her rouge, despite she hadn't been gone from home long. One last glance in the mirror gave her the courage to meet the challenge.

She entered the presentation room to find the company's employees sitting in the chairs lined up theater style. Devon walked to the front of the room where a podium and microphone stood. "Thanks for coming in. I understand how busy you all are." The mike made her voice sound strong and assured. If she only were.

"Some events have occurred I need to inform you about." She drew in a deep breath before hitting them with the news.

"We found the company is missing $500.00." Murmurs met her announcement." Let me assure you, none of you is suspected." Again, her comments were met with the noise of conjecture by her employees.

She raised her voice. "The loss of the money has thrown a wrench into our plan to purchase Swanson Cosmetics. Milly Swanson was disappointed at the news when I called to tell her." She glance in the direction of her head chemist. And we won't move ahead with the production of the new eye cream." The largest response came at this news.

"I'm sorry to tell you there's a possibility I may have to let some of you go. If any of you have other offers," she smiled, "this may be the time to check them out."

"What if we could cut some salaries in lieu of letting any employees go?" Karen suggested.

"Yes, how about that?" one of the chemists spoke up. "Maybe any of us who are prepared to make do with a bit less for a finite period could notify you, and we could avoid losing anyone."

"Oh, my." Devon put a hand to her trembling lips and blinked her eyes which were suddenly wet. The generosity of her employees overwhelmed her. "Well, of course. How wonderful. What do you think, Karen, will this help?"

"Of course." She stood up. "If those of you who can face a short term pay cut will come see me, I'll run the figures and see where we are.

"Okay."
"Yeah."
"We can do this."

The cries of support warmed Devon's heart. Guess it took a crisis to show her how incredibly awesome her employees were.

The meeting ended with hugs, high fives, and a positive can-do attitude. Devon couldn't believe how her employees had stood with her. Now if she hurried, she wouldn't be late to meet Brett.

Twenty minutes later, she parked in the downtown parking garage for Franklin's office. She got out of her car, put the strap of her bag over her shoulder and made her way into the elevator to ride up to the twelfth floor. He'd hated being on this floor. A sigh escaped. When she shouldered her way through the glass doors to his office, she found Brett sitting in one of the waiting room chairs. He rose.

"Good morning."

"Hey. Sorry to be late. The meeting with my employees took longer than I expected." She faced Jessica Lopez, Franklin's secretary/receptionist. "Good morning. Jessica. You remember Brett Townsend. He's helping get Franklin's business interests straightened out."

She smiled. "Yes, of course. I've wondered what you'd be doing, Ms. Moore. I'm assuming you'll be closing the office?" Her voiced lilted up in a question.

"That's correct. I hope you can stay until we've got everything worked out and count on me giving you a five-star recommendation."

"Thank you, Ms. Moore. I'll do whatever you need."

"You're welcome. I appreciate your cooperation. Jessica, do you have Franklin's passwords?"

"I do." She opened a safe behind her and pulled out a folder. "Let me make you a quick copy." She turned to a copy machine sitting behind her desk on a credenza. In no time, she handed over four pages.

"Oh, my, this is a lot."

"Yes, and I suppose it's possibly not all of them, but it's all I had access to."

Devon glanced at Brett. "Okay, let's get busy." They walked through the door to the left of Jessica's desk."

"I expected a bigger operation." Brett glanced around a large room with lots of glass and a view of a row of glass buildings. "He didn't have anyone else working for him?"

Devon shook her head. "He didn't have many people he trusted. It's one of the reasons he worked such long hours, but he loved fiddling with the numbers, investments, and making money."

Brett pulled out the chair behind Franklin's desk. Devon swallowed hard at the oddity of seeing someone else sitting there.

"Let's see what we can see."

She stood a moment as he opened the computer. "I'm heading back to my office if you don't need me?"

"No problem." Brett seemed to already be in the zone.

"I'll tell Jessica it's fine for you to be here. Check with me when you finish."

"Okay." Brett nodded but never took his gaze from the computer screen.

Henry Logan had kept an eye on Franklin's office by hanging out in front of the building. He expected the ex to show up sometime. The redhead rewarded his vigil with her arrival today, but who had she let tag along? Interesting. Yes, indeed, interesting. Maybe they'd be able to get by Franklin's bitch of a secretary who'd stonewalled him and had a no for every one of his reasons for her to allow him to see her boss' computer. He figured once he got into Moore's computer he could get the money he deserved.

He was still bowled over the wimp Franklin had taken his own life. Did he think he'd get his wife and kid off the hook? Stupid man. Henry Logan never lost. He'd get his money back one way or another.

Time to pay a little visit to the gorgeous redhead. Gotta give Franklin credit. He'd married a beautiful woman.

Logan made his way over to parking garage and walked up the ramp. He'd earlier checked out what the ex-wife drove. By the time he reached the 12th floor, he was huffing like an old engine. Needed to get to the gym more. Well, how about that now? Here came the wife. She glanced around a couple of times as if she sensed him there. He reached into his pocket for the ski mask and covered his head. He needed to make sure she got his message. He wanted his money.

Just as Devon reached her car, she fumbled the keys dropping them to the concrete. Stupid. She stooped down to scoop them off the ground, and standing up quickly enough, she got a little lightheaded.

"Let me help you." A muffled voice came from behind her and an arm reached around and snatched the keys from her.

"You're not going anywhere right now. We need to talk."

Devon's blood pounded in her ears. Her heart beat at double time. Her legs barely held her up. God, not again. Hands flipped her around and shoved her hard up against her car. The door handle ground into her lower back.

She gazed into brown eyes with a steely glint in them. No way would she let him rape her. Been there done that. Not happening again.

One arm cut across her throat shutting off her breath so she couldn't scream. No. No. Not again. He shoved one of his legs between hers, taking away her ability to knee him, her first line of defense.

"Just listen, bitch. Your dead husband owes me money. Two million. I want it. I'll call you and set up a time when you can deliver the money to me."

Her fingers tugged at the arm across her neck. His gloves kept her from hurting him. She shook her head, hating the tears leaking from her eyes, hating to show weakness. It's what they liked to see. Made them feel powerful.

"Why are you shaking your head? Don't you understand?" He

loosened the hold he had on her throat.

"I don't have your money." The words came out scratchy.

"Well, darlin', you better figure out a way to get me two million. I'd hate to take out my loss on your sweet daughter."

Devon's legs wouldn't have kept her upright if the masked man hadn't held her tight against the car.

"You get my money. I'll be back in touch." His arm moved from her neck, and Devon sucked in life-giving air. Before she took a second breath, the man's fist connected with her jaw. Pain erupted in her body and stars circled her head. He stepped away as she slumped to the hard concrete of the garage floor.

"Oh." Devon's head pounded. Every part of her body ached like she'd been run over. She blinked her eyes. Where was she? What happened?

"Oh, God," the words slipped out as her memory flashed pictures of the man in the ski mask and his demands for money. Was he still here? How long had she been out? She slowly swiveled her head around, but all she saw were car tires, asphalt, and the sides of vehicles. Using her hands, she levered herself to a sitting position. The garage spun. She put her hand to her head to keep it attached to her shoulders. She had to get up. She had to get back inside to find Brett. Yes, she needed Brett.

With painful movements, she staggered to her feet, leaning against her car for more support. Where were her keys? She couldn't find them anywhere. What about her phone? She patted her pocket, but no phone. It must've fallen out. No way could she get back on her knees for a search. Her head was about to explode. Her jaw throbbed. Her stomach threatened to empty itself. Please not that.

Walking slowly and leaning on each car in turn, she made her way to the elevator, tapped the button, and stepped inside when the doors swooshed open. No one was inside. She pushed twelve and leaned against the wall bracing her hands on the railing. When the doors opened, she staggered through and made her way across the hall to the glass entrance doors leading to Franklin's office.

She pushed, but couldn't get the heavy door to open. Tears streaked down her face. Defeated by those damn heavy doors Franklin had insisted made his office more prestigious.

Just before she slid to the floor, the door opened, and she stumbled into Jessica's arms.

"Ms. Moore. What happened?" She raised her voice and hollered, "Mr. Townsend, come quick."

Jessica helped Devon to a chair inside the door. So grateful, she feared she'd collapse on the floor.

"What's the matter?" Brett's voice filled Devon with a sense of security. He'd know what to do. "Hell. What happened? Devon, your jaw is turning purple and is swollen."

Devon met his gaze, her eyes tearing up again. She had to stop that. She needed to talk with Brett, but without the secretary around.

"I'm okay. Jessica, why don't you take the rest of the day off?"

"Are you sure, Ms. Moore?" But she reached behind her desk for her purse.

Nodding wasn't a good idea, but Devon managed causing stars to dance on a black background. Her voice wasn't reliable.

"Go on, Jessica. I'll see you in the morning." Brett closed the door behind her.

"Can you walk to the inside office." He slipped his arms under hers and urged Devon to stand.

With his help, she stumbled into the office and away from that damned heavy glass door, which allowed anyone to see her. He carefully lowered her to the sofa and lifted her legs up.

"Don't go anywhere."

Devon would've laughed, but couldn't find the energy.

"You need ice for your jaw." He stepped over to the bar and put ice in a towel. He sat beside her on the sofa and gently laid the cold pack on her jaw. She winced. "Sorry. What happened? Did you fall?"

"No." The sound of her scratchy voice scared Devon. "Attacked in the garage."

"What? Damn, woman, you'll have to stay out of garages unless we get you a round the clock body guard."

A smile perked up one the uninjured corner of her mouth, all she could manage. He did have a sense of humor. She liked that about him, among other things.

"I'm calling the police." He moved to get up, but Devon grabbed his arm.

"Please don't."

"Why the hell not?" He glared at her with his arms across his broad chest.

"The attacker wanted me to pay him the two million he claims Franklin lost or stole from him. Can I have some water, please?

"Of course. Sorry." Brett rose and crossed quickly to the bar then returned with a cup of water.

Devon sipped and then related the incident. "So, you see, I can't call the police. Then the story will be revealed, and Bailey will find out about her father."

"But Devon, he threatened your daughter."

"I know, but maybe you can find the money when you get through all his files. I can pay the man, and he'll leave us alone."

"You're nuts, you know?" Brett paced in front of the sofa, running a hand through his hair.

"Did you have time to find anything?" Maybe she could take his mind off the police idea.

"Not really. I did find your ex-husband kept detailed records. If he has more money, I'll find it."

"Good."

"How's your jaw?" He sat next to her on the sofa and lifted the towel from her cheek. "Wow! You've got a doozy of a bruise.

Anything else hurt?"

"Other than my whole body? No."

"How do you propose to explain your injury to Bailey or your parents?"

Devon sighed. Maybe he was giving her a pass on the police. "I'll tell them I fell. They'll worry because they'll imagine I've got some awful disease or I'm getting old." She struggled into a sitting position. Brett shifted, and she wound up with her thigh pressed against his. When the room tilted, she grabbed on to his leg, a muscled leg. Boy, he was right. She was nuts. How could she be reacting to him, with her world turned upside down? Maybe that's what caused the appeal. His solidness and his strength were comforting. She certainly could use that now.

"Here's the thing, Devon." He clasped her hand between his two. "You're in danger. Your daughter is in danger. Maybe your parents are in danger. You should go to the police and report this."

She glanced at the man. So handsome and his blond strength did things to her hormones. Nuts. She was nuts. "Brett, what if I could get Bailey and my parents out of harm's way?'"

"How do you do that?" His thumb rubbed the back of her hand.

"I may have to tell my parents what's going on, but then I can get them to go to their log cabin in the North Carolina Mountains. He didn't respond for what seemed like a long time. Was he ready to wash his hands of her and her mess?'"

"That's not a bad idea. How about we drive over to Fort Worth and run some of this by Addie and Mike? They might have some new ideas or at least confirm we're going in the right direction. An objective third party is always helpful."

"I never turn down an opportunity of seeing Addie. As soon as we get Bailey and my parents out of here, let's do that."

"I forgot to ask. How'd your meeting with your employees go?" Devon teared up. "Despite evidence to the contrary, I'm not normally a crybaby." She wiped her eyes.

"Understandable with what you've been juggling. Were they upset? Did they give you a hard time?"

"Oh, my gosh, Brett. They were wonderful. They're finding a way I won't have to let anyone go. Some of them will take pay cuts. They were positively amazing. Took my breath away and made me proud."

CHAPTER TWELVE

Thursday, September 29

"Mom, Dad, I need you to sit down." Devon had invited her parents to her house because she hoped the talk about what all had happened would be easier in her home, but no, no not so much.

"Devon, whatever happened to your face?" Her mother put her finger under Devon's chin and gently tipped it upwards." Careful application of makeup hadn't been enough to conceal her injury from observant Miriam.

Even minimizing what happened in the garage, explaining the circumstances to her parents cut a hole in her heart. They were shocked and angry. She almost regretted her involvement with Franklin, but then together they produced their wonderful daughter. Bailey made anything worthwhile.

"What do you mean Franklin stole money from your company?" Her father's anger came out as a cold fire. She'd never heard her father's voice filled with so much tension.

"I'm sure he meant to pay me back, Dad." She patted his arm trying to calm him. So much anger couldn't be good for his blood pressure.

"Sweetie, don't you think you should go to the police?" Her mother leaned forward and took Devon's other hand.

"If I do, then Bailey will learn about her father's exploits, Mom. My goal is to avoid her finding out, if possible."

"I get that, dear." Her father rose from the sofa and paced her living room stopping to stare into the empty fireplace. "I hate the idea of you having to pay for Franklin's misdeeds. It's not fair."

"You're right it's not fair, but then life often isn't. Will you take Bailey and go to North Carolina?"

"But what about you, Devon? How do you think leaving you by yourself to deal with all this will affect us?"

"I'm sorry, Mom. But I've got to keep y'all safe and ensure Bailey doesn't learn about her father."

Her dad met her mother's gaze. Something passed between them in that manner of folks who'd been married a long time. He walked to the side of his wife's chair and took her hand. "We'll do this, Devon, but two things. How will you convince Bailey to leave? How will you get the money to pay this man? Well, I lied. The third question is once you've paid him two million, what keeps him from coming back for more?"

Her father stopped talking. Devon rose, crossed to the windows pushing aside the sheers, staring out on their street. She found herself doing that a lot now. Looking for…something…she didn't know what, but any indication of danger.

"It's not like this guy is blackmailing me with something, Dad. No reason he should be aware my desire to keep all of this from Bailey. If Franklin owes him money, then in some way I'm obligated to repay him."

"But you've been divorced for six months. His debts can't legally be considered yours."

"I know, Dad." She let the sheers drop in place and faced her parents.

"How will you come up with the money? We can help some, though I'm sickened at the idea of bailing out your louse of an ex-husband." Her mother was such a kind person always ready to overlook slights others would take exception to, that the venom in her voice surprised and shocked Devon. She swallowed a couple of times. What could she say?

"Miriam, be generous to the dead." Then her father nailed Devon with one of his looks telling her he wasn't stopping until he was satisfied. "Where's the money coming from, Devon?"

"I can sell this house."

"Oh, Devon, no." Her mother's shock resonated with all of them.

"We've had realtors stop by and offer us a million for it."

"Without any kind of sign in the yard?" Her father crossed to the sofa and sank into the soft cushions. "We must live on the wrong street, Miriam." His chuckle, a rueful huff.

"What about the other half?" her mother asked.

"I can sell my business."

"Dear God, Devon, you've worked hard to build the company into something wonderful." Her mother rose and crossed to her. "There must be some other way." She clasped an arm around Devon's shoulders.

"At this point, that's all I've come up with, Mom."

"What about your investments?" Her father's thumbs twiddled, a sure sign he was deep in thought. She'd seen his habit any number of times when he worked out a problem for one of his college students or a family member.

"I hate to use those, Dad. They're what we'll be living on until I can get a new company up and running. I'm sure I'll have to sign a non-compete clause for some amount of time. And," she looked at both her parents, "can we move in with y'all?"

"Of course, sweetie." Her mother's answer immediate. Then she laughed." We've been the only ones in our group whose children have not moved back in for a time."

"Happy we can help you feel like you're on the same level with your friends." Devon hugged them both. She hated to let them go. Finally, she forced herself to step back.

"As for Bailey, her fall break begins next Monday. She's off from Saturday, October 8 through Sunday, October 16. School is back in session the following Monday, October 17. The holiday buys us some time. Hopefully, y'all can come back afterwards, and she can go on to school."

"She'll hate losing the house, Devon. I've heard her say how much she loves this place."

"I'll tell her it's too big for us, and we'll do better to downsize, helping her prepare for her small college dorm room." She forced a weak smile.

"Will you talk with her about your plans before we leave?" Her mother's voice filled with strain and worry.

"Talk with me about what before we leave for where?" Bailey bounced into the living room, giving her grandparents a peck on their cheeks and settling on the arm of the sofa next to her grandfather.

"Hey, Bailey dear, your granddad and I were about to leave." She rose." We'll talk with you soon." Miriam hugged her granddaughter, and hugged her daughter. She whispered in Devon's ear, "We're be-hind you and will do anything you need'.

"Love you, Mom, Dad." She walked them to the front door, peered up and down the street before she closed and locked the door. After drawing in a deep breath to fortify her for the coming meeting with Bailey, Devon walked back into the living room. Her daughter wasn't there.

"Bailey, where are you?"

"Kitchen. I only stopped in the living room first when I got home because I saw Mimi's car out front. I'm starving. How about some popcorn?"

"Great idea. You pop the corn, and I'll melt the butter, because what's the point eating it if you can't put butter on it, right?" Devon opened the door to the refrigerator and removed two bottles of water and the butter dish.

For about five minutes, the sounds of the pan rattling and corn popping filled the kitchen.

"Yumm. Smells almost better than it tastes. So much better than the microwave kind and that doesn't make near enough." Her daughter emptied the popped corn into a large yellow bowl with white kernels of corn on the side and added salt. "Your turn."

Devon drizzled a half cup of butter over the white puffy popped corn and parceled out two servings in smaller matching yellow bowls. "Now this is some good eating. Here's your napkin and water. Can we sit here at the kitchen table? I want to visit with you about some ideas I have."

"Sure." Bailey dropped into one chair and propped her feet on an-other one. "What's up?" She tossed a kernel into the air and caught it in her mouth.

Devon laughed. "Good job, girl." Devon chewed a few of the puffy kernels herself before gutting up and doing what she needed to do. "Here's what I've been thinking. Our house has five bedrooms and a full basement, plus a living room and den and dining room."

"Yeah, Mom. I've lived here for sixteen and a half years. I know how big the house is."

"I've had realtors stop by asking if we'd consider selling—

"What?"

"Yeah. We live in a desirable location. Everyone wants to live here. They figure if they offer enough money, people will sell."

"What are they offering?" Bailey swallowed a couple of gulps from her bottle.

"Over a million dollars."

Bailey spurted the water from her mouth. "No kidding. Wow. That blows me away." She wiped her mouth and then chewed more popcorn and drank more water. "But don't you love this house, Mom."

"Well, I used to, Bailey, not so much anymore. And it's gigantic for only the two of us."

"That's true. We sure don't need all this room." Bailey glanced around at the gigantic kitchen.

"No, we don't."

"But this is a great kitchen."

"I agree."

Bailey chewed her popcorn while gazing at her mother. "Are you checking out my reactions to this idea of selling our house?"

"Yeah, I am." Devon glanced at her daughter from the corner of her eye and ate her popcorn, not wanting to push Bailey for an answer. The salty, buttery taste of the snack, her favorite. "But you don't have to say anything right now."

Bailey ate two more handfuls of corn and washed it down with water. Then she turned to her mother, "No, I'm good with it. But I need you to promise me you don't intend for us to move into one of these Tiny Houses, I see you watching on TV."

Devon laughed, relieved at the resiliency of youth. "I can safely promise we won't look at any tiny houses. I've seen ones big enough from one person and a small dog, to a family of five, but I don't see that working for us. We may move in with Mimi and Granddad, until we find something we like for our own. Would you be okay staying there for a temporary solution?"

"Sure. They've got a great TV room and the backyard patio and pool will be super for my friends to come over and hang out."

"No parties unless at least one of us is there." Devon rose, added popcorn to her bowl. "I'm going to my office to contact a Realtor.

"What are we doing for supper?"

"You're eating right now. Why are you concerned about what

we're having for supper?"

"Because I'm a growing, energetic girl and I need to plan ahead."

"How about we order in pizza, and I'll throw together a salad?"

"I'm good with that."

Devon hugged her daughter and kissed her on the top of the head and Bailey didn't brush her off . What a blessing this girl was. Devon left her contentedly munching her popcorn and scanning posts on her phone.

After settling at her desk in the office, Devon blew out a long breath. Whew, that had gone way better than she'd hoped. Could she pull this whole feat off ? Selling the house should be the easiest part. Next, she had to get Bailey and her parents out of town, elevating her worries about their safety.

Worse than selling the house was the idea of selling her business. Talk about tearing a hunk from her heart. At the thought, her stomach tightened, and the wonderful popcorn backed up in her throat. Finding a buyer was problematical in and of itself. Th en how much could she sell the company for? One million? Could she sell fast enough to satisfy the crazy man Franklin owed money to. What about her employees who'd all rallied around the way they had?

She dropped her head on her hands, humbled by their support. Still, this whole state of affairs had turned into a nightmare. After a few moments, she straightened. A pity party wouldn't get the show on the road. Devon looked on line for the Realtor who'd found her current house. She'd be the best place to start. Her fingers flew over the keys.

Saturday, October 1

Driving to Devon's house, Brett squirmed against the car seat. All the time in front of a computer made his lower back ache, aggravated by his worry about Devon and what she planned. Best results from their upcoming visit with Mike and Addie? Devon deciding to go to the police. Pulling into her driveway, he accepted the anticipation he felt at seeing her again, despite the issues facing her.

Before he climbed out of his car, the front door opened, the gorgeous redhead stepped out on the porch. and pivoted to lock her door. She skipped down the stairs. He hopped out, held open the car door, and she eased in.

"Sorry to keep you waiting."

"You didn't. I'd just parked in your driveway." He walked around and got in beside her. "And I would've knocked on the door. My momma taught me good manners."

She chuckled. "Well, you wanted to leave earlier, and I couldn't because I had a meeting with my real estate agent. Can you imagine she's already got three offers on our house? All above one million."

"That's great. I'm happy for you."

"Finding a buyer for my company will be harder, I'm afraid. Oh, let's not talk about this anymore. I'm excited to get to see Addie and Mike. Thanks for making this happen. We schedule get-togethers every month or so, but I haven't seen her since the weekend I met you. It's about time."

The memory of the first time he laid eyes on the flesh and blood woman warmed Brett's insides. He'd always be grateful to Mike for putting them together. The trip went fast as he and Devon talked about music, movies, and books they liked. Before long, he pulled down the long drive leading to Mike's ranch house west of Fort Worth.

They reached the house, and the door opened. Addie, with her long dark hair loose and flying in the breeze, burst forth.

"Devon. Devon. I'm happy you could get over here." The girls embraced like sisters.

"Addie, I'm always so happy to see you."

Mike followed his wife out, and he and Brett clasped hands.

"Welcome. The girls will be busy for a while and never notice us. Come on in, and I'll get you a beer."

Brett followed Mike into the ranch's open living room, dining room and kitchen, a warm, friendly space. Brett drew in a long breath enjoying the smell of the fire crackling in the fireplace. While the temperature wasn't low, it was cool enough to warrant.

The women made for the stove and several steaming pots, communicating without speaking.

Brett settled onto the large leather chairs in front of the fireplace. "I need your help, Mike. We can't let Devon sell her business to pay off this guy who says her dead ex-husband owes him. I haven't found anything yet signifying Moore owed anyone two million dollars. He did steal $500,000 from Devon's company."

"Can you prove he took the money?"

"Yep. I can. If he were alive, I'd go after him. But Devon is dead set against doing anything to spoil her daughter's vision of her father." He accepted the beer Mike held out for him.

"On the phone, you mentioned she'd been attacked twice?" Mike took a healthy gulp from his bottle.

"Yeah. Makes me nuts her not reporting the attacks to the police. Can you help?"

"I'll see what we can do. Addie and I talked about the issue after you called to clue me in. Addie says Devon has always been careful with Bailey. She'd worked hard never to speak disparagingly of Franklin. Preventing the divorce from ruining Blair's relationship with her father has been Devon's goal."

"That's commendable, but the behavior seems foolhardy given the threats on her life."

Brett glanced at the two women in the kitchen, each beautiful in her own right. Brett imagined the heads they must turn when they were out on their own, Addie with her long dark brown hair and Devon with her red mane.

"Supper is ready if anyone is hungry." Addie set plates full of spaghetti on the table. The aroma of the red sauce made Brett's mouth water. Devon put salad plates on the table. Brett seated Devon.

"Wine?" Mike held up a bottle of red.

"Yes, thanks." Devon nodded.

"I'm sticking with the beer."

Addie put a big bowl of salad on the table.

"That garlic bread smells great." Brett took a sip of his beer.

"Oh, gosh yes. Grab the loaf will you, Mike?" Addie settled into her chair, and Mike got the bread from the oven and set a basket on the table.

"So, Devon, Mike has told us something of your situation." Mike glanced her.

Devon sighed. "Do we have to talk about this now?"

"Yeah, honey. We do. You should've told me as soon as it all went to hell in a handbasket." Addie laid a hand on Devon's arm. "I can't believe you've been attacked twice."

"It worked out okay each time."

Addie rolled her eyes. "Can you hear yourself? All blasé like everyone gets attacked."

"Well, you have been attacked, Addie. And more than once, right?"

"Let's not talk about those times." Mike's jaw muscle jumped. "I get a pain in my gut when I remember what happened to her."

"I'm sorry, Mike, but Addie made it sound like no one else had ever been attacked."

"Okay. Okay. I give. Help yourself to the salad and then pass the bowl please, Brett."

"Sure, Addie, but in your case, I heard you went to the police." Brett took a small amount of the salad.

"Well, of course." Addie placed a generous portion of salad on her plate and passed the bowl to Devon who served herself."

"That's the problem. Devon here doesn't plan to do that." Brett sent a sharp glance at the subject of the discussion.

"I'm here. Don't talk around me." Devon forked her spaghetti around on the plate. What was the matter with these people? "Don't you get I'm trying to protect Bailey's image of her father?"

"We do, sweetie, and your behavior is commendable, but more important is your safety. And Bailey's. Didn't this Neanderthal threaten her, too?"

"Yes, and that's why I'm sending her off to North Carolina with my parents. I'm hoping her being gone during Fall break will give us time to get this settled."

"That's another week off." Addie protested.

"I know. I'm keeping a close rein on her. She's either with me, my parents, or at school.

"What about cheerleading? Don't I remember they're hoping to get to nationals this year?" Addie kept banging away at her.

"Yes, they're working hard for that. Mom and Dad have been taking turns picking her after practice. This would be so much harder if she were driving. We're not taking any chance of her being left alone."

Mike laughed. "I bet she loves that. My memory of those times with Jeremy and Elizabeth...that kind of coverage doesn't go over well."

Addie laughed. "Yes, but you handled them both well, Mike. One of the reasons I love you."

Mike leaned over and kissed his wife. "That's sweet." He glanced at Devon and Brett. "Pardon us. We're still newlyweds."

Devon didn't dare make eye contact with Brett. She smiled and nodded. "I hated not being able to travel up to Maine to see Kate and Jim get married. I had financial concerns but didn't realize how great they were, and I kept hoping they'd go away." Her head-in-the sand technique for dealing with problems backfired.

"We missed not sharing the time with you, Devon. It's a beautiful state, cold and lots of snow, but with gorgeous vistas and delightful small harbor towns. We promised Kate, we'd make a trip up there early next year. Let's get your finances squared away so you can go with us next time."

"We're working on that, Addie," Brett sipped his beer and set down the bottle. "I've got more work to do going through Franklin's computer records. We're trying to find out if I can substantiate any—well, legitimacy isn't the right word exactly—but maybe truth to the claims he owed the money to a client."

"Should you have to pay, Devon, even if it's real? I mean you and Franklin haven't been together for over two years. How can this become your obligation?" Addie sipped her wine and then used her fork, pushing her salad around on its plate.

"I'm sure it's not, hon. Pass me more of that garlic bread, will you Brett?" Mike reached his hand for the basket.

"It's the threat turning the money into an issue, Addie. Here you go, Mike." Brett snagged a piece of the garlic bread before handing the basket to Mike. "Now if Devon went to the police and reported the threat, the police would find this guy, and the problem would all go away. You could forget about selling your house and business."

"I hate to hear you talk about maybe having to sell, Devon. You've put your whole life into to building the company to its present success."

"You're right, Addie, but I love Bailey more than the company. If I did what Brett wants, everyone would learn about Franklin. I don't care about others except for what they'd say to Bailey about him. I can't have her learning her father stole from my company and maybe played fast and loose with someone else's money."

Devon looked around the table. "Do none of you get that?"

"My kids' father was no great shakes as a dad. But they both

120

seem to be okay with him being a jerk while they were growing up and now, too, when he wants nothing to do with either of them."

"Oh, Addie. I'm sorry. I remember what a rough time you had with your ex."

"Can you consider telling her and then the police?" Mike used his bread to sop up sauce from his almost empty place.

"Please." Addie took Devon's hand.

Devon squeezed back. She glanced around the table. "I appreciate y'all's concern. Knowing how well Jeremy & Elizabeth are doing is encouraging. I'll think about what you've said." Not having to sell the company would be wonderful, but Bailey had to come first.

CHAPTER THIRTEEN

Monday, October 3

Brett slipped off his glasses and rubbed his eyes. The work was tedious at best, and at worst, when he didn't find anything, frustrating as hell. Moore must've stashed the money somewhere, or the goon had made it all up. Brett found investments in an energy company about to go under.

Maybe Moore didn't steal anyone's money and hide it away some place. Maybe he invested the guy's money in this company, and the company kept losing money, giving no rewards to Moore or his client.

But that's the breaks of the market. No one can promise an investment will make money, certainly, not in the energy field, which had been volatile for the last several years. Could the price of oil go any lower?

Brett shoved his reading glasses back on and went to search for the clients were Moore had invested money for. Several days had passed since he and Devon had dinner with Mike and Addie. Still, Devon hadn't decided what to do about Bailey. Brett sighed. Having Bailey out of harm's way would sure make this whole situation less stressful.

"Hey, Mom. I'm home. Mimi said hi." Bailey made for the kitchen and a snack. First, she dropped her backpack in the mudroom at the back door then stepped back into the kitchen and opened the refrigerator door. "Oh, good you've got apples." She took one out of the storage bin, rinsed it off , and then dried the apple with a paper towel before taking a bite. She wiped her chin where the juice wanted to drip.

"Hey, Mom. Where are you? I've got a question."

"Bailey, I'm sorry. I was on the phone in the office. I see you've got a snack. How did practice go?"

"We're excited about our chances, Mom, especially if we can all stay healthy. If we make finals, we'll fly to Nashville during the Christmas holidays. We're supposed to stay at the Gaylord."

"I hope you get to go, sweetie. Y'all have all worked hard. My heart sure stops when you toss the smaller girls up in the air."

"They do the hard part, the rest of us are the muscle." Bailey laughed at her mother's expression.

"Do you have some time, Bailey? I'd like to talk with you." Her mother paced the kitchen like something had upset her.

"Sure, but before you start, can you tell me where the picture albums are? I remember looking at them before we kept everything on our computer and phones."

"What do you need the old albums for?"

"We're doing a family project in our sociology class. We need to make a collage using family pictures from when we

123

were little, showing all our family members. So, I need some of Dad, you, me, and Mimi and Granddad. The old ones when I was young."

"I'll get them." Her mother rose, and by the time she returned Bailey had finished her apple. She washed her hands at the sink and dried them on a hand towel. "Here you go, sweetie." Her mother put five albums on the kitchen table, and Bailey flipped open the first one. "Oh, I remember this trip, Mom. You, Dad, and me traveled to Carlsbad Caverns in New Mexico. I didn't like the caves and Dad picked me up and carried me the whole time." She flipped more pages. "This one will do, too." Bailey shoved the album toward her mother. "Dad's surprise birthday party. You were afraid I'd tell, but I kept the secrete."

"You made me proud of you, sweetheart."

"What did you want to talk with me about? This project may take me a while."

"Oh, I, uh, wanted to follow up with you about selling the house and moving in with Mimi and Granddad until we find something of our own. You're sure you're okay with the plan?"

"Yeah, I've told you I'm good, and I haven't changed my mind."

"Okay then. You enjoy looking at the pictures. I've got work in the study."

Bailey nodded, picked up several albums, carrying them upstairs to her room. Sometimes, her mom acted weird.

Devon walked unsteadily to her office and sank into the chair behind her desk. How could she tell Bailey about her father aft er the way her daughter went on about him, the pictures, and her memories? If she'd explained to Bailey about the missing money and the threats, she'd rip up those memories and tear them to shreds. Poor Bailey. What a mess.

She jumped when her cell rang and without thinking, she pushed the receive button before noticing she didn't recognize the number.

"Hello, Ms. Moore. Do you have my money for me?" The low voice with perhaps a hint of a Texas twang sent chills down her arms.

"What's your name? Why do you think my ex-husband owes you money? And more importantly, why should I pay you for one of his debts?

"Oh, Ms. Moore, I'm disappointed you haven't taken our earlier exchanges seriously. What do I have to do to get your attention?"

Devon's fingers clamped on the cell with enough force, a cramp developed around her thumb. "You haven't answered my questions."

"You're a gutsy broad, but stupid. Better keep a close eye on that daughter of yours, until I get my two million."

"Wait, wait. I've got a buyer for my house. I'll get you one million from the sale. Selling my company will take longer. Please give me more time." Devon's stomach tied itself into knots. Her mouth went dry, and her hands shook. What a sickening situation.

"How long until I get your house money?"

"A week to a week and a half at the latest. We're waiting for the inspection, which I don't expect to have any problems with, and then we can close, and you can get your money."

"Okay. Ms. Moore. You've got yourself more time, but after you get me the million from your house sale, I need a specific time for when I'll get the other." Click

He'd disconnected. Tears ran down Devon's cheeks. She wiped them with her hand. She must be a mess. Couldn't let Bailey see her like this. She had to find a buyer for her company. More tears gathered and fell. She'd have to support them, but how without her business? Dear God, have mercy. Something's got to give.

Devon jerked when her cell beeped again. Now what?
She exhaled in relief. "Oh, hey, Brett." Could he tell she'd been cry?"

"Yeah. Were you expecting someone else?"

"Hey, Mom. Will you look at this?" Bailey shouted down the from the top of the stairs.

"Uh, no, no. Well, I can't say right now." She leaned away from the phone."I'll be there in a minute." She turned back to her cell. "Sorry. Bailey wants some help with her homework." She took a deep breath and released her request. "Would you like to come to supper over here? I'd like you and Bailey to get better acquainted. And I do have something to tell you."

"Thanks. I'd like to, and I may have a breakthrough of sorts to share with you. I'll bring a bottle of wine with me."

"Not necessary, but thanks. See you at 6:30 if that works for you."

"Do you mind I invited Mr. Townsend to join us for supper tonight? Using a long mitt, Devon drew out the baking dish from the oven."

"Your house, Mom. I don't care. As long as you planned enough for all of us." She leaned over the pan and wafted the aroma toward her. "The pork chops and dressing smell awesome."

Devon chuckled at her daughter and her healthy appetite. Her years of cheerleading had made her strong, flexible, and easily able to burn lots of calories.

"I hope he gets here fast. I'm starving." The doorbell chimed. She laughed. "I guess he did. I'll get the door, Mom. You get the food on the table." Bailey skipped toward the front of the house.

Devon shook her head. Had she made a mistake to ask Brett to to have supper with Bailey?

Devon hoped inviting him over would help him better understand her intention of protecting her daughter from the truth about her father.

Talking from a low voice and a higher one preceded her guest and daughter into the kitchen.

"Hey, Devon. I hope this Cab is okay with what you have planned for supper."

"Mom's favorite is champagne, but I haven't seen her drinking it much lately." Bailey took the bottle to the counter and uncorked the wine.

"Thanks for bringing the Cab, Brett. I hope you like pork chops. That's what we're having."

"If it tastes as good as what I'm smelling, I'll be delirious. Can I do anything to help?"

"No. We're ready to sit, which will be good news if you're as hungry as Bailey seems to be. Have a seat." She and Brett took seats across from each other.

Bailey set the wine glasses in front of Devon and Brett and took her place with a glass of water at the end of the table.

"Um. This is good, Devon. You're quite a cook. Not sure I've ever eaten pork chops with dressing before. You've got cranberry sauce, too. I love the stuff." He shoveled in a forkful of pork topped with the dressing.

"Thanks. Glad you're enjoying my mother's recipe."

"Mom and Mimi are both super cooks," Bailey added between bites of her salad and the main dish.

"Do you like to cook, Bailey?" Brett leaned back and sipped his wine.

She nodded. "Yeah. I have fun alternating with Mom each night." She speared a bite of dressing with the cranberries.

"Do we have dessert? I'm trying to decide whether to have seconds," Her daughter asked.

Devon couldn't smother the chuckle fighting to pop out. "I picked up a key lime pie from the bakery."

"Well, I'm stopping now then." Bailey put her fork on her plate.

"Would you like seconds, Brett?"

"As a matter of fact, I would. I missed lunch today, studying some data."

When Brett glanced at Devon, she gave a slight shake of her

head. She hoped to put off any discussion about Franklin and the money until after Bailey went upstairs to attack her homework.

By the time they'd all finished a piece of the key lime pie, they were talked out. Brett and Bailey seemed to have found common ground about working out and keeping in shape.

"Great meal, Mom." Bailey kissed her mother on her cheek. "Mr. Townsend, it was nice to meet you. We should go work out together someday. I'm sure I could learn a few tips from you."

"Anytime your mom says okay is okay with me, Bailey.

She smiled and left the room to go upstairs to finish her homework.

"Let me get these dishes in the washer, and we can talk in the living room."

"I can rinse the dishes. My experience with women tells me you have a special way to put items in the washer. When I've filled the washer at my brothers' houses, my sisters-in-law always come along behind and rearrange. By some magic, they can get more in than I can." Brett used a scrubber on the dishes and set the rinsed off ones on the counter above the washer.

Devon struggled with whether to be offended or to find the humor in the man's statements. Ultimately, a chuckle burst out. She set dishes in the washer the way she wanted them there.

It took less than ten minutes to straighten the kitchen, and then they carried glasses of wine to the living room.

Devon sat on the sofa and Brett settled across from her in one of the wingback chairs.

"I hit on a new idea about your ex-husband's money situation."

"Oh, what is that?"

"What if he didn't steal money? What if he lost money on an investment? Whoever his client is, he doesn't understand that's the breaks with investments. Sometimes you make money, but you can as easily lose money. So, Franklin invested his client's money on a bad deal. That's why we can't find the hiding place. There's not one."

"Good and bad news, I guess. I'm relieved to learn Franklin didn't steal from his client, but he did steal from my company. Now we won't find any money to pay this guy off." She set her drink on the coffee table and leaned forward with her elbows on her knees and her head in her hands.

Brett's hand on her back sent warmth and comfort. She glanced sideways to find he'd moved from his chair to the sofa next to her.

"I guess I'd better find a buyer for my company pretty fast then." She wiped at the tear slipping out of the corner of one eye.

"It's possible we can find the guy who's threatening you and Bailey. The police could arrest him, and he'd stand trial. Then you don't have to sell the business."

"But then Bailey would find out about her father."

"He didn't steal from a client though. He made a bad investment the client lost his money."

"He did steal from me, which is crappy. I'd have loaned him the money if he'd come to me." Another tear slipped out.

Brett's finger tenderly wiped the moisture away. "We'll figure this out."

She hopped from the sofa to stand in front of the mirror. "I must be a mess."

"I bet you've never looked a mess in your entire life. Certainly not now. I see a beautiful woman who has a lot on her shoulders, but you don't have to carry this alone."

"I'd like to trust you, Brett, but I've been betrayed before and now again by Franklin. I'm not depending on anyone again. I appre-ciate your offer of help, but for Bailey's sake, I have to do this on my own."

"Why the change, Devon? Aren't we in this together?"

"Yes, but the man called again and specifically threatened Bailey. I promised him one million as soon as the sale of the house closes. I begged for more time for the second million because I have no idea how long before I can sell the company." A tear squeezed out at the idea of selling her baby she'd worked hard to build and given almost everything to.

"I'll do whatever you decide, Devon. However, you decide to handle the situation, I'm with you. I'm leaving now, but call me if you need anything." He about faced and walked out the front door.

CHAPTER FOURTEEN

Wednesday, October 5

Brett paced his office. A file opened on his computer screen had lost his interest. What could he do about Devon? In his opinion, she'd made such a bad, dangerous decision to avoid the police and handle things on her own. What kept the guy from killing her after he got the money?

Crap. Not a comforting idea at all. And what was all her talk of betrayal? He hadn't done anything to make her doubt him, had he? He got how Franklin had betrayed her on a couple of levels, but what else had happened?

Without hesitation, he yanked his cell phone out and tapped in Mike's number. After a brief discussion, Brett arranged to meet Mike and Addie at Addie's theatre because she had limited time for a get together.

He told his secretary he'd be out of the office for several hours and drove the over thirty miles to west of downtown Fort Worth to Addie's theatre located on the edge of the cultural district for a meeting in her office.

"Can I get you a coffee, Brett?" Addie poured herself and Mike one."

"Sure." He took the offered coffee but didn't sit. Addie moved behind her desk. Mike settled into one of the chairs in front.

"Here's my problem. When I first began checking into Franklin Moore's accounts and files, it occurred to me Devon might have information about her husband's mishandling of the funds—

"Are you kidding? She's not like that," Addie stood behind her desk.

Brett stopped pacing and faced Devon's defender, his hands raised in front of him in a surrender position. "I know that now, Addie. What I've found is, other than the funds Moore took from Devon's company, he didn't steal from anyone else. He lost funds in a bad oil deal."

"He wasn't alone in that. Many people lost money in the downturn of the oil prices. Whole companies went under." Mike shook his head.

"But investors make bad investments. The market goes up and down. Surely, no client believes Franklin lost his money on purpose? Losing the money is the risk you run when you invest in the stock market." Addie sat down but tapped a pencil on her desk.

"Apparently, this client plays by a different set of rules. Devon has a buyer for her home. She'll pay the blackmailer one million as soon as the house closes."

Addie made eye contact with her husband. "Can't you do anything to stop this, Mike. It's unfair and dangerous."

"I'm afraid, not, Addie. Devon has limited our options." "And she's still determined to keep Franklin's actions from Bailey, so the police are out." Brett rubbed his forehead. Not being able to help Devon gave him a headache.

"I hate this. Her company means everything to Devon. The only thing she loves more is her daughter." Addie went from tapping her pencil on the desk to rolling it back and forth, where it made a soft clicking noise whenever it hit her ring.

"Devon mentioned betrayals last night. I understand her ex-husband. Not only did he steal from her but he committed suicide and left her with a total financial mess." He sipped his coffee and dropped into the chair next to Mike. "Why this stubbornness to protect Bailey on her own?"

A glance passed between Mike and Addie.

"Well...what do you know?" Brett pushed. He needed all the information about Devon he could get to be able to help her.

Addie sighed. "It's not my place to tell you. It's Devon's story. The only people she told are Kate, Kim, and me. She didn't even tell her parents. When the other girls and I heard about it, we were too young to give her good advice about what she should do."

"What are you talking about?" Brett leaned forward to catch everything Addie said.

"It's why she always wears makeup. Have you ever seen her without her makeup her on?"

Brett shook his head.

"And you won't."

"The other evening when she cried, she went on and on about how she looked a mess. And she looked like a beautiful woman with tears in her eyes. The way she talked...well, it seemed like she thought she was ugly."

"I can't tell you more, Brett. You'll need to get her to tell you. And frankly, I'd be surprised if she will."

"Okay." He nodded. "Thanks for meeting with me on such short notice. I'm worried about Devon and needed to talk with you."

"We're worried, too. Glad you care about her, Brett. Now, I don't mean to be rude, but I have the board coming in soon, so I'm kicking y'all out." She rose from behind the desk and kissed Mike. "I'll see you this evening?"

133

He nodded.

"And you, Brett Townsend, keep me posted on our girl. If I hear anything from her, I'll let you know, too."

"Thanks, Addie. You're a good friend."

"Easy when we've been there for each other for as long as we have."

When Brett got out in front of the theatre, he shifted toward Mike. "You're a lucky guy."

"You're damn right I am."

"Do you know what's behind Devon's issue about looking good?"

"Nope. Addie's never shared that, and I've never pressed her."

His expression said he wasn't going to now, either.

Th ursday, October 6

Devon walked up the steps to her parents' home. Not the home she'd lived in as a little girl. They moved to the current house just after her twelfth birthday. Such a blessing for her. She couldn't have continued to live in the other place after what happened there. This beautiful older two-story home had columns on the front porch. She loved the house for its warmth, charm, and wonderful backyard with pool. Bailey loved it, too, spending lots of time in the house, when Devon and Franklin had traveled or when she had meetings run long in the early days of getting the company up and going.

Several times when her parents traveled, her friends, Addie Greer, Kate Thompson, and Kim Denison had come and stayed for a weekend while Franklin kept Bailey. Addie and Kate came from Fort Worth and Kim from Wichita Falls. They had such good times, reminiscing about when they were children and current experiences in their lives. Good friends were a definite blessing.

And parents. She was lucky in her parents. She unlocked the front door. "Hey, anyone home?"

"Hey, Devon, glad you stopped by." Her mother gave her an especially long hug and then led her back to the large kitchen, which opened into their den. "I have a recipe to share with you. It's for Italian meatballs and uses oatmeal rather than bread crumbs as filling."

"Is that what I smell in the oven?" She pulled in a deep breath. "Umm yummy."

"I'm serving the meat and sauce over spiraled zucchini. Your father's doctor told him he needed to drop five pounds."

"We can all stand to drop a pound or two." She opened the oven door and looked in. "I'll cook these for Bailey and me."

"Would you like a glass of wine?"

"Never turn down an offer of the grape." Devon settled at the large island, a place she'd had many talks with her mom over many years. She raised the glass and took a healthy sip. Her mother's eyebrows rose.

"What's going on, sweetie?" Miriam sipped her own wine.

"So, the *bad guy*," she finger quoted. "That sounds melodramatic, but I don't have another name for him. He's threatened Bailey directly."

"Oh, dear, God. Devon, you must go to the police!"
"Mom, no. I'm trying to protect Bailey from learning about her father."

"Your priorities are messed up here, Devon. Her life is more im-portant than how she feels about her father." Her mother got up and paced stopping in front of Devon and taking hold of her shoulders. "This is harsh, but what I mean is she can learn to deal with issues about Franklin because she'll be alive to do so."

Devon dropped her head. "I hear you, Mom. I really do, but tomorrow is the last day of school before fall break. I'll meet you and Dad at the airport, and y'all fly to North Carolina to stay at your cabin there. You'll be gone for over a week. And you'll be safe. Weather is beautiful now, and did I say you'll all be safe? That's the important thing."

Her mother took Devon's hands in her own. "But what about you? How do you think I feel going off and leaving you to face this on your own?"

"I won't be entirely alone, Mom. Brett will help me."

"Brett Townsend, who's done the accounting research? What kind of help can he be?"

If her mother had ever met Brett, she wouldn't need to question his abilities. He was so not the nerdy accountant type.

"Besides being a forensic accountant, he's an experienced security expert. Addie's husband, Mike, recommended him. I feel safe with him."

"Oh, you do, do you?" Her mother's eyebrows went up, and she smiled. Devon could guess where her thinking had gone.

"When do we get to meet him?"

Yep. She knew her mother well. Just what Devon expected. Didn't take much to push her mother into matchmaker mode. "We're friends, Mom." No reason to comment on the way her stomach did that weird dropping thing whenever she saw him. Time to change the subject.

"So, are y'all ready to leave tomorrow?"

"Yes, and we're happy to have Bailey with us. Your dad and I will do anything for the two of you."

Devon nodded and hugged her mother. Maybe she'd made a mistake all those years ago, not to tell them about what happened. But at a young twelve, she didn't understand. It must've been her fault. Ah, well.

"Mom, I'll talk with Bailey about the trip when she gets home today. I've put off the discussion, but this gives her time to pack, but not too much to make a stink. I can't imagine why she'd kick up a stink about going with you to your cabin in the woods where the leaf colors will be awesome. She loves it there. I confess to being envious." She smiled.

"Wish you'd come, sweetie. I hate leaving you here." She drew Devon in for another big hug. "And I'd feel better if we could meet this Brett person before we leave." A troubled smile showed her unease and her desire to check out the man spending time with her daughter.

"I'll see what I can do, Mom. Maybe he'll have time tomorrow morning." How would she explain to Brett she wanted him to meet her parents? But she had to convince him for her mother's peace of mind.

"Lovely, Devon. Thank you. Your father and I will be here all morning preparing for the trip. Anytime works. Call us when you're on the way."

"Okay. Thanks, Mom." She took a last sip of the wine, kissed her mother on the cheek, and left. On the way to her car, she glanced back over her shoulder. Sure enough, her mother stood on the front porch and waved. A habit they all had.

Driving toward her office, she activated on the board calling system. Might as well get this over with. What would she do if Brett couldn't stop by her parents' house tomorrow? He might be tied up with a job or have a dentist appointment. Geez.

"Call Brett Townsend."

The phone rang and rang. As she prepared to leave a message, Brett picked up at the last moment.

"Everything okay, Devon?"

"Hey, Brett. Yes, thanks. I do have a favor to ask though. Do you have a minute?"

"Sure. What do you need?"

Devon heaved a sigh. "I need you to meet my parents tomorrow morning if that's at all possible."

"Well, sure, I'm scheduled to be in the office tomorrow, but I can get away. I'm happy to meet them, but why the sudden urgency?"

"They'll leave for their North Carolina cabin tomorrow and take Bailey with them. Mom's worried about me staying here by myself." She glanced out the side window and changed lanes. "I told her you'd be here."

"Okay."

"She wants to make sure you can take care of me if need be."

Brett laughed. "I'll be sure to bring my security credentials and maybe the results of my last weapons practice."

Devon chuckled, too. "Well, that probably won't be necessary. What time works best for you?"

"How about 11:15. After we visit for a while, I'll take you to lunch."

Oh, my. Well, lunch wasn't dinner. She should be fine. Shouldn't she?

"Devon. You still there?"

"Uh, yes. Uh. Lunch will be nice. And thanks for seeing my parents."

"Will you be at your office in the morning? I can come by and pick you up and then we'll go to your parents' house."

"That will be fine. Give me a buzz when you get there, and I'll meet you in the garage."

"How long from your office to your parents'?"

"About twenty minutes."

"I'll pick you up at 10:55 then."

"Thanks, Brett."

Why had he asked her out to lunch? Maybe he had more things to talk with her about than the stalker/blackmailer guy. She hoped her problems weren't the only reason he wanted to talk with her. Her tummy did its Ferris Wheel imitation. Not altogether uncomfortable.

"WhooHoo! One more day until Fall Break." Bailey tossed her backpack on the bench in the mudroom. "Let's go someplace, Mom." She skipped into the kitchen. "What do we have to eat?"

Her mother trailed behind her. "How about popcorn? Won't take a minute with the new microwave container I have."

"Okay, but only if you slather the popcorn in butter." She took a soft drink from the fridge and settled on one of the bar stools. The pop and fizzy sound always made her smile.

"Well, that does sort of defeat the purpose of microwaving in the first place, but of course, we must." While the popcorn in the bright red container in the microwave popped cheerily, her mother selected the yellow spread from the fridge. After removing the popcorn container, she slid in a dish with the spread. In just a few seconds it melted, and her mother drizzled it over the popcorn she'd emptied into two small bowls.

"I've got the salt." Bailey tipped the container over the white puffs.

"Let's get back to talking about a trip, Bailey. How about the North Carolina cabin with Mimi and Granddad?"

"You bet. It will be gorgeous there this time of year. Boy airplane tickets will cost a fortune at the last minute if we can even get seats this late." Bailey took a healthy swallow of her soda. "This is yummy, but the little red plastic thingy doesn't make nearly enough, Mom."

"This is not supper, Bailey. Count it as a snack. Your grandparents have already purchased the tickets. I'll pick you up after school tomorrow and take you to meet them at the airport. Can you get packed tonight?"

"Of course. It's the mountains. Jeans, sweaters, and jackets, and I'll be set to go."

"Throw in one pair of black slacks or long skirt, so you'll okay if your grandparents decide to eat at the country club while you're there."

"That jersey knit will roll up easy-peasy. With my leather jacket and good boots, I can go anywhere. I'm glad we can go, Mom."

Her mother eased off the stool next to her. "I hope you won't be too disappointed, Bailey, but I'm not going." She walked around to the sink and rinsed their bowls. "With selling the house, I need to do a lot of cleaning and throwing out and giving away. I'm still looking for someone to buy the company—"

"I don't understand why you need to sell the company, Mom. I get moving from here. This is way more space than you and I need, but your company?"

Her mother stood and walked to the wine rack, slid out a bottle, and used the cork remover Bailey had given her last Christmas.

"I do love the company, Bailey; it's provided me lots of freedom and a feeling of accomplishment. But there are more things I want to do with my life. You only have two more years before you leave for college. I plan to be available for all the events. When you graduate, I'll travel more. Being tied down to the same place every single day of my life doesn't sound as much fun as it once did."

"Huh. Surprised to hear you say that., but whatever makes you happy is good with me, so long as we have money for college. Ending up with tons of debt the way some kids do, doesn't sound like fun."

"You'll be okay. Your father and I set up a separate savings ac-count when you were born."

Bailey scooped the last kernels of the popcorn, and set the bowl in the sink. "When's supper?"

"In an hour. Why don't you see about putting your clothes to-gether for the trip? We have time to wash anything you want to take. We're having meatloaf with mashed potatoes and salad for supper. Sound okay?"

"Great. I hope Mimi cooks a lot while we're there. She's the only one who's better than you, Mom, and she can teach me how to make some new dishes." She laughed as she climbed the stairs.

Devon joined her daughter's teasing laughter as she set a large pot of water on the stove and then washed potatoes before cutting them up. Was she doing the right thing sending her parents and Bailey away? For sure, but she'd miss them all. She did have tons of work to do. Packing up everything to sell the house topped her to-do list. If only finding someone to buy the company could be as easy as selling her house.

Damn, Franklin. Why'd he do this to Bailey and her? She slapped the ground beef on the board and made the oblong shape the way her mother always did, using eggs and Ritz crackers to help it stick together. Her addition to the recipe was to use more onions than her mother recommended and to add red pepper flakes. She added the loaf to the pan and slid it in the oven.

It was one thing to sell the house, but the idea of selling Bailey Moore Cosmetics? Nausea rose in the back of her throat. The company had been her baby for a long time. She'd poured her heart and soul into its development. She'd been pulling in big bucks for several years. More importantly, she'd helped plenty of women with her products. Everyone wears a mask. Some need more help than others with that mask.

She threw together the ingredients for a salad, items she always had on hand in her fridge. The potatoes were bubbling crazily. She turned down the gas and let them go for a while longer.

"Hey, Mom," Bailey shouted from upstairs. "When do we eat?"
"The meatloaf has another twenty minutes, and the potatoes need longer before I can whip them."

"I'll put in a load to wash before I come down then."

Was Devon doing the right thing? She'd do whatever it took to keep her daughter safe. Devon took out her fear and frustration on mashing the potatoes.

CHAPTER FIFTEEN

Friday, October 7

Brett drove into the Bailey Moore Cosmetics Company garage but didn't have to wait for Devon. She came through the office doors before he'd come to a complete stop.

He hopped out and held the car door for her. "You shouldn't have come out until you were sure who was here."

"Well, hello to you, too, Mr. Townsend."

Brett shook his head. "Sorry. I'm in security mode where you're concerned." Of course, if he wasn't careful, he could easily find himself embroiled with more than the gorgeous redhead's safety. "So, can I start over?"

"Please." Devon nodded her encouragement.

"Good morning, Ms. Moore. It's a beautiful day out. Almost as lovely as you." Oops, maybe he'd gone too far. A lovely pink splashed across Devon's cheeks. Had he moved too fast? Yeah, maybe. Eventually, they'd resolve this mess of Franklin's business and then....

"Kind of you, Brett. I wouldn't have expected such poetry from a forensic auditor."

"Guess you bring out my more artsy side." He glanced at her as the pink deepened to a lovely rose. Traffic drew his attention back to the road. Before the lunchtime rush, but Dallas traffic notoriously never slowed down.

He hit the brakes when a black pickup cut in front of them. His arm flew across to protect Devon as they were both flung forward. "Oof."

"Thanks. Do you have kids, Brett? You have a super-affective *mom-save*-move."

"Only nieces and nephews, but my father always protected my mom when he slammed on the breaks by throwing out his arm." Brett's super-affective move produced other results. He'd have difficulty climbing from the car right now. Devon's breasts were firm to his touch and soft at the same time. He needed to use his big head to keep her safe. He drew in a long breath and let it out.

"Tell me something about your parents, Devon." Maybe hearing about them would keep his mind off the gorgeous woman sitting next to him."

"Both my parents were college professors, retired now, spending all their time on charity events. Their schedules gave them the flexibility to help with Bailey when she was young. She loved hanging out with Mimi and Granddad. One time I got to their house to find her on the floor with my father, and they were using screw drivers to take apart the kitchen table."

Brett laughed. "A professor who was good with his hands, huh?"

"Yes, his father had been a builder, and when his company took off and he made a lot of money, he made sure Dad had the skills to handle anything to come along. Mom made sure I knew to be grateful for his skills. He can fix anything."

"What about your mother?"

"She was the first in her family to go to college, and her parents were thrilled when she caught a wealthy man. Stereotypical of them, but those were the times. Mom's an artist who loves teaching. Many of the pictures in their house are hers."

"Impressive."

"Anyway, because I'm an only child, they've always been over protective. Not helicopter parents, but keeping a close eye. This whole mess with Franklin and the *bad guy,* as I referred to him the other day, has made them pretty nuts."

"Understandable. I'll make them comfortable about leaving you here, I promise."

"Thank you."

She rested her hand on his arm for a moment squeezing once. He covered her hand with his and nodded.

"Slow down." She removed her hand from his arm and pointed.

Too bad she took her hand away. He liked the warm feel she'd left, almost as if her hand belonged there.

"Their house is the third on the left."

After parking in the circular drive, Brett escorted Devon up the steps, his hand resting on the small of her back. He liked that feel, too.

The front door flew open. An attractive older woman with hair only a little less red than Devon's stood in the entry.

"Mother, this is Brett Townsend. I've told you about him."

"Hello, Mrs. Bailey." He shook the hand she'd held out to him.

"It's Miriam, Brett. Nice to meet you. Come in. Can I get you some sweet tea?"

"Wouldn't turn down a cold drink, thanks." He followed the two women into a large entryway and then to a den in the back of the house. Large windows showed off a spectacular pool with spar-kling turquoise water. "Wow, that's gorgeous."

"Thanks, we think so." A tall slender man rose from a leather chair. "You must be the man my daughter tells me will keep her safe while we're gone."

"Yes, sir. Brett Townsend." Brett studied Mr. Bailey the way Bailey studied him. Brett would've, too, if the positions were reversed.

"Richard Bailey. Good to meet you." They shook hands. "Devon why don't you go help your mother with the sweet tea."

"But, Dad." Devon glanced between her father and Brett. "We'll be okay. Now run along." He shooed her off with both hands.

With one last glance at Brett and a shrug of her shoulders, Devon left the room.

Richard Bailey gestured for Brett to sit on the sofa, and he dropped onto the plush leather. Devon's father settled in the chair across from him.

"So, I understand you're also the one who found my daughter's ex had been cooking the books, so to speak."

"Yes, sir.

"I never cared for Moore. Not supposed to speak ill of the dead, and he loved Bailey, but he got caught up in the trappings of his wealth. He never could have enough money. For him to have lost him to lose their money...well, I'm mad as hell. Putting her and our granddaughter in danger is inexcusable!" His hand squeezed the arm of the chair to the point his knuckles whitened. He drew in a ragged breath, paused a moment. "How do you propose to keep Devon safe?"

Brett leaned forward and spoke in a softer voice than usual. "I haven't told Devon yet, but I'm moving in with her."

"What?" Moore straightened in his chair.

"Not like that, sir." Brett quickly responded, though he wouldn't object to the living arrangements if they were possible. Hell. An idea he needed to stuff away. "I'll serve as her personal bodyguard. Whoever this guy is, he doesn't stand a chance to get your daughter. It helps for you and Mrs. Bailey to take your granddaughter with you out of the state. I can more easily focus on Devon's safety," and Brett sat back."When are you leaving?" He wanted all the details he could get.

"We'll head to the airport in about two hours."

"What's your security like at the cabin, sir?"

"We're in a gated community with a guard at the entry and security cameras on our cabin. We feel safe there. Miriam used to take Devon when I couldn't get away. I never worried about them."

"Good to hear."

"Could they come after us all the way to North Carolina?" A frown cut grooves between his eyebrows.

"I don't know. Frankly, I've been arguing with Devon, but she's adamant against the idea of going to the police about this. She seems determined to protect her daughter's view of her father. Not the best plan to me, but she's the client."

"Client, huh? You sure there's nothing else going on? She's only a client, Mr. Townsend?"

Well, hell, so much for hiding his feelings. "No, Mr. Bailey, but I've not tried to do anything about a relationship. She has enough to worry about with her ex killing himself and all this blackmail."

"Good to know." Mr. Moore nodded. "Now, I'm sure you'll take care of her."

"Yes, sir. I will."

"So sorry, gentlemen. We had to brew a fresh pot of tea." Miriam and Devon entered the den. Devon held a tray with a tea pitcher and glasses. Miriam held a smaller tray with cookies.

"Now this is sweet tea, Brett. It's the only kind we serve in my house."

"Yes, ma'am." Brett caught Devon rolling her eyes.

Miriam sat with a glass in her hand. "So, did you explain to

Richard how you'll keep our daughter safe while we're gone?"

"He's moving in with her, Miriam."

"What?" Miriam and Devon spoke together.

Saturday, October 8

Devon hadn't recovered from the shock of learning of Brett's plan to move in with her. What was he thinking? What did her parents think of his idea? They seemed to be quite okay with the idea, instead of shocked. And she? What would she do with him in the house with her? Already the time she'd spent with him took a toll on her hormones. They skittered all over the place whenever he stood near. She didn't have time to be distracted. She had to pack, arrange for movers to take her furniture to a storage facility, and find a buyer for her company.

The last task made moisture pool in her eyes. How could she sell the company?

It meant everything to her. Maybe she could convince the *bad guy* to be satisfied with the one million. Yeah, right.

The noise of the mail falling through the slot in her front door drew her to the entrance. Mail delivery had been coming later and later. She stooped to pick up several bill-looking things and a large black envelope. What in the world? She dropped the mail on her desk in her study and picked up her letter opener to see what the intriguing black envelope held. Some sort of society event?

The doorbell interrupted her. She fumed as she returned to the front of the house. Through the glass she recognized Brett and opened the door. She stepped back, and he walked into the entryway.

"Are you sure this is necessary?" Despite her efforts, her hands went into a wringing action.

He dropped a bag in the hall. "Yeah. Despite the attacks in the two garages, you don't seem to realize how vulnerable you are."

"I can take care of myself."

"You didn't then."

"I'll start carrying my gun."

"You have a permit to carry?"

"Yes. I haven't practiced much lately after I got used to Franklin not living at home and it seemed…well, I'm a busy person."

He nodded. "Yes, you are. We'll go out and brush up on your skills, okay?"

"That's not necessary. As soon as I finish looking at the mail, I'll whip up something for our supper."

"That will be nice, but we haven't finished with the gun subject. Glad your parents and Bailey were able to get away okay."

"Yes. I don't have to worry about them."

"Where am I bunking?"

"I'm sorry." She'd left him standing in the entryway. Where was her brain? "It's the first room on the left upstairs." She pointed toward the stairs. "There are fresh sheets on the bed and towels in the adjoining bathroom." He nodded, picked up his bag, and headed that direction. Devon returned to the study.

She slit open the black envelope. Probably a charity invitation. Her fingers grasped the glossy sheet. Oh, God. She gasped and screamed, dropping the picture on the floor.

"Devon. Devon. What's the matter? Are you all right?" Brett burst into the study with a gun in his hand.

She stared silently at him, pointing to the picture on the floor. He stopped and picked up the image of Bailey and Devon's parents with red X's across their bodies.

"Dear God. Devon, I'm sorry." He enveloped her in his arms, close to his body, and she leaned against him.

"I'm glad you're here, Brett." His heartbeat comforting.

"Me, too. Give your parents a call and check on Bailey."

"Yes. Yes." She stepped away from the strong man, wishing

she could stay in his arms longer. Picking up her phone, she punched in Bailey's number. Her daughter answered.

"Hey, Mom. Good timing. We landed only minutes ago. How are you doing?"

"Good. Good. Can I talk to your grandmother?"

"Sure." Muffled noised indicated she handed the phone over.

"Hey, dear. Everything all right?"

"Mom, listen. Don't react. I've received a picture in the mail of you and Dad and Bailey." She paused. "There are red X's across your faces."

Silence for several seconds before Miriam managed, "I see. Well, we'll be sure to watch out for the bad weather, dear." She must've an-gled her head away towards her husband and Bailey because her voice got softer, but still Devon made out her mother's words. "Devon says we might be in for some bad weather." Turning back to Devon. "We'll take precautions, dear. Thanks for the warning. We're about to debark. I'll keep you posted."

"Love you, Mom."

"Me too, you." She disconnected.

"Mom's a rock!" She told him what her mother had said.

"She's quick for sure." He held out his hand. "Come with me to check out your house. See if there is anything more we need to do to upgrade the security."

Devon took his hand, and an instant sense of calm settled in. Scary times, but she trusted Brett to keep her safe.

CHAPTER SIXTEEN

Friday, October 14

"Hey, Mimi, this has been the best week. We hit the timing just right to catch the leaves. They've been spectacular. It's been a gorgeous fall." She arranged a bunch in a vase. "It may be stupid to do this when we'll be leaving soon, but I love them."

"Glad you enjoy yourself here, Bailey. And I agree, New England has nothing on our North Carolina colors! What do you want for supper? Granddad suggested BBQ chicken."

"Sounds yummy to me."

"You and I can go down to the store and pick up what we'll need."

"Okay. I'm picking up a sweater, and then I'll meet you at the front door." Her grandparents surprised her with wanting to cook. Usually, they didn't prepare a meal the night before leaving. They got take out so there'd be less to clean up. Oh, well, she wasn't turning down her granddad's BBQ chicken.

The drive down the mountain took about ten minutes. A person could walk it in about thirty. Going down was considerably eas-ier than coming up. Usually, Bailey and her grandparents had made the walk a couple of times on prior visits, but not this time. Maybe age was catching up with them. She'd have to remember to talk with her mother about their health.

Because they'd been coming to the cabin for many years, grocery store employees were familiar with visitors by name.

"Bailey Moore, you are all grown up. I'd heard you were in town. I've been down with a cold and have missed seeing you on this visit. Tell me you haven't graduated yet." The checker rang up the first of their items.

"No, ma'am. About a year and a half yet."

"Where you planning to go to college, sweetie? University of North Carolina is a pretty special place. That's where my granddaughter goes." The older woman's accent dripped of honey and magnolias.

"I've heard that. I'll probably go to UT. My grandfather went there." She lifted the chicken breasts from the buggy and put the package on the counter.

"The University of Tennessee, huh? Well, I'll be."

"No, ma'am. The University of Texas."

The checker chuckled, "Figured that's what you meant, but I had to ride you a bit." She scanned the corn on the cob. "Y'all having company for supper?"

"No, it's only the three of us, Peggy. Why do you ask?" Mimi pulled out her wallet and grasped her credit card.

"A man showed up yesterday, flashing around Bailey's picture to see if we knew her. He was supposed to meet up with her family, and he'd lost their contact information."

"Did you tell him where our cabin is?" Mimi's voice had a ragged sound, as if the story scared her. What's this about? Everyone knows everyone here. Even the part-timers like they were.

"I told him y'all were in your cabin in the Hunter's Hill development. That he could contact you through the guard at the front gate. Did I do wrong? He seemed like a regular guy. Someone y'all might know."

"Did you catch his name? Can you describe him?" Mimi tapped her fingers on the top of the checkout counter. Something must be bothering her grandmother. She was easy-going and laid-back. Nothing fazed Mimi.

"He didn't leave his name, average height less than 6 feet. Not heavyset at all. Thinish, but looked strong if you get what I mean. He talked the way y'all do. So, I figured he must know you. Did I do something wrong?"

"No, Peggy. Thanks for telling us about the man looking for us. Here, Bailey, you carry the heavier bag." She handed her the blue canvas bag. "I'll take the lighter one." She picked up the green bag. "See you, Peggy."

"What's the matter, Mimi?" Bailey held open the door of the store for her grandmother.

"Maybe nothing. I'm being cautious. Were you expecting any friends to join us up here?"

"No. Several people went skiing, and some went to the beach. I wasn't chancing breaking my ankle on a skiing trip, not after last summer's mess up, and the beach isn't my thing. I like the mountains a lot more. The air is so fresh. That's why I was glad we came up here. Wish Mom could've come, but I've been happy here."

They put the groceries in the back of the 4-wheel drive and then climbed in the front.

"Before we leave, I need to check with Richard if he needs anything else."

"If we don't hurry, we won't get back before dark, Mimi. I know you don't like to drive on mountain roads then."

"This will take a second." She punched in her husband's name on her phone. "Hey, hon. I'm checking to see if you need anything else for supper? Okay then. We'll be home soon."

She disconnected and punched in Blair's mother's face.

"Now you're calling Mom? Mimi, let's go. I'm starving, and Granddad still has to cook the chicken."

"Hold on, Bailey...Oh, Devon, honey. Glad I caught you. We may have a visitor up here. Wanted to let you know...Some man asked in the store about Bailey...no. He'd have to get through the guard and the gate...We're heading back now. I'll contact you when we get there. Love you. We will." Her grandmother disconnected and started up the 4-wheel drive, backed out of the parking space, and headed up the mountain.

"What's going on, Mimi? I'm a big girl. You can tell me. Why were you telling Mom about the person in the store? Lots of folks from Texas come up here."

"You're right, sweetie, but, Bailey, you can't be too careful when you're in a strange area. I've heard of reports about escaped convicts."

"What? I haven't heard that?"

"You don't read the newspaper either, Bailey, dear."

"Well, you've got me there, but I haven't seen anything on the Internet."

Bailey used her phone to surf the web.

After a while, her grandmother spoke. "Bailey, can you read the letters and numbers on the license plate of the car behind us?"

"I didn't find anything about your escaped convicts story, Mimi. And yes, I'm sure I can."

"Don't turn around. Use the side mirror."

She did as her grandmother requested. "Now if I can reverse them...CVE 97478."

"You're sure?"

Bailey looked again. "Sure."

"Can you make a note of the number on your phone

for me please?"

"You got it."

"What can you see of the driver? He's pulled up pretty close." Mimi reached out a hand and stopped her from turning around. "Look through the side mirror like you did for the license plate."

"Okay, but you're acting beyond weird."

"Humor your old Mimi."

"Yeah, right old. You look like you could be Mom's sister... okay, he has salt and pepper hair. Can't tell anything about height."

Mimi took the turn up toward the gatehouse.

"He's followed us, Mimi. He must have a cabin up here."

Her grandmother stopped at to the gatehouse instead of driving straight through when the guard waved her in. "Hey, Dennis."

"Hey, Mrs. Moore. What can I do for you?"

"I'm afraid the car behind me may be following us. If you don't recognize him as a member here, please don't let him in."

"No ma'am, I won't. Oh, looks like he was lost and finally got his bearings. He's reversing and heading back down the hill."

Her grandmother let out a long sigh. "Good. Thanks, Dennis. Have a good evening."

"You, too, ma'am. Good night, Bailey."

"Okay, let's get to the cabin so your granddad can get busy with the BBQ."

"I'll get the corn ready."

"Thank you, Bailey. I can always count on you."

Friday, October 14

"Hey, Mom. I can tell from your pictures, y'all are having a great time." Devon settled the cell more comfortably on her shoulder while she continued to empty the dishwasher.

"Devon, I'm worried we've been followed up here."

The strain in her mom's voice was as scary as her words. Devon juggled her phone and dropped a glass in the process of keeping contact with her mother. The shattering sounds brought Brett running to the kitchen and ratcheted up Devon's heartbeat.

"What happened?"

She waved a hand to shush Brett. "Mom, let me put you on speaker so Brett can hear."

"Oh, I'm relieved you're there, Brett." The tension in her mother's voice relaxed when she realized he was present.

"Mom, tell us why you think someone followed you to North Carolina."

Brett's eyebrows rose, and he moved closer to Devon, draping his arm across her shoulders.

"Bailey and I had gone down the mountain to the store to get supplies for your father to BBQ chicken. While we were there, Peggy—she's the head cashier, Brett, and we've known her for ever—well, Peggy said a man had been in the store showing a picture of Bailey around and asking where she lived."

"Oh, my God, Mom. What are you talking about? Tell me everything." One hand reached for Brett's free hand, needing something to tether her to the room. She wanted to hop a plane and go to Bailey and her parents to make sure they were safe.

"I'll get this out, Devon if you stop talking. I don't have much time before Bailey comes back inside from the deck where she's helping your father with the grilling."

"Sorry."

"Go on, Miriam." Brett's calm tone helped Devon keep a grip.

"Driving up the mountain to Hunter's Hill, I noticed a car behind us, drawing closer and closer. I asked Bailey to read the license plate."

"It's probably a rental if it's someone from Dallas and not a local." Brett inserted. "But give me the info." Her mother repeated the number, and he made a note on a small pad. "What happened, Miriam?"

"I stopped at the security gate and told the guard my concern. While I talked with him, he noticed the car turning around and going back down the mountain."

"Smart move, Miriam. You keep talking with Devon. I'll get my people to check out the plate."

"Oh, Mom. I'm sorry." Devon's heart ached to the point she feared she'd be sick. "I've messed up asking you to go to your cabin, but you should've been safer there than here." Devon paced avoiding the broken slivers of glass on the kitchen floor.

"Sweetie, this is not your fault. Actually, we probably are safer here with the guard at the gate and the large fence surrounding the whole facility." Her voice trembled. "It did unnerve me though."

"Maybe you should stay there for a few more days. How did Bailey react to all this?"

"It's her opinion her Mimi is a bit paranoid." Her mother forced a chuckle.

"Let's put off your returning for another week, Mom. I'd hoped Brett and I could have settled matters here, but we need more time. I miss you, but I want you to be safe when you come home." She nearly gagged talking about her parents and daughter's safety. What a nightmare.

"Bailey is eager to get home to her friends. I've overheard some of her conversations. She's looking forward to seeing everyone, Devon."

"I'm sorry you'll get the brunt of her ire, Mom, but you must stay. After Dad finishes cooking, please go inside and lock up. Check all the windows and put on the alarm. We don't normally take those precautions when we're there, but I'll sleep better knowing you're securely locked up."

"Okay, Devon. You take care. Love you."

"Love you, too, Mom."

Devon disconnected and shoved the cell into the pocket of her slacks. She glanced down at the floor. "Guess I'd better clean up this mess." With a broom from the pantry, she focused on sweeping up the glass. As she worked, tears filled her eyes. She paused to dab at them with a tissue. Her parents and her daughter were in danger. And it was her fault. Well, technically, Franklin's. But as usual, he'd escaped the consequences of his actions.

"Hey, you okay?" The deep tones of Brett's voice when he stepped into the kitchen had a calming effect on her. He'd have ideas of what to do.

Devon emptied the shards of glass into the trash bin and put away the dust pan and the broom. "I told Mom to plan to stay through next week. The compound has a high fence along the boundaries, and there's a guard at the gate. Despite what happened today, they're probably safer there than here. Right?"

He nodded.

She'd have to believe Brett's assessment of her parents' location. "Did you find out anything about the car?"

"Yeah, a rental as we suspected. I don't have the name of the renter yet, but I will. I'm not familiar with the specifics, but can Bailey miss school with no repercussions?"

"I'll have to go in Monday and give them some explanation. Not the truth, but something."

"I'll go with you."

"You don't need to do that."

"Devon, until we get this straightened out, I'm sticking with you like white on rice as they say in the south."

Devon laughed at his exaggerated southern accent. "Thanks for making me laugh and for being here."

"You're welcome. I have some work to do on my computer. Tell me when you're ready to turn in."

Devon had been surprised at how easily she and Brett had worked out their living arrangements. Neither ate breakfast. They

157

carried coffee with them to her cosmetics company where he left her before he continued to Franklin's office where he dug into tracing the money. She stayed in her office building until he came to get her at the end of the day. Sometimes they'd eat supper out. Sometimes they'd cook. Brett was a good cook. His spaghetti was to die for. They acted like an old married couple with one of them cooking and one cleaning and both disappearing behind their computers in the evening. They watched the 10 o'clock news and then worked for an hour longer.

He'd never tried to kiss her, but he touched her often, and sometimes she'd notice something in his eyes causing tension to coil in her middle.

Sunday, October 16

Devon sat in the kitchen sipping her coffee. The mild temperature made her want to go outside to enjoy the patio, but Brett made her promise to stay inside with the alarm on while he went after donuts and to his office for a short time.

Her phone chirped with the sound for her daughter.

"Hey, Bailey. How's the weather there? It's plenty warm here."

"Mom. I don't want to stay here. Mimi says we have to stay, but I have to go back to school."

"Ah, Bailey. I can't explain, but this is for the best for now."

"Mom, what about cheerleading? The squad is preparing for nationals in case we get an invitation. If I miss practice, I won't be able to go, and they'll put in someone from the junior varsity. I have to go home."

Blair's voice trembled with unshed tears. Devon ached for her daughter's pain, but what could she do?

"Sweetie, this is hard, but I need for you to stay in North

Carolina with Mimi and Granddad."

"But why? Tell me why?"

Devon let the silence go on longer than she should've, but what could she say? Not only did your father steal from my company, but he owed money to some scary bad dude who's threatened to come aft er us? Not happening.

"I'm sorry, Bailey. I need you to be a grownup about this. We don't always get everything we want in life. I'll talk with Mimi about registering you in school up there on Monday."

"OMG, Mom. You've got to be joking! I'm not attending a Podunk small-town school. You can't expect me to do that." Her normally low-pitched voice spiraled into the atmosphere.

"Well, I do expect you to." Devon struggled to keep her voice level. "Please get on board with this. I hope you won't be there for longer than a week or two, but I can't have you missing school." Devon's stomach tied into knots and her fingers clenched her cell. This situation made her sick, but she had to keep her daughter safe. No matter what.

"Bailey dear. I love you. Please, I need you to understand." Silence followed her words. What could she do to get Bailey to forgive her and play along? And she had to play along. What else could she do?

"Okay, mom." The connection ended

"Damn, but it's hard to be a mother." She leaned her head on her arms on the center island and sobbed.

"Hey, Devon. I'm back with the best donuts you'll ever eat." Brett entered the kitchen to find Devon sitting at the bar with her head resting on her arms, her shoulders shaking.

"Devon, what's the matter?" He set the sack on the counter, gently faced her toward him, and lifted her chin. Tears ran unchecked down her cheeks. She yanked her head away and used her hands to cover her face.

"Don't look at me. I must be a mess. I've cried off all my makeup." She pulled away from him, but he didn't let go.

"Tell me what's wrong. Is Bailey okay? Are your parents? Tell me. I can't help if I don't know what we're dealing with."

She hiccupped several times, before the tears ended. Still, she faced away from him. What the hell was with that? Did she really think he was so shallow he'd be turned off if he saw her without makeup or with her mascara running? He needed to get her to tell him about whatever had caused her odd reaction, but not now.

"Okay, Devon. If this is not a life and death situation, you go to the bathroom, get cleaned up, and then you come tell me why you were upset."

She nodded and left the room.

"I'll be damned." He had expected her to turn and say no she could talk. But she didn't. The makeup thing must be a big deal. Such a big deal he worried about what caused her reaction. Brett set a cup under the one-cup coffee maker and snapped the small receptacle in place. Taking the crullers from his favorite store out of the bag, he put them along with the sausage rolls in the microwave for a quick warm up. With a plate of the donuts and his coffee cup, he went to the back patio. Good time to enjoy this mild weather.

Easily fifteen minutes had passed before Devon joined him carrying her cup. She looked her regular beautiful self, makeup perfectly in place. Must be a giant hurt to make her keep her shield in place the way she did.

"I'm sorry I fell apart."

"It's okay, Devon. You're under lots of pressure." Brett sipped his second cup of coffee.

"Thanks for bringing the donuts." She sat on the edge of the Adirondack chair before sliding back in a more relaxed position.

"I'm afraid they're cold now."

She shrugged and lifted a crueler from the plate.

"Can you tell me what had you upset when I got here?"

"I'd been talking with Bailey, and she's adamant about not staying and attending school."

"Not surprising. Who'd want to change schools for an indefinite amount of time during their junior year of high school?"

"Gee thanks, Brett. Your words cast this whole situation and me in such a great light." She scowled at him.

"Devon, I'm saying, you shouldn't be surprised, since you're determined to keep her in the dark about what's going on. Which I'll remind you, I've stated on several occasions is such a mistake. You don't' protect kids by keeping information from them. With the information, they can better protect themselves."

She rose and paced to the railing and back. "I appreciate your perspective, but I have to make decisions concerning Bailey I believe are best for her."

"I get that, Devon. Hell, if I had the decision-making authority, we'd be sitting downtown at the police station, asking for all the help we could get with this crazy guy who's determined to take money from you."

She stared at him. "I appreciate you not pushing me to do that, Brett."

He stood, reached out, and took her hand. She didn't pull away. He gently rubbed his thumb over the back of her hand. "I know this is tough, Devon. We'll work out the mess. I need you to trust me." He positioned her in front of him and lifted a h and t o b rush a t a long spiral of her glorious red hair.

He drowned in her beautiful green eyes. Must be some Irish in her background. His hands skimmed up and down her arms. What he wanted to do, he shouldn't do. He wanted badly to kiss her, to hold her, and keep all the bad away from her and her family. Well, he could probably do the last, but that wouldn't satisfy the burning in his gut telling him he wanted to be more to this woman than someone who worked for her.

What was the matter with her? His blue eyes mesmerized her, and butterflies set up a convention in her stomach. A not altogether unpleasant feeling, and it had been a long time since she'd experienced anything like this. She wanted to kiss him. His lips when he spoke tantalized her. His hands on her arms were warm and inviting. Oh, to let go and revel in some mind-blowing sex. Make all the bad go away—at least for a time. Was he interested? She hoped so. Could she gather enough courage to make the first move? Oh, she hoped so.

"Brett." She raised her right hand and ran a finger over his lips. He opened his mouth and sucked on her finger. Her breath hitched. Must be interested. Her left hand glided up his broad chest and over his strong shoulders to join her right, encircling his neck. She went up on her toes and touched her lips to his, gently at first, but he quickly responded, and the kiss deepened causing her heart rate to kick up several notches.

Was she going through with this? He pulled her close. His growing erection warmed her middle, sending shock waves to her nether regions, which clenched with increasing need. It had been so long. Long before she and Franklin finalized the divorce. Her body cried out for Brett's.

Because of her early experience, it took her a lot longer than most to become comfortable with her sexuality, but she had. After losing any interest in the waning years of her marriage, she'd now awakened to needs which she'd been ignoring.

"Devon." His voice roughened, and his breathing became as erratic as hers. "Are you sure about what you're doing? Because I'd hate for you to regret this later if we keep going, and God I hope we keep going." One hand slid between their bodies, and he massaged her breast, gently pinching the nipple through her lace bra.

"We'll have to, Brett, or we'll have two incredibly disappointed and frustrated people." She stepped back and undid the first couple of buttons on her blouse. "Care to help me finish?"

"You better believe it." He stepped toward her then stopped. "Let's lock up and put the system on."

She nodded. "I'll meet you in my room."

'I'll be right there." He closed the back door and went to set the alarm.

Devon wandered toward her room, hoping he wouldn't be too long, giving her a chance to change her mind. She didn't want to change her mind. Brett was a good man, smart, brave, and good looking enough for magazine covers with those broad shoulders, and he'd set her motor humming almost from the instant she'd caught sight of him. As they'd spent more time together, she'd dreamed more and more about them making love. Now hopefully, they'd get their chance.

She stepped through the door to her room, lit five candles arranged around the room, pulled the covers back, sat on the bed, and kicked off her shoes.

"You're the most beautiful woman I've ever seen." Brett stood in the doorway. His gaze roamed over her ravishing her with a look.

"Thank you." She reached a hand toward him. He moved quickly into the room and sat next to her on the bed one arm snaking around her waist. With the other, he proceeded to unbutton the rest of her blouse. He brushed aside the silk, dragging in a breath at the sight of her breasts covered with sheer lace. He dropped his head, smothering them with kisses. Next, he traveled up her neck and Devon arched back, giving him greater access. Her heart beat a rat-a-tat-tat, and she opened her mouth to gasp for more air.

With the gentlest of movements, Brett lowered her back on the bed. One hand continued to caress her breasts before sliding toward her stomach. The zipper of her slacks made a slight hissing sound as he tugged it down. Easing his hand inside, he touched her mound through her panties. Devon arched into his hand, taking in big gulps of air.

"Take it easy, Devon. We don't need to rush, and we'll have a good time."

They did have a good time. Certainly, Devon did, if the number of orgasms she'd experienced counted for anything. And they did. Judging from the way Brett had yelled her name when he came, she hadn't been the only one who'd had a good time. Almost the best part was him curling around her body afterward. His arms around her and their legs intertwined, they'd drifted off to sleep.

Forcing her eyelids open, she drew in a long breath and let it out slowly. Guess they couldn't stay in bed all day.

"I hear your mind working, Devon. What's going on in your beautiful head?"

Her lips tilted up, and she rolled to face him. "I'm wondering if we could stay in bed all day."

A loud laugh burst from deep in Brett's gut. "Well, I'd like that, too. But if I don't get something more substantive to eat than those donuts earlier, I'll be useless to you." He trailed his fingers down her bare arm causing chill bumps to form. "And I'd really hate not being of use to you."

Devon chuckled deep in her throat. "Well, let's get this man some food then." Rolling out of bed, she grabbed her silk robe, slipped into it, and headed to the door.

"Kitchen?" Brett's eyebrows rose in question.

"Yep. Come on, buster. Let's round you up some food to fortify your strength."

He stepped into his jeans, and they padded on bare feet down the hallway,

"Breakfast or lunch?" Devon opened the refrigerator door and leaned in. "Plenty of eggs, bacon, and veggies for omelets if you're of a mind."

Brett came up directly behind her and eased his hand around one breast. "What's the fastest breakfast you can make? Let's eat that and get back to your room. Or maybe I'll take you right here on this giant-sized island."

Devon turned to him, clutching a carton of eggs in front of her, her breath catching. "Talk like that will not get the omelets made quicker. I better give you a job."

Brett chuckled. "I have a job. It's to make love to you all day long."

"Grab the butter and jelly from the fridge. Bread's in the basket on the counter. You're in charge of the toast." If she kept him busy, maybe they'd get the meal eaten, before he could act on the island idea. The heat of a blush spread up her cheeks.

Devon quickly beat the eggs, added a dollop of plain yogurt, and poured the mixture into the skillet where she'd put a couple of teaspoons of olive oil. As the egg mixture sizzled, she cut veggies, spread them on top, and added cheese. Brett had made a batch of toast and gotten them both coffee. In almost no time, they sat at the bar enjoying the meal.

Brett could certainly be a keeper. If he'd never been married, how had he escaped? And how had she been lucky enough to come across this amazing man? She sure owed Addie and Mike. Maybe nothing would develop past a few fun romps in the bed. Based on this morning's activities, she'd enjoy that.

As she sipped the last of her coffee, Brett moved in and sent her hormones into overdrive with kisses he lavished on her neck. He set down her cup and pulled her to him, slipping his hands inside the robe. Devon melted into him. Could this get any better?

The jangling of her cell lying on the island yanked them apart.

"Do you need to get that?" Brett rained kisses on the other side of her neck.

"Maybe not." She kissed his lips. Lips, she found addicting, pulling her back for more and more.

The cell stopped and then started again.

"I guess I better. They're insistent." She glanced at the cell. "It's my mother." She dropped her head on his chest, drew in a long breath before clicking the button on the cell.

"Hey, Mom."

"Where've you been? I've called and called."

Devon glanced at her cell to see that indeed her mom had been calling all morning.

"What's the matter?"

"Bailey is gone?"

"Gone, what do you mean gone?" Devon's gut tightened. One hand grasped Brett's.

"It's a beautiful day here. Warmer than usual. Bailey wanted to go outside. We're in a gated and fenced community with a guard on the gate for heaven's sake. She should've been all right."

Brett took the phone from Devon and put it on speaker. "Miriam, this is Brett. Are you saying Bailey is missing? When did you first notice this?"

"Thirty minutes or so ago. I went outside to call her to come, but she didn't respond. We walked around outside figuring she'd wandered down to the stream. Oh, my god, Devon. I'm sorry." The sounds of Miriam crying cut holes in Brett's gut. Missing kid cases were awful, especially when he personally knew the girl and loved her mother. And he did love Devon. Th e realization hit him hard. Damn no time to process now.

"Miriam, Is Richard there? Can I talk with him?" Brett put his arm around Devon's shoulder and drew her close.

"Hey, Brett. Richard here. I went out and walked all around the land surrounding our cabin, but found no sign of Bailey." His tone sounded like he'd lost his best friend. In fact, he'd lost his granddaughter.

"Richard, if you haven't already called the sheriff, you need to do that. We can't assume she's off collecting leaves."

"I've put a call in, but haven't heard back."

"Call them again. I'll call them, too. Let's keep in touch." Brett disconnected and reached for Devon. She shuffled away.

"We'll find Bailey, Devon." He stepped toward her. She backed away again.

"What's the matter?"

"We were in bed enjoying ourselves while some bastard stole my daughter." She reeled from him. "Agggghhh." The scream came from her gut as she sank to her knees on the cold kitchen floor.

Brett had witnessed this kind of thing before. The parents blamed themselves for actions of others. He moved to her and dropped beside her, gently taking her in his arms. He rocked her as if she were a child with a hurt.

"It will be okay, Devon. We don't know for sure if anyone has Bailey. Maybe she got caught up in nature and time slipped by on her."

"She didn't want to stay, Brett. I should've let her come home."

Her cell buzzed. Devon's eyebrows drew together. "That's not a ring from someone I know."

Brett rose and picked up the phone and showed her the screen. "Unknown."

"Generally, I don't answer those."

"No, I don't either, but maybe you need to now."

They stood close, and Brett clicked the answer button.

"Ms. Moore?"

"Yes. Who is this?

"Ms. Moore. I have something of yours, and you have something of mine. You owe me a lot of money. I've been patient, but no longer. When can you get me money?"

"I'll get the money for you. I promise. Do you have my daughter?"

"I do have your pretty red-headed daughter."

"Let me talk with her."

"You can't make demands of me."

"I'll get the money for you. I need a couple more days."

"Well, I'll keep your daughter with me until you have the money—all two million now. I'm tired of waiting. In the meantime, I'm sure we'll find ways to entertain ourselves."

"Don't you touch her!" White-hot anger and ice-cold fear increased her breathing rate so much she became lightheaded. "I'm getting you your damned money. Don't harm my daughter."

"Don't go to the police. I'll call you again, Ms. Moore." Click. The connection ended.

Devon put both hands over her face and sobbed. "Poor Bailey. This is my fault."

Brett took her in his arms, and she fought him, pounding her hands on his chest. "We were having fun while some stinking asshole stole my daughter."

"Devon, stop. Listen to me. We need to make plans. You want to get Bailey back, right?"

"Of course." She stood still, not moving an eyelash.

"We need to contact the FBI."

"No. Didn't you hear him say no police? I've got to get the money, so I at least have some of it when he calls back."

"You've got a buyer for the house. A clear one million. You can probably access the money in a couple of days. What about your investments? Do you have some? Did Franklin manage those for you?"

"No, he didn't. Guess it's lucky I used a recommendation from my friend Kim Denison. The man is from Wichita Falls where she lives, but he has offices here in Dallas. He handles all my own investments. I told my parents I didn't want to use any of the investments money because I'd planned to live on them after we sell the company."

"Wichita Falls, huh? I have a good friend there, too. Listen, Devon, you'll be able to access the investment money faster than you can find someone to buy your company and get all the details ironed out for a sale. Let me go with you to your investments manager and see what we can do."

"Are you sure that's for the best?"

"Well, I'm certain you can get money faster by selling investments than you can by selling your company. Keeping the company allows you to replenish your investments."

She nodded. "Sounds like a plan. I'll call my parents and tell them not to go to the police, and then I'll get Michael on the phone."

CHAPTER SEVENTEEN

Sunday, October 16

"Oh." Bailey rolled over. Her body ached. Her bed wasn't normally this hard. What had happened? With great effort, she blinked open her eyes. Darkness. Her room had a night light. Crap! This wasn't her room. She blinked a few more times. She ran her hands over her body. She still wore the clothes she'd had on when she left Mimi's house in the mountains for the town store. She'd wanted to check on bus schedules. If Mimi and Granddad wouldn't take her—and there'd been no reason to ask them if her mother had said no—she'd been determined to find a way back home. The bus had been the simplest way to make that happen. A bus stopped in the town.

But that's when things became hazy. After telling the guard she planned to walk to the store, she'd gone several yards past, just out of site of the guard house, when a black SUV swung to the side of the road and stopped right in front of her. She didn't remember much aft er that. Walking through the gate on her own hadn't been such a smart move. Had the man in the black SUV snatched her? Had someone else?

Standing made her head hurt and the room spin. Bailey slumped back on to the pallet on the floor. What had she gotten herself into? A tear rolled out of the corner of one eye. She rubbed her face on a shirtsleeve. Thank God, she wasn't tied up. Attempting to stand a second time proved more successful. She wandered around the small, darkened room, with her arms stretched out in front of her, but couldn't make out a window or door. There had to be a door or else how did she end up in the room? Maybe she hadn't walked all around the room.

Boy Mom would be miffed with her. She hoped she didn't yell at Mimi. It wasn't her or Granddad's fault. Bailey slumped onto the pallet. This was all her stupid doing.

"Michael, thank you for meeting with us on a Sunday afternoon." Devon shook hands with her Financial Advisor. He covered her hand with his other.

"Of course, Devon. I'm sorry for your troubles, but I'll fill out the documents to sell one million of your assets tomorrow. It will take about four days to get the wire transfer done, but you should have access to the money by Thursday morning."

"Can't happen too soon. Again, thanks for letting us crash in on Sunday evening."

"Of course. Brett, I'm glad Devon has you on her side in all of this."

Brett nodded. "Let's go, Devon. Thanks again, Michael."

The same hand that had touched her intimately this morning, now rested on her lower back and both comforted and aroused at the same time. This morning, the same time someone snatched Bailey putting her life in danger.

How would she ever forgive herself? Devon stepped away from his wonderful hand and forced herself to stand on her own two feet. That's what she'd been doing since the divorce. Why should she behave any different now?

Devon rushed down the front stairs of Michael's house, a large stately affair in the center of Highland Park, near her own home. Living here didn't guarantee a happily ever aft er.

Monday, October 17

A door flung open, and light blinded her, sending electricity straight down her arms, making her hair stand up at the base of her skull. How brave could she be? Bailey jerked to her feet as if she could fight off whatever approached. While gymnastics and cheerleading made her strong, still, the person standing in front of her intimidated. Probably a man, tall, but could be a woman. Th e hood covering the person's face would've terrified her if she hadn't already been scared enough to throw up.

"Who are you? Why have you taken me?" Maybe she wasn't smart to ask, but she'd read somewhere not to show fear. A difficult task. Her gaze traveled around the small room. Ah, stairs. How had she missed the stairs? The door must be up there.

"As feisty as your mother. I like that."

Based on the muffled sounds coming from the hood, Bailey as-sumed her captor to be a man.

"You'll be free to go as soon as I get my 2 million from your beautiful mother."

"Two million?" Where would her mother get that kind of money?"

"If your careless father hadn't stolen my money you wouldn't be in this situation." He grabbed her arm and tugged her along. "Come.

I'll take you to the facilities. You can eat and then it's back in your little room. At least three more days. Your mother has promised to have the money by then."

Her father? What did all this have to do with him? And stolen? Her father didn't have to steal anything. He had lots of money. Thoughts swirled in her head, but upper-most now was the idea she could pee and eat. The man shoved her up the stairs. She passed through an open door into what appeared to be a kitchen, not new, but not falling apart either.

"The bathroom is through there." He pointed to her left. "Don't think of escaping. The window is boarded up, and any attempts will be met with harsh consequences." He lifted her hand. "Pretty nails and fingers. I assume you'd like to keep them all."

Nausea rose in the back of Blair's throat. She jerked her hand away and made for the bathroom where she threw up in the commode. She cleaned up then peed. What a relief. The idea of peeing in her pants made her gag. She didn't know how she'd get through the next several days or however long this nightmare lasted. But she determined to do just that.

A pounding on the door. "Get out of there now, or I'll come in and get you."

Bailey turned the door handle and stepped into the kitchen. She wiped her damp hands on her jeans.

"You've got donuts and coffee. You don't like. Don't eat. I don't care. Up to you."

Donuts wouldn't have been her first choice. She liked eggs for the protein, but donuts would suffice. She wolfed one down washing the sugar from her mouth with not half-bad coffee. A second one followed. No telling when he'd feed her again. When she'd finished her coffee, the man took her arm and led her back down the stairs. The idea of being locked up in the dark again made her skin crawl. Dare she make a request?

"I'll be back this evening with supper and another bathroom

break. Enjoy your day." He turned to leave.

"Wait. Please, leave on the light."

"Sure. Knock yourself out looking for an escape route. You won't find one. The door is double deadbolt locked, and the room has no windows." The hooded man climbed the stairs and shut the door. The lock clicked loudly. Almost a relief. If the man wasn't here, he couldn't hurt her. Aside from kidnapping her and knocking her out with something, he hadn't physically hurt her. Bailey was grateful for his consideration and grateful he'd left on the light.

Mimi told her you could find something to be grateful for in any situation. Bailey would have plenty of time to find those things over the next several days. For the time being, she'd walk around the room and do some exercises, keeping up her strength in case an opportu-nity came to escape.

What was the garbage he'd spewed about Dad? She'd been up-set when her mother told her they were divorcing, but her parents hardly talked with each other. Meals when her father had been home consisted of long, strained silences. Because her mother had moved into a different bedroom, the news of the divorce didn't shock Bailey, but she was sorry for both her parents, and sad. Sad for them all and what they'd need to do to get through the messiness of the divorce. Many of her friends' parents were divorced. Her parents' process had been quieter than others.

But stealing? No. Not her father. She stopped pacing. But he had taken his own life…something must've been off-the-charts wrong to make him do that. Bailey hugged her middle where the emptiness made her queasy, and the donuts curdled in her stomach.

Devon picked up her cell. Thank goodness Michael's name showed up and not the unknown number.

"Hey, Michael. Any news?"

"I've got enough shares sold to raise the one million. You'll have the money available on Thursday morning. You'll need to set up an offshore account, so I can transfer the money there before you attempt to pass it on to the kidnapper. It's easier to make these kinds of deals from one of those accounts than from here in the states.

You can show him on your phone the money is there in your account and then give him the account number to make the transfer happen. Are you following all of this?"

Devon sighed. "Yes, I guess he needs to call me again so I can make sure he has an offshore account." One more hurdle accomplished to get her daughter back. "Thanks, Michael."

"Good luck, Devon. I'll email you the information. Get hold of me if I can do anything else."

She sighed again. Thursday seemed like an eternity away. Her imagination was giving her daytime nightmares about what could be happening to Bailey. She had to be all right. If the guy hurt her or God forbid, raped her...no telling what Devon would do. She'd nev-er gotten over what had happened to her when she was twelve. She blamed herself. She'd used her mother's lipstick and mascara. Tall for her age, she'd looked older. But the son of her parent's friends had to have known she wasn't a teenager yet. Snap. Devon shut off the memories. After all this time, they still made her ache.

Despite the experience, she'd gone on to fall in love with Franklin, and they'd had an okay sex life. Nothing as amazing as the morning she'd spent with Brett, but... She shut down those memoirs too. They also hurt. While she'd been in a euphoric state of bliss, a crazy man kidnapped Bailey. No telling what he'd done to her. As a mother, she should've known. Probably would've if she'd not been caut up in the whirlwind of passion that was Brett. He kept urging her to eat, but anytime she put something in her mouth, nausea hit. Was Bailey eating? Was she drinking water? Enough time for Devon to eat and drink after she got her daughter back safe.

"Mom, listen to me. I know what Brett said earlier, but don't contact the sheriff again. Let him think everything is all right. I'm putting together the money, and I'll get Bailey back." Afraid of dropping it, she grasped her cell tighter, which was made more difficult by her trembling fingers.

"Devon, are you sure?" Her mother's voice was fi l led with doubt and fear, shaking and breathy, like she was starved for oxygen.

"I'm sure. Th is guy wants his money. And to get him to leave us alone, I'm willing to give him this money whether it's nonsensical to return funds he lost on a bad stock market deal or not. I'm determined to get him off our backs."

"Do you need help with the money, Devon?"

"No thanks, Mom. I have the money from the house sale and Michael has sold stocks to come up with another one million. Th e only bright spot in all of this is my company is safe. Now, to get back my daughter. Th a t's my whole focus. I've gotta go, Mom. Keep Dad away from the sheriff. "

"Okay, sweetie. You take care."

Tuesday, October 18

The simplicity of setting up an account in the Caymans surprised Devon. She handled the whole thing on line. Afterwards, she sent the account number to Michael as well as transferred the million from the sale of the house so he could arrange for the transfer of all her funds at one time.

Despite the ease of the transfer, Devon paced around the kitchen island while Brett worked on his computer in the study, searching for which of Franklin's clients was the one they were dealing with. She still hadn't heard from the man telling her where to go. Tickets and seats for North Carolina were available for Charlotte on a ten a.m. flight out of DFW on Thursday. The plane would arrive mid-afternoon with the time change. But then what?

She collided with a big solid body. Brett. She hadn't been aware of him coming in the kitchen.

"You're still pacing." He placed both hands on her shoulders, and she stopped. The warmth of his grasp comforted her, but she couldn't let her feelings for him distract her now.

"Yeah. Can't sit. I've got enough energy pushing through my body I might explode."

"That's normal, Devon. Waiting to act is hard. Once we get the word, you'll feel more in control."

"Like I'm in control of anything," she flung away from him, taking jerky steps to the other side of the island. "Ever since I learned of Franklin's deceit with my company's funds, my life has spiraled out of control. I don't mind selling the house. I don't mind moving in with my parents. I would've sold the company if you hadn't pointed out a better way.

"Knowing I'm powerless to protect my daughter makes me ill and makes me angry. I want to get the gun Franklin used to kill himself and blow off the head of the guy who took Bailey."

Her tirade depleted some of the energy, and she stopped walking. Her breath was ragged, and she heaved in a couple of big gulps reaching for the control she valued.

"You feel better now?"

"Yes. I do. And I'm getting the gun."

"Can you use one competently?

"I told you I have a concealed handgun license, right?"

"Yes, but that doesn't mean you know how to shoot."

"I can, and I'm a damn good shot."

He looked at her as if seeing her for the first time. "You weren't carrying when you were attacked either time."

"No. I've never felt the need to carry."

"Why do you have the CHL then?"

"Addie got hers, and she encouraged the rest of us to get ours. So, we all did. We'd meet up at a shooting range and practice together and then go have lunch together."

"Interesting group of women friends you have."

"Yes. We've done things together like that since the summer after second grade."

He held out his hand. "Come with me. I have papers to show you."

Devon hesitated then took his hand. How good to have a strong masculine hand to grasp in the middle of her heartache. She walked with him into the study.

"I've narrowed down the suspects to three of Franklin's clients. Devon, he was shuffling a ton of money all around to make up for some losses in the energy investments. Your company's $500,000 in funds was a small part." He slipped into the desk chair.

"Who'd you find?" She rested a hand on his shoulder as she leaned closer to see the screen. His scent, masculine and strong enveloped her.

"Henry Logan, Carlton Sheffield, and Harvey Henderson. Do you recognize any of these names?"

"I recognize Henry Logan's name. I met him at the country club once or twice about five years ago. The other two names don't mean anything to me, but Franklin had lots of clients."

"Yes. He did, but these three men all lost big in the downturn of the oil and gas business. Franklin had invested a great deal of their money with the Triple X Energy Company. Triple X went under because of mismanagement of funds by the chief executive and lots of people lost tons of money."

"But that's not like stealing, Brett. The guy on the phone says Franklin stole his money."

"Most sane people understand when they invest their money in a risky business with the potential for high rewards, there goes with it, hand in hand, the risk to lose everything."

"So maybe the guy who has Bailey isn't sane?"

"Let's assume he doesn't have the same kind of world view you or I do. Let's also assume he only wants the money he lost returned, whether this makes sense or not. We'll get your daughter back, Devon. Never doubt that."

Devon's phone buzzed. The screen showed an unknown number. "Brett, this may be him."

"Answer it on speaker." Brett stepped closer.

Her fingers trembled as she tapped her phone. "Hello?"

"I hope you've got good news for me, Ms. Moore. Do you have my two million?"

"I'll have your money by Thursday—all two million. How do I get Bailey back?"

"You're getting a little ahead of yourself. Once I have the money in hand, then you can have your daughter back."

"Here's the problem. You don't get the money until I've got her back. I'm prepared to come to North Carolina Thursday afternoon. Do you have an offshore account? I'll need your bank account number so I can make the wire transfer. I'll set up an account in the Caymans. I'll set up for the transfer of the money from my account to yours. As soon as I see my daughter, I'll push send.

"When precisely do you get the funds?" His muffled tones drove her nuts and set her teeth on edge because of how hard she gritted them each time she talked with him.

"I'll have access early Thursday morning and ou—my plane

179

leaves at ten am that day."

"Well, good news finally. We're close to a deal, Ms. Moore. I'll call you Wednesday afternoon to set up further arrangements." The phone went silent.

Devon let out a long sigh. "This is killing me."

"I know. You're doing great. You stumbled in telling him about the plane. What happened?"

"I nearly referred to *our* plane. Didn't seem a good idea to let him know I have help." She faced Brett. "And I'm grateful for your help. I truly am. I'm sorry I've been gritchy of late."

He draped his arms around her waist and tugged her to him. She didn't resist.

"You've been juggling a lot for quite a while now. You entitled to steam up now and again."

She rested her head against his chest; his heartbeat strong and steady. She had confidence he could do what he said.

"When we've got Bailey back, I'm going after this bastard. I'll have enough on him to take to the police and the DA."

"But—

"Don't start with the business of not wanting Bailey to find out about her father. Doesn't she have some good memories of her father?"

"Yes."

"Those will have to be enough to cushion the blow of learning he wasn't perfect."

"But—"

"We're nailing this bastard." The expression on his face convinced Devon not to argue anymore.

CHAPTER EIGHTEEN

Thursday, October 20

The door banged open. Blair's heartbeat kicked into overdrive.

"Get up. Time to go."

What did this mean? Go where? Would he kill her? He'd taken care of her in the three or four days she'd been his captive. Got her to the bathroom. Fed her. Had provided her a blanket when the temps dropped one night. Was she still in North Carolina? How long had she been here? She kept track of the days as best she could by marking on the wall with a rock she'd found the times he fed her and took her to the bathroom, but he could've changed his pattern. With the upstairs windows boarded up, the light was always the same.

Mimi and Granddad must be worried out of their minds. And her mother? She'd never be able to make up for causing her mother to experience all the worry and heartache.

"Come on. Come on. You don't want to keep your mother waiting, do you?"

Bailey walked toward the man with the hood. Was he taking her home? What had all of this been about anyway?

He marched her up the stairs. Yanked her hands together and secured them with a soft rope. He didn't hurt her, but she couldn't loosen the bonds, which she tried to do immediately he turned his back. He blindfolded her by throwing a large what looked like a dark colored pillowcase over her head. Now she depended on him for being able to get around. He shoved her up the staircase ahead of him. Doors slammed and judging from the temperature of the cooler air, he led her outside.

"I covered your eyes so you can't lead anyone back here after I turn you over to your mother." He guided her down a short stairway, then opened the door of what because of its heavy sound, seemed like a big vehicle. He held her head to keep her from bonking herself. Maybe she'd get out of this in one piece. If she didn't have a heart attack first, a real possibility, the way her heart raced, beating against her breastbone.

She straightened in her seat when the hooded man climbed in. "Where are we going?"

"To meet your mother and to get back my money." He put the key in the ignition, and the vehicle roared to life.

They bounced along in silence. Bailey flung against the door one time when he took a turn quickly.

"Are you okay?"

"Yes." She righted herself.

"Should've buckled you in. It's not much farther."

Bailey was thankful to be out of the tiny prison of a room but terrified about what lay ahead. Where was he taking her? What was next? Would her mother be there? Would he kill them both? She blinked against the moisture forming in her eyes. She had to be brave, no matter how scared she was.

"How close are we?" Devon leaned forward searching for the land-marks she'd heard mentioned by the voice on the phone. A large red sign on the right-hand side of the road and then a sharp turn to the left .

"Up ahead." Brett hit the brakes and twisted the steering wheel hard.

"A little earlier than I'd expected." The car bounced along a rut-ted road. "I wish you'd let me call the police or sheriff's office"

"No. The plan is to get Bailey and give him the money. I don't care about anything else. Once we have her, you can contact the authorities."

"Thank God you've finally come to your senses. I wish you had earlier, and we'd get the guy now."

"Now I just want Bailey."

"But you've sold your house and a million dollars in stocks. You may never get the money back."

"But I'll have my daughter. I'm praying she's all right, and he hasn't hurt her like…." Her voice trailed off. She wasn't going there anytime. She especially couldn't have that discussion with Brett.

"Like what?"

Of course, he didn't miss anything. She should've kept her mouth shut.

"Look. There's a car."

Brett slowed. "We'll talk about this later."

As soon as he came to a stop, Devon jumped from the car.

Brett followed her. "You were supposed to stay inside until he showed himself."

She ignored him and hollered, "I've got the wire transfer num-ber. Where's my daughter?" She was proud her voice didn't waver. She'd show this man no fear. Her hands clamped into fists at her side.

"Mom."

Devon's stomach clenched. Bile rose in the back of her throat. "I'm here, baby. Hang on."

A man in a hood with holes for the eyes and the mouth stepped from the large black SUV. "You have numbers for me?"

"Yes. Let me see, Bailey."

He walked around to the passenger side of the car and helped her daughter out.

"Bailey." Her first word soft as a whisper. Then louder, stronger. "Are you okay, Bailey?"

"Yes. I want to go home. Can we go home?"

"You bet, sweetie." She aimed her gaze at the hooded man, the man who'd thrown her world into chaos. "So how do we do this?"

"I'll give you my Caymans account number. You make the transfer happen. As soon as I see it's begun, Bailey's yours.

"Okay." She started toward him.

"Be careful, Devon." Brett's words followed her as she moved step-by-step closer to the man who held her daughter hostage.

God, please let me get her back safely. She walked on shaky legs, but each step firmer as she got closer to her daughter.

Within feet of the Hooded Man, she stopped. "I'll pull up my account." She typed on her phone. "See." She held it in his direction. "Give me the number of your account."

Hooded Man gave her a paper. She typed in the digits and clicked Send. "The funds are moving."

He dropped his hold on Bailey, took Devon's phone from her.

She eased closer to Bailey who must be terribly scared not to be able to see what was going on. Devon grasped her daughter's hands where they'd been tied in front of her body. "It'll be okay," she whispered. With an arm around Bailey's waist, Devon eased her away from the car.

"Yes. I've got it." The triumph in Hooded Man's voice stopped Devon in her tracks. She glanced behind.

"You did good, Ms. Moore. Made up for the whacked up work your ex-husband did. Here. I don't need this." Her phone landed at her feet. She stooped to retrieve her cell, and she and Bailey kept moving.

No telling what Hooded Man was about to say, and keeping Bailey from hearing more about her father made her walk away from him faster.

The man stepped to his SUV, climbed in, spun the vehicle in a tight circle, and drove offint he opposite direction.

Devon yanked off the pillowcase covering her daughter's eyes. "Did he hurt you? Please tell me he didn't rape you."

"No, Mom. He didn't."

"Thank God." She hugged her daughter.

"Let me get the restraints off your wrists." Brett cut through the smooth rope with his knife.

His arms came around them both. "Let's go home to your parents' cabin." He shepherded them to his SUV. "Call them, Devon, so they can tell the guard to let us through."

From the back seat where she sat with her arm wrapped about her daughter, Devon did as he directed. In no time, they were through the gate and pulling up to her parents' log cabin. The large wrap-around porch. The beams. The amazing trees. All brought comfort, but who knew how long before she'd get back the control she was used to having.

The front door flew open, and Devon's parents rushed down the porch stairs. Miriam pulled Bailey into her arms. Her father gathered Devon in for a hug.

Brett took Richard's outstretched hand.

"Thanks for bringing them safely home." The tremble in his voice showed the strain they'd all been under.

"It wasn't me, Richard. Your daughter took care of everything. Devon controlled this situation. She wouldn't let me do more before we had Bailey home safely." Finally, with Bailey safe, he could do his thing with his computers, and he'd nail the SOB who harmed this family he'd come to care for.

"Let's go inside." Miriam let go of Bailey long enough to briefly hug Devon then she ushered them all into the stately log cabin.

"Log cabin, huh? This isn't like any log cabin I've seen before." His gaze skimmed the high ceilings with giant beams in the rafters. The giant fireplace held a roaring fire. Instinctively, they all gath-ered in front for the warmth and the comfort brought by the roaring flames.

"I've got coffee and hot cocoa. Anyone like something?"

"Thanks, Mimi. The hot chocolate sounds heavenly. I may never drink from a bottle of water again. On the other hand, I guess I'm lucky he gave me anything to drink."

"I'll fix the coffee." Miriam walked purposefully toward the large open kitchen. Richard followed her. They must've taken comfort to have a concrete task on which to focus. When they returned, Richard carried a tray with cups, and she held one with the cream and sugar.

Devon hadn't moved from her daughter's side where they'd settled on the large leather sofa with Devon's hand in continuous movement over Blair's hair, almost a match to her own.

"So, you want to know how this happened?" Bailey rolled the cup between her hands.

This excursion into the dark side seemed to have matured Bailey, who'd always appeared more mature than her age. But at 16, who's mature? Bailey sipped her cocoa, making a marshmallow mustache. She swiped the back of her hand across her mouth.

"If you feel like telling us what happened, dear, we'd listen."

Devon sipped her coffee and set the cup back on the coffee table, which appeared to have been made from reclaimed wood. Fitting for this rustic, yet elegant cabin.

"I was mad you wouldn't let me go home. The cheerleading squad is important to me, and we have to prepare for finals. I wanted to carry my share of the load, so I hiked down the hill and told the guard I planned to walk to the store. I wanted information about when the bus arrived so I could go home. Linda would've let me stay with her."

"Did you call Linda?" Her mother brushed a hand through her daughter's long, tangled hair.

"No. She's not good at keeping secrets. Once I was there, she'd be okay. I'd walked out of sight of the guard station when a black SUV appeared. Hooded Man jumped out and started for me. I ran, but he caught me. He must've drugged me because I don't remem-ber anything until I woke up in a dark place." She sipped her hot chocolate.

"I never saw him without the hood which gave me comfort, since I couldn't ID him, maybe he wouldn't kill me."

"Oh, dear God." Devon's voice quivered. She sipped her coffee, giving Bailey a chance to drink more of her cocoa.

Miriam sat on a matching leather chair, and Richard perched on the arm to hear their granddaughter tell her story.

Slowly, and with much detail, Bailey explained what she'd experienced. "Aside from drugging me and taking my freedom, he didn't hurt me. He made sure I had bottled water and gave me packages of those cheese crackers with peanut butter. They got a little old, and I won't need to eat them for a good long time, but I didn't go hungry. I guess I'm lucky." She tipped up her chocolate cup and swallowed several times. She moved the cup from her mouth and made eye contact with everyone gathered there in her grandmother's cabin.

"What did the man want? Why did he take me? What did you do to get me back?"

"That's a lot of questions, Bailey?" Devon glanced at Brett and then her parents.

"The time has come to tell her, Devon." Her mother had claimed the title of the most persuasive of any of them. Brett had been trying to convince her to tell her daughter for a couple of weeks. Maybe if Devon had told her daughter in the first place, none of this would've happened. Bailey wouldn't have tried to run off , and the kidnapper wouldn't have had an opportunity to take her. Brett decided to not mention the idea to Devon. She'd been through enough already and carried enough guilt.

"Tell me what, Mimi? What's she talking about Mom?"

Devon rose from the sofa and paced into the kitchen area. She poured herself another cup of coffee. She held up her cup. "Anyone else?"

No one responded.

The silence was broken when Bailey rose. "Tell me what, Mom." She stood with her hands on her waist, demanding an answer.

Devon lifted her cup and took a quick gulp, burning her tongue. She'd been trying to protect her daughter and preserve Bailey's good opinion of her father. Devon was about to pour mud all over that opinion.

She cleared her throat and walked back into the living area. "Sit down, Bailey."

"No. Not until you start talking." Her daughter planted her feet shoulder-width apart.

No avoiding this. Devon straightened up. "Okay. Do you re-member when I told you I wanted to sell the house?"

"Sure. Too big for the two of us."

"That's right, but I wouldn't have sold i f I hadn't needed the money"

"Why'd you need the money? For my college? Don't we have a separate college fund you and dad set up when I was born?"

Devon crossed to her daughter, taking her hand in her own. She so didn't want to have to speak the next words. "Bailey, you father lost money on some investments and tried to cover up the loss by taking money from my business.

"What? What do you mean he lost money? He didn't steal it, did he?" She jerked away her hand and backed up a step.

"Brett has found evidence an energy company your father invested other people's money in went bust, and all the investors lost their shirts. He tried to cover up the loss by using my company's money." Devon dropped onto the sofa.

Bailey's gaze cut to Brett and back to her mother. "So, he lost a million dollars? That's the amount we sold the house for, right?"

Her daughter was a smart young woman. "Yes, we sold the house for over a million, but Hooded Man, as we've called him, wanted more. Two million."

"Oh, my God!" Bailey dropped down beside her mother. "That's a lot of money. Did Dad do something wrong with the investments?"

"Brett, can you explain what happened to her?" Maybe she wouldn't be hurt as much hearing someone else explain what happened.

"Sure." Brett walked to the end of the sofa and sat on the edge of the coffee table facing Bailey. "Investors take their clients' money and put it into companies. The idea is they'll make a lot of money for their clients. Your father invested much of his clients' money into Triple X Energy Company."

"I've heard of them. They went out of business or bankrupt or something."

"That's right. Generally, people who play the stock market

understand the risks they're taking. If there's a chance for big gains, you can count on there being a chance for big losses. One of your father's clients blamed your father for the loss."

"That doesn't seem fair."

"No. But this man contacted your mother and demanded she pay him the money your father's investments lost him to the tune of two million dollars."

Bailey looked at Devon. "Did you go to the police? Cause that's not legal, is it?"

Devon shook her head. "No. I didn't go to the police. And I accept full responsibility for that decision. Everyone--your grandparents, Brett, Addie and Mike, all told me I should, but I...I didn't want you to learn about you father taking the money from my company. Now it's all come out anyway. I messed up, Bailey and put you in danger. I'm so sorry."

"Mom. I've always appreciated you not badmouthing Dad after the divorce. The parents of many of my friends haven't been as controlled."

"I should've told you, maybe you would've understood better when I shipped you off with Mimi and Granddad, and you wouldn't have taken chances. Maybe Hooded Guy wouldn't have kidnapped you. I'm sorry, Bailey. It's my fault." She brushed at the moisture in her eyes.

"Mom, I'm the one who's sorry. It's my fault for not doing what you asked me." She threw her arms around Devon, and they both cried.

After a moment, Brett stood. "Neither of you is at fault. It's only the fault of Hooded Guy. You don't need to take on the guilt, either of you."

"Mom, Mr. Townsend, Brett, is right." She wiped her eyes with a tissue Miriam handed to both Bailey and Devon. "I don't blame you. I appreciate you trying to protect Dad's memory. Where are we now money-wise?"

What a practical kid. Pride for her daughter warmed Devon's heart.

"I sold the house for over one million, and I took one million from my investments. I have my company, so we'll still have money coming in. Over time, I'll pay back the investment accounts. We'll live with Mimi and Granddad until we have enough money to buy a small place of our own."

"What about my college fund money?"

Her super-smart daughter had circled back to that subject. Devon sighed. "The college fund seems to be empty, too."

"Oh, wow." What color Bailey had in her face drained away.

"I'll figure out something, Bailey. You will be able to go to college. Worst case we get a loan."

Bailey nodded. "Okay. Can we go home now? Before Hooded Guy, I had a good time with you in the mountains, Mimi and Granddad." She gave them both hugs. "But I want to go home and be normal."

"Yes, baby. We can go home. We can all go home."

CHAPTER NINETEEN

Monday, October 24

Brett removed his reading glasses, raised his hands over his head, and stretched. God, he'd been at the files for hours. It was tedious work, but he'd finally figured out which of Moore's three clients he'd earlier focused on was the most likely suspect. He studied the picture of Henry Logan. His suit looked as expensive as it probably was. Brett's research revealed Logan had grown up poor. The only way he got into SMU was on athletic and academic scholarships where, hanging out with his wealthy friends, he'd learned to appreciate the finer things in life.

The funds were easy to track once Brett figured out what to look for. The man hadn't lost the two million he'd been asking for from Devon. The amount was closer to the $500,000 Franklin stole from her company. Guess the greed monster made Logan ask for the larger sum. And Devon had given the money to him. Totally upended her life to make good on a debt not hers, nor real.

He slid copies of the files into a folder to show her and insist she go to the police. She couldn't resist now since her reason not to talk to them was gone. Despite Devon's concerns, Bailey seemed to be managing the news her father was a thief surprisingly well. "Okay, Devon. Let's get this guy."

Brett drove his car to her office, parked in the garage, and made his way to her office. "Hello, Liz." He smiled at Devon's secretary. "Does she have time to see me?"

"Hey, Brett. I'm sure she will. Let me check." Liz picked up the phone on her desk. "Devon, Brett Townsend is here. Do you have time to see him?"

Liz smiled at him. "She said come right in."

The door swung open. "Brett, hey. Good to see you."

There she was in a black dress and white jacket with a large turquoise pin on the lapel. Her glorious red hair hung down her back, held back from her ears with clips. He walked toward her. "Hello, Devon." The door closed behind him.

They stood looking at each other for a moment before he reached for her and she moved into him close. He touched his lips to hers, and she gasped, opening to his tongue. He wanted to go on kissing her, but this wasn't the place, and they didn't have time to put out the fire. Finally, he let her go. "I've missed seeing you."

She smiled. "Me to you. Can I offer you coffee?"

"No thanks. I have info to share with you."

"Okay." She didn't let go of his hand but settled on the sofa pulling him down beside him. "What do you have?"

"I've discovered who the blackmailer is." He laid the folder on the coffee table in front of the sofa and removed the picture of the suspect along with the documentation about the money.

Devon gazed at the picture; her eyebrows tilted into a frown. "I Remember this man. Hugh, Hank?"

"Henry Logan is his name."

"I heard Franklin refer to him as Hank." She glanced at Brett. "He's the one who's been aft er me and kidnapped Bailey?" A shudder shook her whole body.

Brett slipped an arm around her and drew her in tight. He rested his head on hers and whispered comforting words. "You're okay, Devon. Bailey is okay."

She nodded.

"Now he may not be the one who physically attacked you. He could've hired someone." He faced her. "Here's the deal. We need to go to the police with the evidence I've collected. Th ey will arrest him. There will be a trial and ultimately, I hope you'll get some of your money back."

"Well, I—

"Don't give me any arguments, Devon. Bailey knows about her father which was your only reason—though a weak one—that kept me from insisting we go to the police earlier."

She pushed away from him. "If you'd let me speak, I was about to say, I agree. It's time." She smiled at him.

"Okay, you got me." He chuckled. "Can I set up an appointment with the police?

She nodded, rose from the sofa, moved to her desk, and picked up her cell. "Let me give you several times that work for me. If they don't work with the detectives, I'll make whatever arrangements they need. Let's get this done."

Wednesday, October 26

Brett clenched his teeth together as Detective Hernandez chewed out Devon for not being forthcoming about the cause of her husband's suicide from the beginning.

"Ms. Moore, do you realize we could arrest you for obstruction of justice?" The Hispanic man's mustache bristled.

Devon bristled too. She straightened her shoulders. "You do what you have to do, Detective. I did what was best for my daughter."

Brett raised his eyebrows and made eye contact with the Detective. The man needed to get the message he'd better dial back the pressure he put on Devon. Best not to take on a Mama Lion.

"Okay, Ms. Moore. I get you had, what to you, was a reason important enough to keep quiet about your husband."

"Can you arrest Henry Logan with the evidence I've provided, Detective?" Brett was certain they did, you never could tell what else the police were focusing on.

"I'm afraid we can't, Mr. Townsend. However, what you've provided gives us enough to get a search warrant." He rose from his desk and walked around to sit on the front corner, close to Devon.

"What would help is if we could get Logan in his own words. Could you help us with that, Ms. Moore?

He and Devon both spoke at the same time.

"Yes."

"No." Brett glanced at Devon. "What? Are you crazy? Detective Hernandez is talking about you wearing a wire for them."

"I understand, Brett."

He rose. His hands clenched into fists and leaned toward the detective. "How can you consider asking her to do this. You could get her killed."

Devon stood and placed her hand on his arm. "Brett, please. I can't let this drag on and on, never knowing what will pop up next. That's not a way to live. Bailey and I need to be safe."

"I can keep you safe, Devon."

"I know you'll do your best, but I owe Bailey to take this next step. The man can't be allowed to wander around loose. If I can do something about it, I must."

Brett ran a hand through his hair and paced the small office with what looked like standard, state issued furniture. He gazed out the lone window, which looked out on another red brick building. Bleak. Like this situation.

"Detective Hernandez, I'm offering to help you with this. What do we do and when do we do it?" Devon's voice rang with strength and resolve.

"This is nuts, Devon." Brett stopped in front of her. "You could be hurt."

"Yes, I could be, Brett. But I could be hit by a car crossing the street. Nothing is guaranteed."

Brett walked away and drew in several deep breaths. Apparently, he couldn't change her mind.

"Okay. How can I help?" If she were undertaking the stupid challenge, he'd be there for her.

Over the next hour, Detective Hernandez and Devon went over options for how to pull off the action. Brett wasn't happy about the plans but made sure they understood he'd be there.

"Mr. Townsend, you need to chill here and let us do our job."

"I understand you can do your job, Detective, but I have skills you shouldn't dismiss."

"Brett," Devon took his and squeezed it once before letting go. "Detective, why couldn't Brett observe with you? He can listen in, and if he notices anything seeming off, he can clue you in. He knows a lot about this situation."

Brett held his breath. Would Hernandez agree? Whether he agreed or not, Brett determined to be close to help in any way needed.

"Okay, Ms. Moore. Let me run this by my boss, and we'll set up a time for the meet."

"Devon. Devon." He wanted to scream at her.

"Brett, you need to be okay with my decision." After a stonily quiet drive from the police department to her house, she closed the front door. She dropped her purse on the entryway bench.

Screaming at a client wasn't his normal reaction. Then again, Devon was much more than a client. The feeling had been there from the beginning despite his efforts to maintain a professional position.

"Let me get you a drink, and we'll talk. I want you to be okay with this." She took his hand and led him to the kitchen.

"All right." He paced while she got a bottle from the refrigerator and placed his beer on the white quartz counter. She poured a glass of wine for herself.

"Come on." Carrying her wine glass into the living room, she paused to click the switch making the fire blaze in the fireplace. "The temps have dropped low for late October. Weather this cool normally arrives in late November."

"Devon." He set his bottle on a coaster on the coffee table then took her hand and drew her to the sofa. "I don't need a weather report. If I want to find out what the temperature is, I'll check my iPhone."

She settled in next to him with a soft chuckle. "It's my go-to subject when I'm nervous."

"You're nervous?" He rubbed his thumb across the inside of her wrist. Her pulse jumped.

"Well, yes. It's not like I've ever done this kind of thing before. I'd be a fool not to be nervous."

"Please reconsider this move, Devon. What if I met with him?"

"Brett, what makes Logan agree to meet with you? No. Me, he'll see when I tell him I have Franklin's papers with his name on them, and I believe Franklin may owe him money. He's greedy. He'll jump at this."

Brett sucked in a breath. What she said was true. He took a couple of gulps of the beer, the cold liquid stinging his throat. Okay, one last shot at changing her mind. A low blow, but he was desperate.

"Devon, what if something goes wrong and you're injured or, God forbid, you're killed? What about Bailey?"

Devon shivered. Brett slipped his arm around her shoulders and drew her close. She sank into him for a moment then retreated. She set her glass on the table, stood, and crossed to stand with her back to the fireplace.

"Brett, I've got to do this for Bailey. I can't leave this man out there hanging over our heads. How do we ever feel secure... safe? How do we live our lives productively with a chasm waiting to open under our feet? And what kind of model am I being for her? I don't run away from problems. No. I have to do this."

Brett sighed, stood, and walked to Devon's side. He enveloped her in his arms. "As much as I hate you doing this, I won't keep fighting you."

She hugged him. "Thanks. I appreciate your change of mind."

"I'll put together some documents you can use when you talk with him, okay?"

"Thank you."

Her hand came up and cupped his cheek and Brett tilted his face to kiss her palm. She sucked in a gasp. He put both his hands around her face and lowered his lips to hers. When she opened her mouth, he dived in, pulling her close, letting her feel how much he wanted and needed her.

He ran his hand over one breast feeling the nipple harden through the silk blouse. Her breath shortened as she tugged, loosening his shirt from his waistband. He fumbled with the buttons of her blouse. He wanted, needed to touch her skin and let his hands caress her skin.

"Bye, Mimi."

The door-opening chime and the slam played back in Brett's mind like a recording. He jumped away from Devon. Dear God, they'd forgotten Bailey was coming home.

Devon looked at him as if she were a deer caught in the

headlights. He almost chuckled but refrained. He stuck his shirt back in and helped her button her blouse. She ran her hands through her mussed red ringlets. Ah, he'd like to be doing that.

"Hey, Mom. Hi, Brett. I ate at Mimi's, and I'm heading up to my room. Got a test tomorrow. Good night."

And she was gone. He looked at Devon and they both burst out laughing. He drew her close, inhaling the scent of her hair and then set her away from him. He ran a finger down her nose. "I'd better get going. What say when this is all over, we get away for a weekend?"

"I'd like that."

Tuesday, November 1

Devon asked her parents to pick up Bailey from school, but she didn't tell them about the plan for her to wear a wire to get evidence against Henry Logan. No need to make them worry, and they would. Besides, she'd probably be able to pick up her daughter as usual. But the cliché "better safe than sorry" applied here.

What about Brett? Who would've dreamed they could have developed a relationship given how they'd met. She hadn't been looking for any kind of relationship. Whenever memories of their weekend away crossed her mind, her tummy butterfl ied up, like the log ride at Six Flags. The rush as you went over the top.

She'd be satisfied with a weekend with the man every so oft en. How would Bailey react to anything long-term? Whoa, she'd gotten ahead of herself, since Brett hadn't indicated he wanted anything long-term. If she were honest, she'd have to admit, yes; she'd like to have many more weekends with the man.

But first, she had to nail Logan.

Her phone chirped and glancing down, she read Hernandez' name on the screen. "Hello?"

The low voice with the slight accent greeted her. "Ms. Moore. I've got approval. You set up a meeting with Logan, and we'll get you suited up with a wire. We'll be near. You'll be safe. You must get him to admit he took the money or your daughter. Either will be enough for us."

Her hand gripped the cell. Her heart raced. Saying you were prepared to go through with this and doing so were two different things.

"Ms. Moore, are you still there? You haven't changed your mind have, you?"

She shook herself and straightened her shoulders. She'd do this for Bailey and for herself. "No, Detective. I haven't changed my mind.

"Thanks, Ms. Moore. We appreciate you doing this. You'll be fine."

"Okay, Detective. I'm holding you to that."

"We'd like you to place the call from headquarters. When can you get here?"

"I'll be down in about thirty minutes."

"See you in a while then, Ms. Moore."

Devon let out a long breath then took a couple of swallows of her coffee. Only after the third sip did she realize the coffee was cold. She emptied the rest of the cup in the sink. Best to get on with this. She threw on a jacket, walked out to the garage, got in her car, and headed downtown. After driving through twice, she found a space and parked in the visitor section before walking into Detective Hernandez' office.

"Hello, Ms. Moore. I'm glad you came in to make the call."

Devon shook his hand. "Sure. I figured at ten-thirty in the morning, Logan should be in his office."

He nodded. Let me get the experts in to set up your phone hook-up so we'll have a recording of this call. In only a short time, a flurry of activity she didn't understand resulted in making sure the police could hear both sides of her conversation.

Detective Hernandez smiled at her. "Any time you're ready, Ms. Moore.

She nodded and punched in the number Brett had found for Logan in Franklin's files. She held her breath.

"Who is this?"

"Mr. Logan, my name is Devon Moore. I'm Franklin Moore's ex-wife."

After a slight pause, "What can I do for you, Ms. Moore? I'd offer my condolences, but considering Franklin was an ex, they probably aren't warranted."

"I'm not calling about what you can do for me, Mr. Logan, but what I can possibly do for you. I'm executor of Franklin's will, and in going over his papers, I found some files with your name on them. I'm no expert, but I'm wondering if he possibly owes you some money."

"Oh? How much?"

"I'm not entirely certain. I'm not a numbers person, Mr. Logan. Could be $500,000 or maybe as much as a million. Anyway, I'd like to talk with you, show you the papers, and see if this was something he paid you or maybe still owes you. Will you meet with me?"

A long silence followed her request.

"I don't believe he owes me any money, Ms. Moore."

Her breath stopped.

"But, I'll meet with you to alleviate your concerns."

Devon let out a breath of relief. He could've blown off her attempt to contact.

"How about the Franklin's country club, Ms. Moore? We can have lunch and then talk business in the gardens after."

Glancing at Hernandez, she shrugged her shoulders at him in question. He shook his head and scribbled a note—*not lunch*—*for a drink after. You have an appointment.*

"Ms. Moore are you still there?"

"Mr. Logan, I'm sorry, I had to check my calendar. I have an appointment at lunch today. How about a drink at two?"

"Very well, Ms. Moore. I look forward to visiting with you. Thank you for following up on this issue."

He disconnected, and after a glance at Hernandez who nodded, Devon did, too. She gulped in a large breath. Apparently, she'd hadn't been breathing. The room tilted for a moment before she dragged in more oxygen.

"You did well, Ms. Moore. I'll have my technicians meet at your house and get you wired for your meeting at the club. We'll set up surveillance in the gardens. We should have visual and audio contact at all times. Nothing to worry about. Don't mention your daughter if you can avoid it. Let's get him on the blackmail, then, if we can, we'll get him on the kidnapping."

Devon nodded, feeling a little shell-shocked. Was this the kind of thing Brett did on a regular basis? Brett. She needed to see him. Telling Hernandez good-by, Devon walked to her car and climbed in. She flipped down the visor mirror to check her make-up. After applying a touch more lipstick, she nodded and drove straight to Brett's office, parking in a visitor spot. She couldn't stay long, but she wanted to see him and tell him what she was doing.

His offices were in a modest building on a corner lot. She opened the glass door and made her way to the receptionist's desk.

"Hey. I'm Devon Moore. I don't have an appointment, but I'd like to see Brett Townsend if he has time."

"Let me check, Ms. Moore." She called into Brett's office, and he immediately came out.

"Hello, Devon. Come on in." His hand rested on her lower back as he ushered her to his office.

"Is everything okay?" He closed the door.

Devon's eyes glazed over as she took in all the computers in his office. "My goodness, Brett. Do you use all of those?"

He nodded. "You bet. At one time or another." He drew her to him and nuzzled her neck. Chill bumps pebbled her right side, running up and down her arm and leg. He drew back. "I'd like to do more of this, but I'm guessing you came to see me about something." He led her to the sofa and settled her there with his arm around her shoulders.

She nodded. "I called Logan today, and we're meeting at the club at two today. Hernandez' technicians will wire me up at home before I go there. I wanted you to know."

He squeezed her shoulder, rose, and paced in front of her. "I wish you'd let me do this, but—" he held up his hands. "No, I won't try to convince you to change your mind, but I will be there." He reached into his desk draw and pulled out a file folder. "Here are documents you can use when you meet with him. I'll go over these to help you know how to use them. And remember, I'll be right there."

She smiled. "I'm glad. Your being there will give me confidence to carry this off." She took the folder from him. "These will help, too."

"Have you talked with your parents about this plan?"

"No, better not to worry them. I told Bailey I loved her this morning, but then I always do."

"Ah, honey, you'll be safe. Hernandez and I will both be there. We'll keep you safe." He hugged her. "How about we eat lunch?"

"Not sure I could keep anything down. Logan wanted us to meet for lunch. Hernandez realized I'd have a hard time being with him for a whole meal, and he wrote me a note telling me to say no, drinks only in the afternoon."

"Drinks, huh? Let's get you some cheese and crackers anyway. They will help sop up the alcohol. You need to have your head on straight."

She smiled. "And how about a fizzy water." Maybe the drink would help settle her stomach.

CHAPTER TWENTY

Tuesday, November 1

“**M**s. Moore, thank you for meeting me here. Franklin didn't lie. You're a beautiful woman.” How could Franklin bear to lose this woman?

She smiled at him and dipped her head. “You're too kind, Mr. Logan.”

“I'm going to have a glass of champagne. Can I get you one?”

“Yes, thank you.”

He got their drinks at the bar. “Is it too cool outside for you? I love the gardens any time of year.”

“The gardens will be fine. My jacket is warm enough. I appreciate your consideration.”

He held the door for her, eyeing her shapely rear. Franklin was a wuss to let her get away. Henry set down his drink on the white wrought iron table and held her chair. They settled in, and he took a sip from his glass. “Drink up, Ms. Moore. It's 5 o'clock somewhere.”

Chuckling at his comment, she raised her glass.

He set his on the table. "So, tell me about this money you say Franklin owes me?"

She reached for her large purse and removed a folder. "Let me show you what I'm talking about." She put papers on the table. The breeze touched them softly.

He looked at where her classy red fingernail pointed. He gulped when he realized she had documented the monies Franklin had lost in the oil price debacle. He glanced at her and then back at the papers. What should he say? Before he figured out what, she went on.

"Did you lose all this money, Mr. Logan?

"Yes, I did, Ms. Moore. One of the worst years I've ever experienced." He sipped his champagne. Best to stick with as much truth as possible.

"How did you manage? Were you able to make up the difference somewhere?" She flipped a couple of pages and pointed to another section of the report. "Oh, look at this line."

How did she have this? He checked out the date on the corner of the page. Recent.

"This report suggests you not only made up the $500,000 but got ahead by one-and-half million, Mr. Logan."

As the saying goes if looks could kill.... Devon Moore's gaze drilled holes through his head. He'd better keep his distance from her, or she'd jab her spike heel into his balls.

"Mr. Logan? Did you get an extra one-and-a-half-million? Where did that money come from?"

He leaned close to her. "Lady, you better not go there."

She leaned in closer. Her gaze shooting arrows at him. "No?"

He didn't respond. She leaned back and crossed one leg over the other, swinging it as if she had no worries at all.

"You see, Henry Logan, I know exactly where the money came from."

"You couldn't possibly." His fingers squeezed the glass hard enough he expected to hear crystal shattering.

"Oh, but I do, and I can prove what I'm saying. Shall I show you what I mean?" She flipped the pages of the report.

Logan had had his fill. He reached for his gun, his fingers caressing the handle.

"I have you covered." He glanced down at the table. "You should destroy those records and forget you ever saw them."

"Or what, Logan. Will you attack me again or kidnap my daughter?"

"You bitch." He stood, keeping the gun at his side. "No wonder Franklin dumped you."

Devon stood and stepped closer to him. Was she totally nuts?

"Let's you and me go for a little walk, shall we?" He leveled the gun at her.

"I don't think so. Staff and guests are inside the door there. I'd be crazy to leave here with you."

"I can make it appear like you killed yourself." He stepped closer.

"No. You can't." Despite her brave words, Devon's heart was about to jump out of her body. For crying out loud. This was a white-collar crime. Logan wasn't supposed to have a gun. While terrified, she determined he wasn't forcing her away from the garden. Besides the people in the club, the cops were near. And Brett was near. They had a future, didn't they? She had to be alive to make being together possible.

"Come with me, you stupid broad." He hand grasped her upper arm and squeezed.

"Not happening." She had a daughter to return to." With that, she yanked her arm and jammed the spike heel of her shoe into his instep as hard as she could. He yelped and waved the gun at her. She scrambled for the weapon at the same time she kneed him in the nuts. As he doubled over, the gun went off.

Brett's heartbeat clattered inside his chest. Sweat broke out on his hands. His breathing became erratic.

"Hernandez?"

The report of a gun exploding galvanized them all into action. Officers came out of everywhere, but Brett got to Devon before the others. If anything happened to her because he didn't act soon enough, he'd never forgive himself.

She lay crumpled on the ground with Henry Logan sprawled on top of her. "Devon." Blood. Everywhere he looked, he saw blood. On her face and seeping out apparently from her side. "Dear God." His hands shook as he stroked her forehead.

An officer rolled Logan off her. He had a hole in his chest.

"Devon. Devon. Are you okay. Tell me you're okay."

"I'm okay. It's Logan's blood. I told you I knew how to shoot."

CHAPTER TWENTY-ONE

Tuesday, November 15

"**B**ailey honey . Come on. You'll be late if you don't get a move on." Devon waited by the front door of her parents' house. She'd already taken her bag and iced tea to the car.

"I'm here, Mom." Blair's voice preceded her as she gambled down the stairs, her backpack slung over one shoulder, a banana in her hand. "Let's go." And she flew through the front door. "What are you waiting for?"

Devon laughed at her daughter and gave thanks she seemed to have come through the kidnapping ordeal healthy and whole. After buckling her seat belt, Devon steered the car into the street and toward Bailey's school. "That's not much for breakfast."

"I've got a peanut butter sandwich tucked in a pocket."

"Glad to know."

"So, Mom, Brett Townsend has been coming around a lot. Is

this a serious thing?"

Devon's hand on the steering wheel grew clammy. Was it? She loved being with Brett. She didn't think her feelings were formed from gratitude for him helping her out of the tough situation with Franklin and the money. Well, and with the police, too. She had shot a man. Thank God, he didn't die. He did bad things, but he didn't deserve to die and certainly not by her hand.

"Hey, Mom. Did you drift off? Not safe when you're driving." Bailey snapped her finger.

"What?" Where had she gone?

"Are you and Brett serious?"

"What if we were? And I'm not saying we are, but what if we had a… relationship?"

"He seems to care about you, Mom. And if you care about him, that's the important thing."

"It doesn't appear to be too soon?"

"You and Dad were estranged from way before you were divorced, and he's dead. You deserve a life of your own. I'll be a senior next year and off to college after that. Then no telling where I'll end up. I'd like to know you had someone of your own."

"That's mature of you, Bailey." Devon was a bit taken aback at her daughter taking on something of a maternal position, but that's what she'd done.

"Now, I want to finish at my high school and go to college and not come out with a ton of debt. Other than that, go for whatever you want." From her backpack, she retrieved the flip over peanut butter sandwich and chomped a big bite.

Devon smiled at the woman child beside her. "Well, how about I set up appointments for us to check out prospective places for us to live. I'm glad we've been able to stay at Mimi & Granddad's, but we can't be there indefinitely or we'll wear out our welcome."

"I don't care where we live, Mom, so long as I can stay in my school and have my own room." She finished the peanut butter sandwich. "Where does Brett live? Could we move in with him?"

Devon jerked the wheel and hit a speed bump nearly losing control of the car.

"Hey, easy. I'd like to get to school in one piece." Her daughter grabbed Devon's iced tea and took several swallows. "Thanks. I forgot to bring along one of my own."

"Okay, we're here. Mimi is picking you up this evening."

"She doesn't have to. I can catch a ride with Linda."

"Okay, sweetie. I love you."

"Love you, too." She blew Devon a kiss. "See if you can't work something out with Brett." With that said, Bailey slammed the car door and waved before turning away, hurrying to meet her friends.

Devon shook her head, stunned at her daughter's words. When a car behind honked she put the car in gear and pulled away from the curb.

Thursday, November 17

Devon had been at work in her office all morning when her phone rang. Her heart jumped into her throat. Sudden noises still made her jittery. The fact that Logan was locked up and awaiting trial didn't seem to matter. Glancing at the screen, the appearance of Brett's name brought butterflies to her stomach. Especially after her talk with Bailey this morning.

"Hello, Brett."

"Can I take you to lunch?"

"I'd like that. Thanks."

"I'm in the parking garage."

"Oh, like right now? Give me a couple of minutes, and I'll be right out." Devon disconnected, stepped in to use the restroom, and applied a bit of fresh lipstick."

She stopped at her secretary's desk. "Liz, I'm heading out for lunch. May be gone for a while."

"Have fun." She wagged her eyes at her and Devon laughed.

The door to the garage opened, and Brett stepped through into the entry.

"Sorry I kept you waiting."

"You didn't. I'm used to making sure you're all right. Kind of a habit of mine." He dropped his hand to her lower back and ushered her out to his car. Warmth spread through Devon's body from the contact with his hand.

"Where are we going?"

"I picked up salads and sandwiches from Joe's Deli. Wanted you to see where I live. We've never had a chance to go there."

"Sounds lovely and not as hectic as a restaurant busy with the racket of lunch time patrons all in a hurry."

"You sure?" Brett squeezed her hand.

"This will be great." She squeezed his hand in return.

"I live in a much smaller home than yours, Devon. My aunt lived here for over fifty years."

"I'm sure it's charming."

They made the trip caught up in their own thoughts. Devon kept replaying Bailey's morning comments. Goodness. Did she want something to come of whatever was going on with Brett and her? Yeah, she sure as heck did. At least she thought she did. Guess she'd play this experience by ear and see what happened.

"Here we are." The red brick bungalow had black shutters. Brett pulled into the long, narrow driveway and stopped the car in front of the garage.

"Normally I go in through the kitchen from here, but let's walk around and use the front door, so you can get the full effect."

He unlocked the door, and she stepped into a living room/dining room combination with a fireplace on the left-hand wall. The kitchen was past the dining room.

"Beautiful crown molding, Brett, and I love the fireplace. Did you update it?"

"Yes. Besides opening the wall between the dining room and the kitchen I kicked out the back wall adding French doors to the terrace."

"How many bedrooms?" Heat rushed up Devon's cheeks. Good grief.

'Three, but I combined the smaller one with the bathroom to make a master suite. Then I added another bathroom at the back of the house."

"Did you do all the work yourself?"

He laughed. "Not a chance. Hired contractors. I'm handy, but this was beyond my abilities and my time. Let's eat then I'll give you the grand tour." He settled her at the kitchen table and spread out the food. "I got you a salad and one of their giant baked potatoes."

"Don't you wonder where they get these?" She unwrapped the potato. It had to be at least five inches long and about four inches around and stuffed with butter.

"I'm a big guy, but I never eat the whole thing. I figured we could share."

"I like that." She cut off a third of the potato and added butter, cheese and bacon bits, but left off the chives and sour cream. He added everything but the chives. They ate in companionable silence for a while.

"How's Bailey doing? Any side effects from the kidnapping?"

"An occasional nightmare, but mostly she seems amazingly fine. She's focused on her school work and practice for nationals."

"This is cheerleading, right?"

"Yep. We still haven't heard if they've gotten an invitation yet. If they do, we'll be in Nashville over the Christmas holidays."

"Could I come along?" He put down his sandwich and took her hand. "Would Bailey mind?"

Devon smiled remembering the morning's conversation with

her daughter. "No, Brett. She won't mind at all. She'd be pleased. And so, would I."

"Good. Changing gears, I've found most of your money."

"My money? What money?"

"What you paid in ransom to get Bailey back."

"Oh? How much?"

"The two million.I found the offshore account where he'd stashed the money. The DA will use my findings in his trial, but when the trial is over you'll get back your cash."

She nodded, not knowing whether to be happy or sad. The money was tainted with Franklin's blood and Blair's kidnapping experience.

"You won't get it back in time to stop the sale of your house."

'Thank you, Brett, but that's a done deal, and even if not, I wouldn't stop the sale anyway. Someone needs to love the house make good memories there. Bailey and I don't need much space. I've got an appointment with a realtor tomorrow to help us find a smaller place."

"You'd be welcome to stay here." He glanced up at her and then away. Almost as if he were shy.

He was the least shy man she'd met, always in control and confident.

"It seems I'm always thanking you, Brett."

"It's small, but we could rearrange to make room for everyone."

"Bailey needs to be in her school attendance zone. We'll stay with Mom with Dad while I look for a smaller house in the attendance zone."

He nodded.

She patted her mouth with a napkin and rose. "Can I see the rest of the house?"

Brett stood. "Sure." He held her chair. Let's look out back first. I'm proud of what we did there." He opened the French doors onto a large terraced deck with pots of flowers in all the corners and a bench running around it.

"This is beautiful, Brett. You must spend lots of time out here in the spring and fall. Love the fountain." She pointed toward a stone waterfall at the back of the property.

"Glad you like it. I did lay the stone floor for that. A labor of love. My aunt loved fountains and had always wanted one."

"What's the building at the back?"

"A guest house. The folks who originally owned the property had live-in help, and that's where they stayed. Complete with a kitchen and bath."

Devon shivered in the wind.

"Let's get you back inside." They went through to a den-like room with another fireplace off the kitchen.

He wrapped his arms around her, and she cuddled in. Like she belonged there.

A long sigh escaped. "This is lovely, Brett."

"Wait until you see the master conversion." He took her by the hand and led her down the hall. "As I told you, I combined a small bathroom with the smaller room, but you've got to see it to understand." He gestured toward a large bedroom with two windows and decorated in soft blues.

"Lovely." She glanced around the large room before moving into the bathroom. The fixtures and tile sparkled. "And oh, my gosh how beautiful. And look at this closet! Nice." She gazed at the two wood rows for clothes and the shelf units for shoes and purses. Well, he didn't have purses, but...

"I'm pretty proud of the results, and Auntie would be, too."

Devon spun around to find Brett right next to her. "Oh."

His hand ran up and down her arms. "Devon, I care about you." He kissed her. "And Bailey." He kissed her again, longer this time. Her heartbeat galloped. She was like a schoolgirl around him. After they'd made love last time—when her daughter had been kidnapped, guilt had swallowed Devon, and she figured she'd never have sex again—but now was different.

She stepped in closer, returning his kisses. "Brett, I care about you." She sucked in a breath. Could she say the words first? "I may be falling in love with you."

"I'm glad to hear that." He took her hand and maneuvered her into the bedroom with the king-sized bed.

He nuzzled her neck, and one hand trailed down the front of her blouse loosening the material from around her waist. Shudders ran through her. She wanted this man. Wanted to make love to him and have him make love to here. She'd be happy if they never stopped.

He unbuttoned and then drew the blouse off her shoulders and down her arms. Never stepping away from her. Then he undid the button on her slacks, sliding the zipper down and trailing a finger across her belly. Shivers followed his fingertips. She kicked out of her slacks.

She unbuttoned his shirt, dropping it on the floor. His pants followed his shirt. He lowered her to the bed and came down on top of her. Every inch of him pressed into her. She raked her nails down his back. He kissed her until she lost her breath and they breathed the same air. Becoming as one. His fingers made her cry out for him. Her being yearned for them to be closer. He entered her and they began a slow ascent to the heights tumbling over together to a vision of rainbows, mountaintops, balloons and a twenty-piece orchestra with soaring music.

Later as she came back down, surrounded by Brett's body, she realized she was complete. Did he experience the same? Did they have a future together? Was this a relationship and not two people who just had the hots for each other?

CHAPTER TWENTY-TWO

Friday, November 18

Devon set out the cheese, crackers, veggies. and dips, for her guests. She sang an old camp song as excitement bubbled up at the idea of seeing two of her best friends who were scheduled to arrive at her parents' house soon. Addison Greer Riley had driven from Fort Worth earlier and was setting out the wines and glasses. Kim Denison, coming from Wichita Falls, had stopped by DFW Airport to pick up Kate Thompson—uh Donavan. Devon needed to remember her friend's new married name. She hadn't been able to get to Maine for Kate's wedding and could hardly wait for all four of them to be together.

Straightening a chair in her mother's living room, Devon decided they'd made a good decision to move in with her parents. She and Bailey each had their own space. Bailey loved spending more time with her grandparents. A year-and-a-half and she'd be off to college.

"Do you miss them, Addie?"

POP "Miss who?" Addie walked in with two glasses and handed one to Devon.

"Your kids." She took the glass of Champagne, the bubbles tickled her nose.

"Yes and no."

"We're starting before the others get here?"

"We're celebrating." Addie clinked Devon's glass. "Since you didn't get to Kate's wedding, this is the first time all four of us have gotten together since the B & B in Irving a couple of years ago." Addie sipped her Sauvignon Blanc.

"We've got to do better."

"There's a car in the driveway. Are they here?" Addie dragged back the drapes and squealed. "They are." She set their glasses on a table and grabbed Devon's hand pulling her toward the front door.

"Yea." Devon swung open the door and skipped down the steps. Kate stepped out of the car, and Devon gathered her into a giant hug. "I've missed you."

"Me, too, you. I was glad Kim could pick me up at the airport."

A flurry of hugs all around ensued.

Addie with one arm around Kate said, "Oh, you did not do all the catching up without us, now did you? You'll have to repeat."

"Everyone grab a bag, and we'll have things inside in no time." Devon linked her arm through Kim's, but she winced. "Sorry did I squeeze too hard?"

"No, It's nothing." They made their way up the stairs into Devon's parents' house.

"Feels like old times to be back here." Kate stood taking in the familiar and the new.

After everyone took their luggage and settled in their assigned rooms with Devon and Kim sharing Devon's old room and Addie and Kate in Blair's room. After unpacking, they met back in the living room.

"I'm sorry to miss seeing your parents and Bailey." Kate sampled the artichoke and cheese dip.

"I told them they could stay, but Bailey wanted to check out the San Antonio sites, in case she ends up attending Trinity University down there.

"This is yummy," Kate dipped another chip into the artichoke dip. "So, is this supper or appetizers? The info will affect how much I can eat now." She sipped her Merlot. "My favorite."

"Addie and I thought we'd have Italian for supper. I've got this special little place you'll love."

Murmurs of agreement followed.

Kim settled on the love seat with Devon. "This is like when we were in college, and we'd come stay at your parents' place. They always welcomed us and never gave the impression we were in the way." She sipped from her glass of Chablis.

"They loved having us here. Said we kept them young." Devon patted Kim's knee. "I'm sorry about your parents."

"Thanks. Such a shock. They were riding in the Wichita Falls retirement center van on the way to the museum in Dallas. A drunk driver broadsided them. Mom and Dad were killed. Others were badly injured." Her voice trembled. "Of course, I'd insisted they move to the retirement center." She dropped her head.

"It wasn't your fault, Kim." Addie's words were firm.

"I know, but I miss them and hurt. I'm glad Robert had already moved out with his own life. Not as hard on him this way."

"Where's your son living?" Kate took a bite of grapes.

"Colorado. I'm afraid he's a ski bum. Oh, he uses his accounting degree, but mostly he skis." Kim stood and leaned over to put another couple of crackers and cheese on her plate. When she did, her sleeve scooted up. She hastily shoved down the silk material.

"Good grief, Kim. How'd you get that ugly bruise?" Devon frowned. "Did you see her arm?" Her gaze connected with Addie and Kate who also showed signs of concern.

218

"Were you in a wreck?" Kate sipped her wine. "You should've told us."

"No. No wreck." She rose and moved behind the love seat. "I...I fell. No biggie."

The afternoon passed with women sharing stories of their families. Kate told how much she enjoyed the small town of Griffin Harbor with Jim. "Of course, we could be anywhere, and I'd be happy."

"We're pleased for you, Kate. We wanted you to be able to go on." Addie scooped the dip with a cracker. "Now if we can get Devon settled, we'll all be happily married."

Devon smiled, but didn't say anything.

Back home after a delicious Italian dinner, the women gathered in the living room again for more wine.

"Can we drink too much wine?" Kate tipped her glass and then stood to replenish the Merlot.

"Not as long as we keep eating." Devon stood. "Addie brought her wonderful chocolate sheet cake. I'm sure it's past time for us to dig into that."

She and Addie served the cake, and they settled around the coffee table.

"Oh, my gosh, Addie. This is truly sinful." Kim took another bite of the luscious dark chocolate. "I'm glad you still make this." She licked the frosting off her fork. "Brings back fond memories of times long ago." She washed the bite down with a sip of Chablis. I shouldn't indulge. The pounds creep up without noticing."

"You don't have to worry, Kim. In fact, you could stand to put on a couple of pounds. Anyone prefer Champagne? That's what I'm having." Devon rose and poured herself a glass.

"Glad you think so. Not everyone does." Kim's voice was almost a low mumble.

"I see you're drinking your favorite spirits again. We'd all noticed you'd stopped." Addie sipped her Merlot.

"I had to when I didn't know where all the money was going. But thankfully, Brett straightened out the problem."

"Tell us more about this forensic accountant of yours." Kate walked to the bar where the various opened wine bottles sat. She refilled her glass.

"Addie knows him. I met him through Mike. I'll always be grateful they introduced me to Brett Townsend."

"What's he like?" Kim asked.

"He's tall, blond, handsome in a rugged, not pretty boy way. Exceptionally smart. Quiet. A good listener."

"Is he a good kisser?" Kim asked.

Devon chuckled. "Well, yes he is."

"So, is this going anywhere? Or are y'all just having a good time?" Addie licked the chocolate off her fork.

"I don't know. But I enjoy his company. He and Bailey get along. He's kept his aunt's house and lives there. It's a small bungalow and quite charming."

"Is there a money thing keeping you separated?" Kim asked.

"Boy, you guys are full of questions. Let's have more cake and wine. Then tomorrow we can walk around White Rock Lake to make up for our overindulgence."

Saturday, November 19

Devon glanced around at all the women bundled in jackets sitting on the back patio. "Anybody need a throw." Devon held out a couple.

"No, thanks. I'm good. Between the walk and this cup of coffee, I'm toasty." Kate stretched out her legs on the lounge. "I heard from Jim this morning. They had a giant snow storm overnight. He's afraid the weather will interfere with my plane on Monday. You may have a guest longer than planned for."

"Not a problem, sweetie. You can all stay for as long as you'd like. Even after my parents and Bailey get back. We've got a couple of air mattresses if it comes to that. You know, you're always welcome." Devon refilled everyone's cup. "I love having y'all here. We're lucky broads, aren't we?"

"Maybe not all of us." Kim struggled out of the lounge chair with a couple of moans. "Y'all have all gone through your bad times. Seems to be my turn now."

"Why honey. What are you talking about?" Addie swung her legs to the side of the lounge.

"I'm thinking about leaving my husband." Her lip trembled. "I've only stayed with him this long because of the money to help care for Mom and Dad, but they're gone now."

Devon jumped off the lounge and walked to Kim. "I'm sorry, honey. You don't love him any longer?"

She shook her head. A tear escaped and rolled down her cheek. Addie and Kate gathered around, and all three women hugged Kim. "It will be okay, Kim. We'll be here for you."

Kim sniffed and nodded. "I know. It's one of the reasons I was excited we could get together. I wanted to tell you how much I love you and what our friendship means. In case."

"In case what?" Kate leaned back to study Kim better.

"In case something happened to me."

"You don't mean your husband might hurt you, do you, Kim?"

"It's a possibility. No one has ever divorced in his family."

"Has he abused you before?" Addie's mouth firmed into a straight line.

Kim nodded but kept her chin down as if she was ashamed to look them in the eye, and her lips trembled.

Devon tipped up Kim's chin. "Honey, if he touched in any way that you didn't want, that's not okay. And it's not your fault, but his."

"You don't have to put up with that, Kim." Addie patted Kim's shoulder.

"You need to get an attorney," Kate added.

"Do you even have an attorney, one representing only you?" Devon asked.

Kim shook her head as she brushed at tears sliding down her face.

"I'm going to get you the name of a friend in Wichita Falls, and when you get home, you call him immediately. Okay?"

Kim nodded. "Yes, thanks. I knew I could count on y'all."

"Of course, you can, sweetie. Now what about we go get those donuts I spoke about earlier?" Devon hugged Kim. The other two women hugged their friend, too.

"We'll eat donuts and then go walk around the lake." The others all laughed and they trooped inside.

CHAPTER TWENTY-THREE

Sunday, November 20

Devon smiled to see Brett's name on her phone. "Hey."

"Can you take off several days?"

"What are you talking about, Brett? I'm busy catching up on everything we put on hold while we were working out the mess Franklin made of my money."

"We should go to the Caymans."

"I can't say I wouldn't enjoy going there, but not now. It's almost Thanksgiving."

"What about if we could get Blair's college money back?"

"Oh my gosh, Brett, what are you talking about? Franklin took that money."

"At my request, one of my employees continued researching all of Franklin's transactions, because the letters he'd sent you kept bothering me. Was he becoming maudlin as he got close to taking his life?

It didn't seem so. My guy spent many hours, but using your birthday numbers Franklin mentioned in the letter, we've identified a bank and an account on Grand Cayman which might have Blair's college money."

Devon flopped down in her father's desk chair in his office. Was it possible? She'd never forget the look on Blair's face when she learned her father had taken her money. She'd been devastated. If they could find the money, what a difference it would make to her daughter. Maybe recovering the money would allow her to keep alive the good memories she had of her father.

"Devon, are you still there? It's awfully quiet on your end."

"This would be wonderful, Brett. I guess, yes. We must go. When did you plan to leave?"

"Sooner is better than later. Technically, we don't have to go there, as you know from your experience setting up the account on line to handle the kidnapping money. We could probably get the money transferred to Bailey, as she is Franklin's beneficiary. This seemed a good opportunity to take off for a few days and to assure you get the money."

"I can go tomorrow. My friends all leave first thing in the morning. I'll make sure Mom and Dad can take over with Bailey, which should be easy since we're living here now, but it's only polite to ask them."

"I'll get the tickets. Bring Franklin's will showing you're the Executor."

"Okay. Wow, you've blown my mind, Brett. Not sure how I'll get the work done I'd planned for today. I want to tell Bailey, but I'm afraid to get her hopes up."

"It's totally up to you, Devon. I'm tying up loose ends on another project. I'll text you with our flight schedule."

"Thanks, Brett. Much too small a word to express my appreciation."

"If we get the money, I bet I can come up with a variety of ways you can thank me."

Heat bloomed in Devon's cheeks. "Oh, you bad man. What am I going to do with you?"

His deep laughed was followed by him disconnecting.

Devon chuckled and then called her mother. "Hey, Mom. How's San Antonio?"

"Lovely. We're eating our way through all the restaurants along the Riverwalk. My tracker is having fun racking up all the steps as Bailey and I shop. Your father is people watching from the bar."

"Glad y'all are having a good time. I called to tell you, I'm going to the Caymans."

"You are? Your father and I had such a wonderful time on our last visit. It's a beautiful place, but why are you going right now? You've been saying how busy you are at work."

Devon paced as she talked with her mother. One part of her brain cataloging what all she had to do to be able to leave. "Brett suspects Franklin may have moved Blair's college fund off shore. We're going down to see if that's true and if we can get the money."

"Oh, Devon. How wonderful. Not just finding the money, because we can always make sure Bailey goes to college, but this will mean so much to her."

"I agree with you, Mom."

"When are you leaving? It's such a long trip. Never has made sense to me why they can't find a more direct way to go. Always a lay over some place."

"Brett's purchasing the tickets, but sometime tomorrow."

"Well, I'm excited for you, sweetie. Your father and I have always found the Caymans to be romantic. Perhaps, you and Brett will, too.
"

"Mo-ther."

She chuckled. "Gottta go. I'm meeting your father and Bailey to take another ride on the river taxi. See you when you return."

"Whew." Her mother was entirely too much. She was right. The Cayman's were beautiful, but she and Brett weren't going for romance.

They were looking for Blair's college money. But...if romance was in the air, that'd be okay, too. She couldn't help smiling as she went back toward the kitchen to finish fixing the salads for her friends' supper. They'd all decided if they wanted more cake, and they did, perhaps salads would be best for the evening meal. All except Kim, of course, who needed to add a few pounds. Maybe when she got through the divorce, she'd start eating again.

Tuesday, November 22

After an exhausting trip, Devon and Brett arrived on Grand Cayman and settled into a beautiful suite in the Ritz Carlton.

"Oh, wow, Brett! This is stunning." She dropped her purse and walked straight to the sliding door to the balcony. She stepped out to be met by soft breezes and the sweet scent from all the flowers they'd seen everywhere on their drive to the hotel.

He came up behind her and pulled her against him. "Yes, you are stunning."

Devon laughed. "You are so quick with a line, Mr. Townsend." She tilted her head back and kissed him on the cheek. "Have you been here before?" She walked away from his embrace to lean her hands on the railing for a better view of the gorgeous aquamarine waters.

"Once about five years ago for a client." He stood next to her and drew in a long breath. "Ahhh. I've always fancied myself more of a mountain person than a beach person, but this is gorgeous."

The beach was dotted with chairs with umbrellas and cabanas. The "beautiful people" wandered in and out of the sea, embracing, kissing, chatting, and sipping, tall colorful drinks. "It's like a movie set. Makes me forget why we've come." She angled her body toward Brett.

He drew her close. "It's okay for us to have a good time while we're taking care of business, Devon. We can play and work at the same time."

She nodded. "When can we go to the bank?"

"Let's get lunch downstairs on the patio and then we'll head to the bank. I've made an appointment with one of the managers there. I worked with on my other case. I was glad to see Calvin Baird still worked here."

"Lunch sounds good. I was too sleepy to eat much on our layover in Charlotte." She walked back into the room. "Let me unpack, and then we'll go down."

It didn't take them long to put things away. They hadn't planned to stay long. Devon loved the intimacy of Brett's shaver sitting on the bathroom counter along with her makeup bag. It gave her ideas.

They were seated close to the edge of the expansive patio, cooled with fans and the winds off the water.

"Would you like champagne? I remember Bailey saying that was your favorite wine."

"That's thoughtful of you to remember, Brett. Let's save the celebratory bubbly until we get hold of Blair's college funds, so maybe just iced tea, and the shrimp salad sounds scrumptious."

When the wait person arrived, Brett placed her order and ordered the fish tacos for himself and a beer.

"Assuming we find the money, Devon, what are your plans? Leave it here or transfer the funds to your bank in Texas?"

She sipped her iced tea. "Home, I guess, but I haven't considered what to do with the money. I'm afraid to count on the funds being there and then end up being disappointed."

"Your mother mentioned y'all could afford to pay for Blair's college even if her fund is gone, but what would you do?" He drew pics in the moisture on the large pilsner holding his beer.

The waiter returned with their food.

"Thank you. What a lovely presentation." She speared a piece of the shrimp. "Yumm, and I'm so hungry." She took several more bites. "How are your tacos?"

"Different from at home. This is the freshest fish and quite tasty. May ruin me for what we have in Dallas. What about the college fund?"

"Sorry, I got caught up in appreciating this gastronomic feast." She set her fork in the conch shaped salad bowl. "We'd probably have to cut back on some vacations and pull out investment funds, but we could manage. Really this is more about showing Bailey, her father didn't take advantage of her and loved her."

"I get how important this is for her. I'm just worried about your money situation. If you need help, I'm here for you."

Devon reached across and took his hand. "Oh, Brett, that's the sweetest thing. Thank you."

"Dessert?"

"Gosh no. I ate every bite of the shrimp salad and a roll. Maybe later."

"You ready to hit up my contact at the bank or do you need to wait until tomorrow. I've got an appointment, but we could rearrange."

What a kind, considerate, smart, and let's not forget handsome, man Brett Townsend was. She was grateful Addie and Mike had put him in her life.

"Let's go now." On the way to the front and the rental, Devon stopped in the ladies' lounge. She touched up her lipstick and blush. She straightened to her full five feet six inches and smiled. Life was good, whether they got back Blair's money or not.

"Oh, my gosh, Brett. You're a miracle worker!" They'd just entered their beautiful suite, and Devon couldn't contain her excitement any longer. She flung her arms around his neck and kissed him soundly then spun him around the room and out on to the patio, practically jumping up and down.

"I like how you say thank you." He laughed at her.

Finally, she flung herself into one of the lounge chairs, raising her hands over her head. "Finding out her father didn't steal her money will mean everything to Bailey. As I told you before we left, we'd have managed, but this is wonderful."

"I'm sorry the transaction took us so long."

"Oh, no, no. I'm sure having the contact with Mr. Baird expedited the whole process for us."

"Are you ready for dinner yet?"

"I'm ready for the bubbly you mentioned earlier." She giggled. "Though I'm almost high on excitement now."

Brett picked up the room phone and ordered a bottle of their best champagne. "It will be here shortly."

"Oh, good. Then we can really celebrate." She couldn't believe she was coming on to him the way she was, but she was nuts about this wonderful man.

He drew her up off the lounge. "I hope you have the same idea I have for celebrating."

"I'm pretty sure." Looping her arms around his neck, she drew his head to hers and simply kissed his lips, then his eyes and his cheeks before nuzzling his neck. He pulled her close, so close his arousal pushing against her sent her senses south. He brought his mouth to hers and began to drink her dry.

The knock on the door made them both jump and then laugh. "Guess that's the bubbly." She shoved him toward the door.

The server wheeled in a small table with a silver server with ice holding the champagne bottle. He deftly opened the bottle and poured a small sample for Brett who sipped and nodded. "We can manage from here."

Brett smiled at the man thanked and tipped him.

"Of course, sir." He nodded and closed the door softly behind him.

Brett poured her glass and filled his up the rest of the way.

He toasted her, "To a beautiful, caring, brave woman who I'm proud to know and have in my life."

The glasses made a tinkling sound as they clicked and the bubbles ticked Devon's nose. "Oh, yes. This is good. Really good." She took a second sip.

Brett sat on the loveseat in their room and tugged her down next to him, sliding an arm around her shoulders. "Are you in my life, Devon?"

Devon took a small sip and rested her head on his shoulder. "It would seem so."

"Good. Hearing you say those words makes me very happy."

He set his glass and then hers on the coffee table and proceeded to show her how happy she made him.

Thursday, November 24

"Bailey. Bailey. We're home." Devon dropped her small bag and purse in the entry hall of her parents' home. "Where is everyone?" Brett followed her in with her larger bag. "Aren't they supposed to be home? You texted your mother and Bailey when we landed."

"I know. They must be back in the den with the TV on. I've no-ticed my parents turn the volume up higher than they used to." She tugged on his hand and hurried in the direction of the den.

Loud explosions came from the latest action movie playing on TV. Devon was always surprised her daughter and her mother too, enjoyed those awful shows.

"Hey, y'all. We're home. Any pumpkin pie left?" Her loud voice got through to her family. Her daughter squealed as Miriam put the movie on pause and Bailey flew into her mother's arms. "I'm sorry we missed out on the Thanksgiving Dinner with y'all." Devon hugged her daughter.

"Glad you're home, Mom. We've got news." Bailey nodded at Brett. "Hi."

"Hi, yourself."

"You do?" Devon kissed her mother on the cheek while Brett and her father shook hands. "We have news, too. You go first."

"Our cheerleading squad qualified for nationals!" Bailey's fist pumped into the air. "We're going to Nashville after Christmas!

Devon hugged her daughter and they swung around in circles. "Congratulations, sweetie. Y'all worked hard to be selected. Proud of you. As I said, we've got news, too. Do you want to hear?"

"Sure."

Devon led them to sit on the curved sofa, keeping Blair's hand in hers. Brett sat next to her on the other side.

"You remember we told you your father had lost your college fund?"

Blair's excitement fizzled, and her mouth turned down at one corner. "Yeah."

"We were wrong, sweetie."

"What?" Bailey looked at her mother, then Brett and then her grandparents. "What do you mean?"

"Your father looked after you to the very end. He moved your money into an account in Grand Cayman."

"Really?" Bailey looked at her as if she were afraid to hope what she was hearing was true.

"Really, baby. You can go any place you want to for college."

"And I know Dad loved me." She hugged her mother and sobbed.

Devon patted her daughter's back and whispered soothing words. She glanced over her to meet Brett's gaze, and her lips mouthed thank you. He nodded.

CHAPTER TWENTY-FOUR

Wednesday, December 28

Brett held Devon's hand as the plane landed in Nashville. She was glad he'd been able to arrange to come on the trip with her to see Bailey compete in the Cheerleading Nationals. He'd been out of town from since just after Thanksgiving through Christmas on a major case. She hated missing going to church with him and her family Christmas Eve and him being with all of them for opening presents and the Christmas Day Dinner, but she accepted that was the way his work operated.

All the cheerleading girls had flown on an earlier plane. After Brett picked up the rental, they drove toward the Gaylord where everyone was booked. The hotel was also the venue for the competition.

"What a beautiful drive." Devon looked out the window. "The road carved out of the stone this way, it's like we're riding in a tunnel with the top cut off."

"Must've taken a lot of dynamite to blast through the rock to build the highway. Wow, there's the hotel." Brett pulled into the long, lighted driveway.

"Oh, it's more beautiful than the pictures." Devon angled her head toward him. "I'm happy you came to be a part of this. It's a big deal in Blair's life."

"That's one of the reasons I'm glad to be here." They stopped under the portico. He tipped the valet attendant. The bellman helped get their bags inside. "Impressive." Brett's gaze zinged around the expansive area covered with greenery, walking paths, and lights. "You stay close. I could lose you in this maze of walkways." He pulled her arm through one of his and drew her next to him.

She laughed. "There seem to be a lot of entrances and exits. We could easily get confused. Good thing we always have our phones with us."

Brett got them checked in and they found their room, a small suite, on the third floor with a king bed, a separate couch, coffee table, and desk with windows overlooking one of many atriums.

"This is lovely, Brett." Devon whirled around the room. "What a fun view from the balcony. Different than the Ritz Carlton in Grand Cayman, but lovely."

"I love the view right here." He pulled her into his arms.

She hung her head. "I'm sure I'm a wreck after the long day and flight." She struggled to get out of his arms. "Let me spruce up a bit."

But Brett didn't let go. "Hey. How come you can't understand that to me, you're beautiful right now? I don't care whether you're decked out in something for a fancy ball, or wearing a baseball cap working in the garden with dirt smudged on your face. You are a beautiful woman. Why's the makeup thing important to you?" Would she answer him? He wasn't sure, but he'd keep digging to find the answer. It's what he did, who he was. He found answers.

"Let's go see if we can find Bailey. I'm eager to see her. Then we can eat supper and afterwards…I'll tell you."

He nodded and kissed her forehead. "A deal."

It took them a full twenty minutes, but they finally located Bailey.

"Hey, Mom."

Devon hugged her daughter who'd opened the door to a room brimming with lots of teenage girls and lots of giggles.

"How many of you are sleeping in here?"

"Just two of us; the others are hanging out." She gave Brett a quick hug. "I'm glad you could come. Hope it's not too boring for you."

"I doubt I'll be bored watching you and being with your mother."

"Mimi said to tell you how sorry she was she and your grandfather couldn't come. She felt like she needed to stay with him after he fell and broke his ankle the day after Christmas."

"I'm disappointed, but I was afraid when that happened, Granddad wouldn't be able to come."

"If it hadn't just happened, he'd probably been able to make it, but he's still getting the hang of the crutches."

"Will you send them pictures?"

"You bet'cha, sweetie." She hugged her daughter.

The noise in the room grew and Bailey pressed them into the hall and closed the door behind her. "In case you're wondering, I'm okay if anything develops between you, too. I may only be 16, but I'm not blind, and I've seen the way you cast glances at each other when you think no one is watching."

Devon's face heated with embarrassment. "Well, Brett and I… well, we're not…I can't imagine what—"

Brett leaned over and kissed Bailey on the cheek. "Thanks for those words. They mean a lot."

"What time do you practice tomorrow, sweetie? We'll stop by."

It seemed best to ignore her daughter's comments.

Bailey told them when and where, and Brett made a note in his phone. "We'll see you then. Right now, I'm starving, and we're heading to one of the restaurants for a late supper." Brett took Devon's hand. She blew a kiss toward Bailey and walked along with him to the elevator, her fingers entwined with his.

"What would you like to eat?" Devon had to say something, but Blair's words had melted her brain, and she couldn't come up with any more inventive words.

"The first thing we come to." Brett swiveled his head, searching for a likely spot. "Look. Let's try The Conservatory Café." They entered. A server took them to a table. Brett settled her in a chair at a table overlooking a jungle like setting.

"This is stunning. It's like we're dining outdoors only we're inside and warm." She leaned back and relaxed for the first time since rushing to get off. The turquoise cushion made the wrought iron chair comfy. Work was back in full swing at her cosmetics company, and Brett had picked up on his own projects. Their flight was delayed because of weather, but now, they could rest, enjoy each other, and Blair's competition.

A server appeared with a glass of champagne for her and a beer for him. She must've zoned out for a few moments because she didn't remember Brett ordering drinks.

"What are you having?" Brett glanced at her around his menu.

"Maybe the coconut shrimp. Haven't eaten those butterflies in a long time, and it's one of my favorites. What about you?"

"I'm considering the pork chops with baked potato." When their server appeared, Brett, gave him their orders. After the server walked away, Brett sat back and sipped his beer. "You've never come to Nashville before? Seems like your kind of place."

"No, most of my traveling except for family vacations has been about the company. I've never attended a cosmetics convention here, but what a great vacation spot. Your first time, too?"

"It always seemed too frou-frou to me, too family oriented. Not having a family, I didn't see the appeal."

Devon nodded. "Oh." And sipped her champagne.

They made small talk while waiting for the meal to arrive. Devon filled Brett in on the finer points of cheerleading so he'd be able to better judge the activity when they attended the practice on Thursday. "After the rehearsal tomorrow, you'll have a better idea."

Supper arrived and they shared bites of their meals with the other. "These may be the best coconut shrimp I've ever eaten. Love the pineapple sauce." Devon practically drooled.

"We'll have to come again before we leave. Give you another chance to eat your fill." Brett winked at her and she smiled back. Then they wandered around the facility to get their bearings, finding the room for tomorrow's practice locating other restaurants. There were many.

"We won't starve here, for sure," Brett laughed.

Finally, they made their way back to their suite.

"How about a drink?" Brett opened the small fridge. "Looks like we don't have champagne, but they have a decent chardonnay and an adequate beer."

"Sure. Thanks." Devon settled on the sofa. She hadn't forgotten she'd promised to tell him about the reason for her makeup. She didn't look forward to this. She'd only told her friends and a counselor. Maybe he'd forget.

Brett handed her a wine glass with light colored liquid then dropped down near her on the sofa and took one of her hands in his. "So why do you think you need to have on the makeup all the time?"

He hadn't forgotten her promise. Devon took a sip of wine and set the glass on the coffee table. Time to come clean. If she wanted them to have a life together and she admitted she did, he deserved to know.

"When I was twelve, my family had friends over to the house.

Not the one they live in now, but another place. Their friends had a son who was fourteen. We went off to hangout while the parents visited and played cards." Her heart rate tripped up as she remembered what happened.

"We were playing hide and seek. The lights were off. Every time he'd find me, he'd reach for my boobs. I was an early developer and they embarrassed me. He must've thought I was older because of them. Anyway, he got me in a dark corner, yanked down my panties, and…"

"Dear God, Devon. He raped you?"

She nodded. "Yeah. Then he told me the experience had to be our secret. Between the two of us. He wiped my tears and told me only really good friends got to do it." Devon nearly gagged at the memory. "Such a betrayal. I'd known him for many years."

"Saying *I'm sorry*, doesn't seem to be enough." Brett drew her closer to him, resting his head on hers. "Did you tell your parents?"

She shook her head. "His parents were great friends of Mom and Dad's. Our families had traveled together. The boy had never acted in any way to make me uncomfortable before. I figured no one would believe me."

"What did you do?"

"I threw away my dress, and when I got to camp in the summer, I told my friends. We decided we didn't much like boys after that, but we all went on and later fell in love. In high school and college."

"So why do you wear the makeup all the time?"

"I did some counseling in college. I was having trouble with my weight. I'd gained a lot and couldn't lose the pounds. Someone recommended I try counseling. The story came out. The counselor suggested I held myself responsible for what happened. The makeup acted like a mask to the world. No one could see the real me, the one who must have done something wrong for the boy to treat her the way he did.

"After some more sessions, I lost the weight, but I still clung to the makeup. My mask."

Brett sat with a stunned expression on his face. After a moment, he leaned forward and took her face between his two hands. "Thank you for sharing with me. You are and always will be beautiful to me. And you're so brave." He kissed her gently on both eyes.

She smiled at him. "They say good comes out of bad. My need for makeup resulted in my company, and I can't be sorry for that. Nor am I sorry about marrying Franklin. Yes, he betrayed both Bailey and me, but thanks to Franklin, I have my lovely daughter. Don't forget, because of all the mess he made, I've met you. You can almost always find a silver lining."

"Well, you can for sure. You are one strong woman."

She leaned in to him. "Not so strong I don't need others."

He took her hands between his. "I hope I'm one of those people you need."

She kissed him on the cheek. "I'll always be grateful Addie and Mike introduced us."

"Me, too. Listen, about what Bailey was saying."

"My precocious daughter?"

"I've wanted you since I met you at Mike and Addie's. Told myself to cool it. You had too much on your plate to make time for me. Besides, I was working for you. I like to keep those things separate. But that's changed.

"We're good together, Devon. I want to have a permanent place in your life and in Blair's. It's a package deal, I realize. I don't have regular hours. That won't change. Sometimes, I'm gone for weeks like I was during the holidays, and then I'm home at odd times."

"Brett, are you asking me to move in with you?" Her heartbeat had picked up at the prospect. Could she do that?

"No."

"Oh. I'm sorry." Heat rose in her cheeks. What a fool she'd been. She put distance between then, but her pulled her back.

"You misunderstand. I'm trying to ask you to marry me. Guess

I'm not doing a good job. I've never done this before. Didn't see my-self ever needing those lessons. Damn, I don't even have a ring for you. But I love you, Devon, please marry me."

Devon brushed at a tear spilling out. "Oh, Brett, what a lovely proposal. No practice needed."

"I promise no more betrayals."

"I love you, too, and yes, I'll marry you." She spent the rest of the evening showing him how great was her love for him.

Thursday, December 29

Devon squeezed Brett's hand, watching the team go through their routine.

"I sure am glad Blair's not one of the ones to go up on the pyra-mid." Brett gasped at a girl being tossed high in the air.

"How do parents let their kids do this crazy activity? Even the bases, isn't that the term you used for the girls on the bottom? Th e y can get badly hurt."

"Did you get hurt playing football?" Devon cut him a quick glance before redirecting her gaze on the pyramid.

"Well, yeah, sure. My brothers did, too, but that was—"

"Different? What's different? Because you were boys and you played football?" She punched him in the arm. "Don't let Bailey catch you saying anything like that."

He laughed. "I guess I've got a lot to learn."

She kissed him on the cheek. "I'm pretty certain you'll catch on fast."

Devon and Brett stood close aft er practice when an excited Bailey came flying up to meet them. Her long, reddish blonde hair tied into long pigtails slightly untidy from the routine.

"Did you see us?" She looked from her mother to Brett. "We

nailed the routine. Hope we can do as well on Friday."

"Y'all were great, Bailey. Gotta admit I didn't realize how athletic cheerleaders had to be. You're strong, kiddo. Like your mother." He draped his arm around Devon's waist.

Bailey smiled. "Y'all seem to be making progress."
Devon glanced at Brett and then shot her gaze back to Bailey. "I hope you're okay with the progress we're making. Brett asked me to marry him and I said—"

"Yes. You said yes, right?" She threw her arms around Devon and hugged her and turned to Brett jumping on him, he swung her around before setting her on the floor. Their laughter so loud, others turned to stare.

"You're okay with all this, sweetie?" Devon patted her daughter's shoulder, a niggling worry scratching at her heart. A lot had happened in a short time.

"Absolutely. Now I won't have to worry about you when I go off to college. Say, where will we live? I don't want to change schools."

Brett patted her back. "We don't have everything figured out yet, but we promise you can stay in your school.

"Well, I'm cool then. Hey, I've got to get back. I'll see you Friday after the competition." She hugged them both again and tore across the floor to be with her friends.

"She's pretty special, you know?" Brett hugged Devon close and kissed her on the forehead.

She nodded, swallowing back tears. Tears because Bailey would be leaving the nest soon. Tears of love for Brett. Tears because she believed in her deepest heart, that with him, she'd have no more betrayals.

The End.

OTHER BOOKS BY
Marsha R. West

VERMONT ESCAPE

Jill Barlow has lost everyone she cared about except her grown children. Caught in her father's fight to keep casino gambling out of Texas, her husband and dad are murdered. She'll do what it takes to ensure her kids safety even if it means leaving Texas and moving to Vermont.

Jerrod Phillips has come a long way in the 20 odd years since his wife abandoned him and their two children. With no room in his heart for love, he'll do anything to keep his family from being hurt again, especially when the threats come packaged in the form of the attractive Jill Barlow who he suspects is involved in murder.

Forced to trust each other when trouble follows her, they'll battle, not only killers intent on ending her life, but the attraction drawing them together.

Review

Marsha R West hits a home run with her debut novel, Vermont Escape. She combines danger, love and family into an intriguing story. The fact that her protagonists are over forty only added to the enjoyment for me. I loved Jill. She fights seemingly unbeatable foes in a battle for the safety of what's left of her family. I can't wait for Ms. West's next book. *Stephanie Berget*

TRUTH BE TOLD

Looking forward to a peaceful Christmas visit with her Fort Worth family, Meg Bourland is shocked to discover someone is blackmailing her father. When he rebuffs her offer to help, the Atlanta SWAT team member enlists her LA police officer brother and his former partner to uncover the truth. She fights her attraction for Scott McClaine and the immediate tug to her heart caused by his sacrifice. Her life is in Atlanta, and his is in California.

Scott McClaine, medically retired homicide detective, came to Fort Worth to recuperate from life-threatening bullet wounds he received saving the life of Meg's brother. Hard enough to accept his new physical limitations, but they make him unacceptable for strong Meg. Regardless, he commits himself to helping her stop the blackmailer. Working closely with her, a bond forms. Could she feel the same?

In the search for truth, they uncover pieces of the puzzle, which threaten to ruin her father's career as mayor and destroy the family she holds dear. Will Meg and Scott find their way through the maze of family secretes? Will they find the strength to make the sacrifices required for real love before the blackmailer makes good on threats to kill?

Review

I totally enjoyed this book. I got involved with the characters from the first page and was pulling for them to solve the crime, overcome their hang-ups, and finally find each other throughout the book. Way to go Ms. West! *Katie Crow*

SECOND ACT, Book 1, The Second Chances Series

When a board member of a non-profit arts agency in Fort Worth turns up dead, the homicide detective assigned to the case looks at everyone involved in the organization, including the executive director.

Addison Jones Greer, divorced mother of two teens, is the executive director of Cowtown Theatre. When someone murders a member of the board in the costume room, suspicion rests on everyone involved with the theatre, including Addie. She has angered some board members because she wants to fire the artistic director. Although she's warned him several times, he continues to go over budget for productions.

Mike Riley, Fort Worth homicide detective, hates that he caught this case. His sister-in-law dragged him to a theatre fundraiser where he met Addison, the first woman he's wanted to pursue a relationship with in a long time. Not about to happen now.

Addison hasn't ventured into romance since she caught her now ex-husband in their bed with his secretary. Trust isn't something she's good at. How could she trust someone who seems determined to think she's capable of murder? Or worse, thinks that her kids might be involved?

Review
Romantic suspense at its best...likeable, multi-dimensional protagonists, a truly detestable villain, well-developed secondary characters, fast-paced and filled with enough twists and turns to keep us reading well into the night. Ms. West has introduced an intriguing new series that will appeal to anyone contemplating a second act or hoping for a second chance at love. I read this book in

two sittings and had trouble putting it down. Well done, Ms. West!
Joanne Guidoccio

ACT OF TRUST, Book 2, The Second Chances Series

A widow since 9/11 and a mother of a grown daughter, Kate Thompson wants to keep her and her daughter safe, but an unexpected inheritance of land in Maine pushes her out of her comfort zone in Texas and into the arms of a Maine lawyer.

Maine lawyer and environmentalist, Jim Donovan wants to protect Aunt Liddy's land and keep it from falling into the hands of developers, but first he must convince Kate Thompson she should hold on to the family land when she doesn't even want to go look at it. However, he's unprepared for the attraction each feels for the other, but denies exists.

Will they be able to settle the land deal before anyone else is murdered or they break each other's hearts?

Review
It begins as a tender love story as these two strong characters with opposing goals are drawn together. Sparks fly. But wait, things are not what they seem. I don't want to spoil the story here, but I will say that as the mystery behind Kate's aunt's death becomes clear, the momentum of the story picks up and it becomes a page turner. I rooted for Kate all the way. A great read. If you believe in second chances, you'll love this story. *Jo-Ann Carson*

THE THEATRE

Forty-year-old, never been married stage and TV actress Kelly Lawson returns to her Texas home to choreograph and star in the Glenview Theatre summer season. Kelly's mother has made a hobby of trailing out every new man in town for Kelly's inspection, hoping she'll fall in love and use Glenview as her home base, especially now that Kelly's father has entered the beginning stages of Alzheimer's. Two years ago, Kelly broke off an engagement shortly before she discovered her former fiancé dead, a gun in his hand and a hole in his head. Reason enough to guard her heart.

When Kelly accuses a Glenview police officer of harassing two of the theatre's gay actors, Police Chief Josh Kincaid, her mother's candidate for this trip, becomes involved in the investigation. Incidents pile up, making it clear someone has it in, not only for the theatre, but for Kelly as well. Josh searches for clues to the person behind the attacks and the reason for them, all the while trying to ignore his developing feelings. How could he trust his heart to a New York actress?

Review
Kelly is a famous actress that leaves New York for the summer break to act in the summer theatre program in her Texas hometown. There she meets Josh, the police chief of the small town. Sparks fly but a long-term relationship seems impossible considering their two different lifestyles, in two different parts of the country. As if that's not complicated enough, Kelly finds herself caught up in a dangerous conspiracy that threatens not only her life but also the cast, crew and even the theatre itself. Lots of suspense keeps one mesmerized by the intrigue, danger and action. When summer ends and the mystery is solved and the dust settles, Kelly and Josh face an even bigger challenge, the fate of their hearts. Wholeheartedly recommend this story. I voluntarily reviewed an advanced reader copy of this book. Five stars.—Dee Archer

ACKNOWLEDGEMENTS

The number of people it takes to bring a book to publication still amazes me. The small and large tweaks that happen with the passing of each new gaze upon the pages continually shapes the manuscript. Many writer friends over the years have looked at my writing and given me feedback. Thanks to my daughter, Laura West Strawser, for suggesting a series based on four friends who met at summer camp.

Thanks to my editor Joy Clintsman, my cover artist Charlotte Volnek, and Stacey Blake with Champagne Formatting. I could not manage without them, but formatting errors are now all mine.

While Margie Lawson hasn't looked at any of this book, what I learned from her led to publication of my first book and thus to this my sixth book. Always grateful, Margie.

None of this would be possible without the support of my wonderful husband Bob West, who shares his time so generously to edit my books, talk plot points, and make suggestions to improve the story, not to mention helping with the business end of things.

Thanks to Michael Moynihan for his contributions to the financial aspects of this story and for the use of his first name, but as always, any errors are my own. I hope you enjoy ACT OF BETRAYAL.

ABOUT THE AUTHOR

Marsha R. West, a retired elementary school principal, is also a former school board member and theatre arts teacher. She writes Romance, Suspense, and Second Chances. Experience Required. Marsha lives in Texas with her supportive lawyer husband. Their two daughters presented them with three delightful grandchildren who live nearby. Charley, a Chihuahua/Jack Russell Terrier mix recently adopted them.

MuseItUp Publishing e-released her first book, VERMONT ESCAPE, in July 2013, and her second book, TRUTH BE TOLD, in May 2014. In the fall of 2014, Marsha formed MRW Press LLC to provide a print version of her first two books and then e format & print of the rest of her books, all of which are available in e-format and print from Amazon, and in e-format at Barnes & Noble and KOBO.

SNIPPETS OF SUSPENSE, Anthology #1 by the Sisters of Suspense, published in November 2015, contains the first chapter of SECOND ACT as well as nine first chapters by other romantic suspense authors. It's **FREE** on Amazon, KOBO, and Barnes & Noble. Great way to find new authors. Marsha is a contributor to ROMANCE AND MYSTERY AUTHORS ON WRITING, compiled by JQ Rose and LOVE TEXAS STYLE, AN ANTHOLOGY, also **FREE**.

Sign up for her NEWSLETTER on her website

marsha@marsharwest.com

Sign up for her blog: authormarsharwest.wordpress.com/

sisterhoodofsuspense.com/blog/

https://www.facebook.com/?ref=tn_tnmn

www.twitter.com/Marsharwest @Marsharwest

www.pinterest.com/marsharwest

She'd appreciate a review and love to hear from you.